A PAGAN'S
NIGHTMARE

RAY BLACKSTON

A PAGAN'S NIGHTMARE

A NOVEL

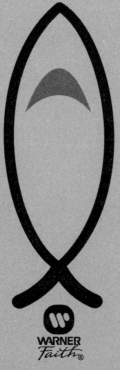

WARNER
Faith®

NEW YORK BOSTON NASHVILLE

Warner Faith
Hachette Book Group USA
1271 Avenue of the Americas
New York, NY 10020

Visit our Web site at www.warnerfaith.com.

Book design by rlf design

Printed in the United States of America

First Edition: October 2006
10 9 8 7 6 5 4 3 2 1

Warner Faith and the "W" logo are trademarks of Time Warner Inc. or an affiliated company. Used under license by Hachette Book Group USA, which is not affiliated with Time Warner Inc.

Library of Congress Cataloging-in-Publication Data

Blackston, Ray.
    A pagan's nightmare : a novel / by Ray Blackston.— 1st ed.
        p. cm.
    ISBN-13: 978-0-446-57959-9
    ISBN-10: 0-446-57959-9
    1. Screenwriters—Fiction. 2. Christianity and culture—Fiction. I. Title.
    PS3602.L3255P34 2006
    813'.6—dc22   2006006838

"They exchanged the truth of God for a lie,

and worshiped and served created things

rather than the creator. . . ."

ACKNOWLEDGMENTS

Special thanks to Beth Jusino for finding a home for this project, and to my editors, Anne Goldsmith and Chip MacGregor, for their keen insight and advice.

The voyage at sea was influenced by the author's reading of *The Pirates! In an Adventure with Scientists,* by Gideon Defoe.

Assistance with the (admittedly few) Spanish words courtesy of Susanne Leland and Ana Mejai.

Early test reads handled by the talented Annie McCarthy.

With apologies to Sister Sledge, ABBA, the Bee Gees,
the Beatles, R.E.M., the Who, KC and the Sunshine Band,
Wild Cherry, the Dave Mathews Band, and anyone else
who has ever produced original music.

A PAGAN'S
NIGHTMARE

Larry Hutch—all lanky, six-feet-three of him—bounded into my downtown Atlanta office at 10:45 Monday morning and dropped a screenplay on my desk. *Thwack.*

"This is it?" I asked.

Larry folded his arms, pressed his lips together in a kind of triumphant smirk, and nodded. "Done."

He looked as if he'd run across Georgia to get there; he was sweating through his madras shirt onto my best chair. This was August, however, so I kept my composure and read his title page. Larry looked on, silent and self-assured.

I thumbed the inch-high stack of paper—thicker than the average screenplay—and felt a tiny breeze tickle my nostrils. "This is what you said I just had to read . . . your best yet?"

"Done," he repeated. Larry sat sprawled in the guest chair and gazed out of my 22nd-story window. "I still may tweak the ending a bit, Ned. And it's not a screenplay. I wrote it in novel form."

I thumbed the pages a second time and noted the coffee stains on chapter one. "Does it have drama?"

He nodded. "By the boatload."

"Adventure?"

"Gobs."

"Romance?"

"Of the highest quality."

I read the first page with my usual dose of skepticism. "You have got to be—"

"Nuts?"

"Completely."

Larry interlocked his fingers behind his head and smiled the confident smile of a creative. "After you sell the movie rights, we'll get the book deal. We'll do this in reverse."

And just like that, Confident Larry rose from his chair and

departed. He left my door ajar, and seconds later I heard his muffled voice from down the hall.

"Just read the first ten pages, Ned, then go visit a McDonald's." His booming laugh followed, a laugh more appropriate for a Halloween gig than an agent/writer meeting.

Nine years earlier, Larry had graduated from film school. Twenty-two years earlier, I had graduated from the University of Tennessee—which is why so many of my shirts were orange. Larry called me Agent Orange, most likely because I killed his previous idea, which was terrible. Aliens invaded a Billy Graham crusade and, well, I'll spare you the rest.

I spent the afternoon on other business. Calls to other authors. Ten other manuscripts to skim through and reject. I badly needed to sell something.

Around 5:30 p.m., just before I left the office, I read Larry's title page again, shook my head in bewilderment, and stuffed his inch-high stack into my briefcase.

It was August 14th, a sunny afternoon as I walked to my car. My Saab sat next to a city park; I remember that clearly. I also remember jingling my keys, unlocking the door, and recoiling when I touched the hot blue paint.

I climbed in and buckled my seatbelt. Traffic was horrendous in all directions, so I figured the thing to do was to stay put, to climb back out and go sit in the park and read Larry's stuff. Like unearthing something rare and unexpected in your backyard, I had that feeling of discovery, the urge to dig further. A shaded bench looked welcoming beneath a burly magnolia, so I hurried over and took a seat and began reading.

A half hour later, I had coined a new phrase for my profession. In my small circle of agent friends, a manuscript that we cannot put down is now known as a "bencher." This is one that keeps you glued to a park bench and causes your spouse to question your whereabouts.

In my learned opinion, Larry had written a bencher. Or at least the beginnings of one. And by the time I had finished his third chapter and darkness was descending on muggy Atlanta, I was experimenting with the term "double bencher." That's when you employ a flashlight and end up spending the night.

Oh, I should also mention that I was married, that Larry was single, and that my wife, Angie, was a devout Baptist.

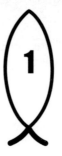

1

SUFFICE IT TO SAY that a certain people—some would call them the fortunate ones—took over.

Well, *took over* is too strong a phrase. Actually it was more like an inheritance. No, actually it was more like they were sitting at a very long table with many strangers, and in mid-course all the strangers left without finishing their strawberry cheesecake, so the fortunate ones just helped themselves.

How shameless—helping oneself to the early departeds' dessert. The gall!

Lanny Hooch will be our hero, or anti-hero—or perhaps an innocent bystander—depending on your perspective. You see, Lanny was in the right place at the right time: in a church, in northwest Atlanta, on a Monday morning, on his knees, atop hardwood floors, facing a baptismal.

He'd been here once before—the previous Friday—and on that morning he'd assumed a similar posture.

And you think Lanny was repentant?

Repentant? Hah!

Lanny owned Hooch Contracting, and on this day he was on his knees with his trusty Craftsman cordless drill, removing rusty wood screws from a ruined baseboard. The baptismal had sprung a leak, and the Baptists had summoned Lanny. He was a good worker. Punctual, with reasonable rates. Sometimes he cursed loudly if he hit his thumb with his hammer, and by 10:00 a.m. he had done this twice. He was alone in the sanctuary however, so no one heard him.

Or did they? During his break he visited the men's room. He washed his hands at the sink, reached for a paper towel, and spotted a sign next to the dispenser. *SOMEONE ALWAYS HEARS,* it read. The blue lettering was still wet, and Lanny returned to his work, wondering who had painted the sign.

Perhaps it was because Lanny was on his knees, down front in an empty sanctuary on a Monday morning in August, that he was picked. Though at this point he was thinking only about lunch, and of course the forty-mile drive to his next work site, an elementary school on the south side of Atlanta.

After he finished the repairs to the Baptist baseboard, Lanny climbed into his sage green Nissan Xterra and headed for the school, where he was to install a kiddie commode, the kind that force adults to sit all squished, with their knees up to their chins. But first Lanny had to stop for gas, so he took exit 57 and turned into a BP station. He stopped at this BP often; they usually had the lowest price.

In a hurry, he paid no attention to the price as he filled his twenty-gallon tank. For several minutes he stood staring out at the traffic, thinking about Miranda and sniffing the fumes. Miranda was his girlfriend. She was twenty-nine, and her flight back from Orlando was due in at 1:30. She had gone to visit her parents and had taken Monday as a vacation day. Lanny could not wait to see her again.

After he replaced his fuel cap, Lanny blinked his confusion as he finally read the sign above the pumps:

UNLEADED: $0.12 PER GALLON FOR THE REDEEMED
$6.66 PER GALLON FOR EVERYONE ELSE

"No way!" Lanny shouted to the pump. He looked around to see if someone were holding a camera, filming him as part of a joke.

He saw no one. At that moment, he was the only one pumping gas.

Surely someone is messing with my head. But what if they're not?

To Lanny, such price gouging seemed positively satanic, not to mention awfully unfair. This pit stop was also his first warning that something—he thought the air smelled funny, never mind the fumes—might be different about this particular Monday. But what could he do? He chalked it up to a practical joke and kept his composure. And composure was a trait he needed, since he had to hurry to south Atlanta to install the kiddie commode.

Lanny had only thirty-two dollars in his wallet, so he walked inside and asked the clerk in the Nike hat what the real price of gas was today.

"For you it's $6.66 per gallon," said the clerk, blank-faced.

"But that's outrageous." Lanny pushed away from the counter. "I won't pay it."

The clerk shrugged and pointed to the hidden camera mounted in the corner. "We have you on tape, and the gas is already in your truck. Don't make us call the authorities."

"Then I'll siphon the gas back out into your storage tank."

"We cannot take it back, sir. The gas is now tainted."

In no mood to deal with the police, a frustrated Lanny wrote out a check for $126.54.

Intelligent persons might pause here and say, "Wait, that does not compute! Twenty gallons times $6.66 equals $133.20."

Intelligent persons would be mistaken. Even blue collars like Lanny know not to drive till their tank is empty. He still had one gallon left in his Xterra.

Hungry and feeling ripped off, he drove across the street to a McDonald's. Everyone behind the counter was smiling the pasted-on smiles of those who have endured fast-food training but are still uncomfortable greeting the customers. Yet Lanny was confused by the uniforms, which, though still the basic red and yellow, possessed no golden arches but instead golden crosses—one on each sleeve.

Perhaps this was Lanny's second warning. But he was hungry and still mad over the satanic gas gouging, so he ordered a cheeseburger, a fish sandwich, large fries, and a Coke.

He hoped that the smiling blonde cashier girl would not tell him that his total was $6.66, and he felt relieved when she said, "That'll be seven dollars and thirteen cents."

Lanny was superstitious about the number thirteen—and normally he would have ordered something else just to change the total—but he was flustered by all the golden crosses and quickly forked over the money.

The cashier girl handed Lanny his change. "Enjoy your meal, Mr. P." she said.

Lanny looked at her with his head cocked funny. "My name is not *Mr. P.* My last name starts with an H."

Counter Girl smiled politely. "Today we're referring to you as Mr. P."

Even more confused, Lanny shook his head, picked up his tray, and sat in the far left corner, next to the window. He felt like he was being watched, so he munched his fish sandwich and avoided eye contact with the fast-food workers. He was still eating, staring out the window at the traffic on I-285, when he noticed the billboard:

How Does It Feel to Be the Last One?
~God

Nervously glancing around the restaurant, Lanny gobbled his cheeseburger before starting on his fries. Imagine his shock when he withdrew the first fry from the pouch and saw that it was curled into one long word, *Pharisee.* He frowned at the wordy potato and stuffed the entire thing into his mouth. Then he read the slogan on the cardboard pouch: "McScriptures—a new kind of french fry, pure as gospel."

Lanny tucked his fries into the bag, grabbed his Coke, and left his trash on the table for the smiling blonde to clean up. "I'm outta here," he mumbled to himself as he pushed open the glass door.

Lanny was a self-professed pagan. Mannerly, sure, and usually a patient fellow, but he had wanted nothing to do with religion ever since eighth grade, ever since he'd found out that his neighbor, an associate pastor, had been convicted of trafficking drugs and adult magazines. That summer Lanny had made up his mind to use Sundays for golf. He would be a low-handicap pagan.

Perhaps that's why Counter Girl referred to me as Mr. P., he thought as he climbed into his truck. *How ironic. But I'm still ticked about the gas thing.*

Traffic was horrible, and Lanny grew frustrated at the conges- tion, even more so when he reached the on-ramp to I-285 to south Atlanta. No one would let him merge. Here traffic was worse than bumper to bumper; it was religious bumper sticker to religious bumper sticker. They were all reading each other's spiritual plati- tudes and giving each other the thumbs up.

In contrast, Lanny's only bumper sticker read "Sometimes I wake up grumpy; other times I let him sleep."

Miranda put it there. She read novels on Sundays while Lanny played his golf.

Annoyed at what the day had wrought, Lanny waited for some- one, anyone, to let him merge onto crowded I-285. But everyone ig- nored him, so he called Miranda's cell, hoping to reach her before she boarded her flight from Orlando. He wondered if she, too, was experiencing the religious weirdness in the South today. There was no answer, so he tried her work number. That number went unan- swered, so he called her cell again and left a message for her to call him as soon as possible.

The temperature was already near one hundred degrees, and Lanny turned his AC on high. Still no one would let him merge. Not the SUVs, not the minivans, not even the redhead in the silver Audi. Her bumper sticker read "Traffic Is My Mission Field."

But the redhead would not look his way, even though Lanny was motioning for her to lower her window so that he could ask her what was going on today in Hotlanta. He hoped the religious weird- ness was a regional thing. In fact, he almost *prayed* that it was a re- gional thing, but then he remembered that he never prayed to anything but his golf clubs, which he tended to slice.

So Lanny sat waiting to merge, fiddling with the radio and eating his McScripture fries. He thought they tasted very much like regu- lar fries, only with less salt.

Lanny had installed satellite radio in his vehicle and figured his best move now was to tune in to a station out of L.A. It was his favorite, as their mix of oldies and modern rock suited his worldview just fine. So he tuned to the station and increased the volume, only to hear the Beatles singing their greatest hit, "I Wanna Hold Your Tithe."

Lanny slammed his fist into his seat. *Someone is even changing the song lyrics,* he thought to himself. *That's sacred territory.*

Minutes later a little old lady in a Volkswagen Bus honked, waved a brochure that read "Repent of Bingo," and allowed Lanny to merge.

He waved with no sincerity at all, then tried Miranda again on the cell phone.

But again he got no answer. *Maybe she's already on the plane.*

He tried her parents in Cocoa Beach—where they'd retired and where she'd been visiting.

Again, no answer.

He tried Miranda's sister, Carla, in Augusta.

No luck there, either.

His father and mother had passed away two and four years earlier, respectively, so the next closest persons he thought about were his golf and poker buddies.

He tried all five of them.

Nothing.

Rolling along on congested I-285, sandwiched between zealots, Lanny felt very alone. In fact, he was beginning to feel like the lone yellow M&M in a bag full of reds. But not quite like that, since feeling alone in the world is much worse than being a solitary piece of chocolate, which has no feelings at all, even when it melts in your mouth instead of your hand.

The smaller shock to Lanny was that religious people seemed to be the only ones inhabiting the state of Georgia. The real shocker to him—it was more like a revolving question—was, where had everyone else gone? Who had taken these people? And how did he—or she? *it?*—manage this?

Lanny's thoughts ran wild. They ran in circles. They even ran all the way back to his childhood, when he had sat in the back during Sunday school.

Surely there's no such thing as a reverse rapture? Is there? Did I miss that part?

Surprise, surprise.

2

MAGINE A SATELLITE VIEW of Florida, especially the sun-drenched peninsula that divides the Atlantic from the Gulf of Mexico. To the far left side of the screen, in swirling bands of white cloud, a hurricane spins four hundred miles away, heading due east from the Gulf, on a beeline for Tampa and Orlando. For all we know, this zephyr may or may not turn out to sea.

Now picture a broadcast booth, and inside, a radio talk-show host. This man is bearded and pudgy and usually jovial. Behind him on the wall sits a plaque on which is centered a set of scales, golden in color, the two cups aligned at a perfect horizontal. For fifteen years this man's hospitable manner has fed America's quest to voice its every opinion, and his show has grown into a meeting place for those with extremist views, stupid views, boring views, and no views at all.

Known affectionately to listeners as DJ Ned Neutral, he leaned into his mic, glanced through Plexiglass at his producer, and cleared his throat.

The producer readied himself behind a soundboard and counted down the seconds on his fingers:

Three . . . two . . . one.

"Hurricane Gretchen is still a category three, traveling east with winds at one-hundred-twenty miles per hour. At its current pace it will make landfall along our coast in approximately four days." Ned's voice boomed friendly and deep, an intelligent voice that he'd parlayed into one of the nation's most popular call-in shows. "Welcome to Fence-Straddler AM radio, where I, DJ Ned Neutral, serve not only as arbiter of American argument, but this week go far beyond the call of duty. . . . I'm doubling as your weather man."

Ned paused, checked the time, rubbed his beard. He glanced at the row of red lights on his phone, lights that signaled incoming calls. All five were lit. Before taking a call, however, he addressed his audience again.

"Good morning to the fruited plain. This is DJ Ned coming at you live from wind-whipped Orlando. Tropical Storm Felix missed us by forty miles, and still I have limbs down all over my yard. And now, *now* we've got a bigger storm on the way. So before we get into which special-interest group hates which and for what reasons, does anyone care to share how they're preparing for a third August hurricane?" Ned pressed line 1.

"Yo, Nute. This is Crackhead."

Ned smiled above his mic. "Yo, Crackhead. Didn't you call in last week?"

"Yeah. I'm the guy who—"

"I remember. You got your name from cracking your head after falling off your skateboard."

"You got it, Nute. I never done no drugs."

"Honest?"

"I swear, Nute. I'm a health guy."

"Right. So, what do you have to say to America today, Crackhead?"

"First I want to say that all these hurricanes could be God's judgment on Florida."

"No kidding?"

"Some pastor said so."

Neutral rubbed his chin and winked through the glass at his producer. "Okay, Crackhead, and just what denomination are you a part of?"

"Some kind of Redeemer Fellowship thing. . . . I've only been twice."

"And you're absolutely sure about this judgment from God?"

"That pastor said so. Said too much drinking and fornication goin' on in Florida."

Ned struggled for words. "Okay, Crackhead, since you've got the

Sunshine State covered, now tell us what kind of natural disaster is going to crush the drunks and fornicators in land-locked states like Kansas and Iowa."

"Um ... I dunno, man ... Maybe all their peas and corn will shrivel and die."

Ned hit the red *End Call* button on his desk. "Thanks for the call, Crackhead."

He restrained a grin and leaned once more into the microphone. "One warning from last week, folks. Although we give voice to most anyone, I'll not tolerate any more Nazi Skinhead versus Lutheran Senior Ladies Book Club. You all wore me out last week. Now, who's my next caller?"

Ned pressed line 2.

"Neutral?"

"Welcome to Fence-Straddler AM."

"Hi, Neutral, this is Nancy from Wichita. That last caller was right about the judgment, but wrong about the reasons. It's the materialism that will cause our destruction. Everyone wants the big house on the golf course."

"Well, Nancy, I happen to live in a big house on a golf course. And I bought it by working hard for fifteen years to give America an outlet to speak their mind."

"Is your house over six-thousand square feet?"

Ned rolled his eyes and gripped the mic. "Is six thousand the cutoff size for God's wrath?"

"I think so. How big is your house, Ned?"

"Five-thousand, two-hundred square feet."

"You see, Ned ... those limbs that fell in your yard were a warning not to expand."

Neutral hit the red button. "Alrighty, Florida. Who else has limbs down in their yard? Welcome to Fence-Straddler AM."

"Neuuuutral! You rock, man."

"Thank you. What's on your mind?"

"My name's John, and I called in to say that I have it worse than just limbs down in my yard."

"And how big is *your* house, John?"

"I live in a trailer, man. Just a single-wide. And now it's turned on its side and leaning up against my neighbor's place."

"And is your neighbor okay?"

"Yeah, my neighbor is Crackhead, who called in earlier. We're about to hitch his four-wheel drive truck to my trailer and tump it back over."

"*Tump* it back over? Where're you from, John? Or should I call you John-boy?"

"South Georgia, originally."

"And do you think your trailer getting *tumped* over by Tropical Storm Felix is a judgment from God?"

"Definitely, and it ain't got nothing to do with house size."

"I see. Then to what do you attribute the cause?"

"Online gambling, Nute. I slipped up and clicked on a Web site that I shouldn't have."

"And does Crackhead know about this?"

"Crackhead told me to click on it. . . . It's how he makes his living."

Ned considered his audience, saw that all five red lights on his phone bank were lit, and cut John off. "Next caller," he said.

"Neutral, this is H. Bernard Randolph."

"Welcome to the show, H. Bernard."

"Thanks, Neutral. I'm on my lunch break up here on Wall Street, and I just have to say that I disagree vehemently with both Crackhead and his neighbor John."

"That so?"

"According to the blonde on the Weather Channel, the percentage of storms hitting Florida is no different today than it was back in the fifties . . . back when America still had its innocence."

Ned paused and considered H. Bernard's factual tidbit. "So Fonzie and Ralph Malph were never in any danger of getting walloped by a tornado for lusting after Richie's sister?"

"No, never. But Joanie was a babe."

DJ Ned hesitated, wanting the caller to continue. "Is that all you had to say, H. Bernard?"

"That's it."

Just as Ned cut the call, all five red lights went dim.

DJ Ned stared at the row of vacancies and shook his head. "That's never happened before," he muttered to himself. "Sorry, folks. All the lines just went dead. This show never has empty lines."

After ten minutes of waiting for the lines to light up again, Ned raised both hands, palms up, and shrugged the big shrug, a silent signal of give-up to his producer.

But his producer was no longer in sight.

Ned looked out through the glass surrounding his booth and tried to spot him. But only Ned himself was in the room.

He figured his producer had run to the men's room. *But while broadcasting?* He glanced back at his phone bank and saw that all five lights were still dim.

By the time his show ended at 2:00, DJ Ned Neutral had not received a single call since H. Bernard phoned in from Wall Street. Ned rose slowly from his radio booth and peeked down the hall of Fence-Straddler AM.

No one else was in sight.

He looked into all the offices, but all were empty.

He called out, "Hey, anyone want to join me for lunch?"

No one answered. Just the clock, ticking off the seconds. He'd never noticed the ticks before.

Next he retrieved his cell phone from his jacket and tried to call his own show, but the call would not go through. "Please check with your phone company," it said.

Confused and a bit freaked out, Ned rushed from the building and into bright sunlight. He tried to calm himself, took deep breaths. He even walked a block down the sidewalk of the business district. In seconds Orlando seemed normal again—humidity high, shade low. The only thing he noticed that looked odd was that fewer people were on the streets. *Maybe everyone went to the beach today.*

Food always helped Ned relax and clear his mind, so he entered The Streetside Café, one of several local eateries he frequented.

Ned was a big eater—and had a habit of ordering dessert along with his entrée—so when a middle-aged waitress arrived to take his order, he pointed first to the dessert menu. "Got any more of that Devil's Food Cake?" he asked her.

She promptly pulled out a Sharpie pen, leaned down to the plastic menu, and marked out the word *Devil's*. Then she wrote a new word in its place. "Management just changed the name to David's Food Cake," she said. "One slice could fill Goliath."

At first Ned could only blink at her.

The waitress smiled politely, pointed to the menu. "Would you like a piece of David's Food Cake, sir? It's already quite popular in Tucson, Dallas, and Chattanooga."

Blank-faced, DJ Ned stared at the waitress, hoping that she was kidding.

But she just waited patiently with pad in hand, ready to take his order.

Ned had yet to connect his lack of callers with the renaming of Devil's Food Cake, but it seemed to him that a strange form of religiosity was sweeping across America from west to east, just like the latest fad from L.A.

3

WHEN LANNY ARRIVED at Southside Elementary on the south side of Atlanta, he parked his Xterra in a visitor's spot and unhitched his seatbelt. By now he had convinced himself that he was simply the victim of a huge practical joke, and over the past half hour he had given little thought to the odd happenings at McDonald's and the BP station. The billboard, however, still troubled him.

Skies were sunny and winds were mild as he got out and grabbed his toolbox from the rear hatch. Whiffs of honeysuckle drifted past, and for a moment Lanny stood and sniffed. The sweet scent restored a sense of normalcy to his day, and around him everything looked in place: grass freshly mown, windows adorned with Crayola drawings, tricycles in the playground, bicycles lined up and parked beyond the sidewalk.

"I remember my little purple bike, back when I was seven," he said to himself. He shut the hatch to his truck and toted his toolbox toward the front entrance.

On his way toward the school, Lanny heard an intercom blaring some kind of announcement from inside the building. He could not make out the words.

As soon as he pushed open the lobby door, he smelled Pine-Sol. But he found no one at the front desk to greet him, so he continued down the hall to room 12B, where he had been instructed to knock before entering. He knocked twice, but there was no answer, no sound at all from inside the room.

The intercom system crackled to life, and from down the hall an emotionless male voice said, "Go to 12D. You're at 12B."

Lanny wondered why no one was talking to him in person, and

how they even knew he was in the building. He loped down the hallway, his toolbox heavy in his hand, his mind suspicious once again.

This is Monday. Surely there are kids here on Monday.

The door to 12D was also closed. Instead of knocking, Lanny almost left to find the school principal. But he went ahead and tried the door, and it opened to an empty classroom. Desks were pushed to the sides, and masking tape was arranged on the floor in the form of a big boat. Drawn skillfully on the chalkboard to his right were colorful fish and a huge octopus.

In the rear, just outside the restroom, he saw the shiny porcelain. An uninstalled kiddie commode sat against the back wall, its lid up, as if inviting him to get to work. Lanny toted his toolbox to the back and read a note taped to the commode handle:

> **Please try to have this installed by 2:15. The kids**
> **have their juice and cookies at 2:30, and we will**
> **need our restroom to be functional.**

Lanny glanced at his watch and saw that the time was already 1:28. Curious as to where everybody had gone, he went to the window and peered out at the schoolyard. It too was empty.

Then the intercom voice said, "Better hurry."

Lanny muttered, "Mind your own business," and opened the restroom door. He was relieved to see that the old commode had already been removed.

He finished the installation in thirty minutes, and as always, he gave the commode a test flush. The swishing sound was immediately followed by the impatient voice on the intercom.

"The children are waiting to return to their classroom."

Lanny paused from arranging his tools in his box to glance up at the gray speaker mounted on the ceiling. "Why can't I meet the kids? I'm not dangerous, ya know."

The voice was monotone and robotic. "We cannot risk them becoming tainted."

"Tainted?" This was the second time today Lanny had heard that word.

"Thank you for the new commode," the voice said.

Lanny frowned and shut the lid. "You're . . . welcome."

Five seconds passed before the voice sounded again. "But you are not allowed to use it."

This time Lanny stood on his toes and stared at the speaker, perturbed at the lack of humanity. He decided to humor whoever was doing the talking. "Why can't I use it? Because I'd have to sit all squished with my knees up to my chin?"

"No, because you're not one of us. You're Mr. P."

At that instant Lanny knew that today was no practical joke. No way would two different strangers, on two sides of Atlanta, call him that. Fighting nerves, he muttered, "So I'm Mr. P., eh?"

"Leave within the next ten seconds or we summon the authorities."

Defiant, Lanny waited twelve seconds. And through the speaker he heard sirens wail.

His complexion paled as he grabbed his toolbox and fled room 12D. His footsteps echoed in the empty hallway, and the intercom offered nary a good-bye.

When Lanny reached his Xterra, he flung the toolbox in the rear, jumped into the driver's seat, and left skid marks in the Southside parking lot. Two miles down the road he tried again to reach Miranda on her cell phone. It was 2:15, and he knew that her flight should have landed by now. But again there was no answer, not even her friendly, recorded message.

He tried the radio, searching for a breaking news story, hoping he was not caught in the middle of some strange invasion. Instead he discovered something far more personal—he heard Atlanta's traffic reporter utter his name.

The female reporter's voice grew excited. "I repeat, Marvin the Apostle is offering a second *Big Reward* for the capture and conversion of Georgia's last remaining holdout, Lanny Hooch. He was last seen leaving the building of Southside Elementary."

Lanny jammed the accelerator. *A reward to capture and convert me?* He swerved around a pair of minivans and paid no attention as his speedometer soared passed 80. *What is happening to Atlanta? And why me?*

At the on-ramp to I-285, Lanny again had trouble merging. But by now he had lost patience with the zealots. Again he jammed the accelerator. Then he pulled onto the shoulder and sped past an endless line of religious bumper stickers. He drove straight to I-85, took exit 99, turned left over the bridge, then hung a right into Miranda's apartment complex. He parked in front of building G, hurried to her door, and knocked.

No answer.

She's a smart girl. Maybe she knows about these zealots, missed her plane on purpose, and is hiding out at her sister's.

However strong his panic, however anxious his thoughts, what Lanny wanted most was to get out of Atlanta. He ran back to his truck, climbed in, and started the engine. But he left the gearshift in park—at the back of the lot he'd spotted an old Camaro with its front wheels up on blocks, and this car offered the subtle disguise he needed.

Two minutes later, Lanny had swapped license plates. In survival mode, he drove out of the gate and turned back toward the interstate. His instincts told him to floor it and flee. But first he knew he should call customer service at Delta Airlines. He fumbled with his cell phone, dropping it on the floor mat. His truck swerved back and forth over the center line as he grabbed the phone from under his ankle. He dialed the number, took deep breaths, and waited for an answer.

Finally a female voice greeted him. "Welcome to Detour Airlines, earthly flights for the heaven-bound."

Lanny nearly crashed his truck. "*Detour* Airlines?" he shot back. "What is that?!"

But he was too shaken to wait for a response. He slammed his phone shut and veered into the exit lane, turning south onto I-85, then back onto I-285. Traffic flowed now, and he felt safest in the middle lanes, driving and thinking, driving and fighting panic, driving and fearing the worst.

He looped around Atlanta in a stupor, trying his golf buddies over and over on his cell but getting no answers. He turned on the traffic report again and heard the reporter giving details of the reward offer: ". . . This offer has a three-day time limit. . . . The first Big Reward was claimed in Athens at 11:00 a.m. today, a deft capture of holdout number two. . . . He is now en route to the containment area. . . . And now one holdout remains. . . . Lanny Hooch last seen leaving Southside Elementary. . . . Believed to be driving a forest green Nissan."

Containment area? What is that?! At least they got the color of my truck wrong.

Someone behind him honked, and out of sheer panic Lanny swerved across three lanes. In minutes he was on I-75, aiming his SUV for Florida. His plan evolved quickly—he changed his mind and took Highway 81 to I-20, wanting to make a stop in Augusta, since Miranda's sister, Carla, lived there. And if he could not find Miranda in Augusta, he would continue on to Cocoa Beach, to her parents' house.

Now doing ninety miles per hour on I-20 east, Lanny tried his best to be optimistic. *Perhaps Augusta and the Sunshine State are immune to the religiosity.*

At a minimum, he hoped to find a few more yellow M&M's.

On Thursday Larry came walking into my office in blue argyle socks, loafers dangling from his fingertips. He walked over to my window and, as was his habit, gazed down at Atlanta in non-stop commute. We had yet to greet each other. I just watched him watching the traffic and wondered why he was carrying his shoes.

"Agent Orange loves it?" Larry asked, still mesmerized by the freeways. "Tell me you love my story."

I pushed away from my desk but remained seated. "The religious right is gonna shoot you."

"Nah, they're gonna love me."

"You mean there's some sort of conversion in this story?"

Larry turned from watching the traffic, and his face went blank. "*Conversion?* You mean like when someone switches from debauchery to chastity? Nah, I don't really deal with that issue, Ned."

I shoved a stack of manuscripts aside and motioned for Larry to sit in my guest chair. "You're not gonna make me ask why you're carrying your loafers in your hand?"

Larry glanced at the shoes dangling from his left thumb and forefinger, as if he'd forgotten he was holding them. "These loafers?"

"Those loafers."

"Just bought 'em yesterday. Italian shoes. You've probably never heard of the brand."

"Probably not. So why—"

"Why am I not wearing them? Because they're tight and my feet hurt. Italian shoe designers must have skinny feet."

"Why don't you just take them back?"

Larry rolled his eyes. "Image, Ned. I need the right shoes, regardless if they fit."

"Didn't they feel tight when you tried them on?"

Larry dropped the shoes to the floor and came over and tapped his index finger hard on my stack of papers. "The manuscript, Ned. Are multiple offers on the way?"

From my briefcase I pulled out Larry's first three chapters and pointed to the title page. "In the story, you're Lanny Hooch, right?"

Larry tugged the sock on his right foot and smiled. "That's correctomundo."

"And I'm . . . I'm DJ *Ned Neutral?*"

"We're quite a pair, aren't we?" He switched to his left sock. "My therapist says my childhood affects my writings, but I won't bore you with what happened. Can you sell this?"

"Possibly. But the religious right . . . Well, I'm not sure if they're ready to laugh at themselves." A tangent flashed into my head, and I tried to steer our chat in a new direction. "You don't have much experience with theology, do ya?"

Larry shook his head as nonchalantly as if he were refusing an offer of gum. "Nah. Very little."

"I see." Another flashing tangent; they were coming too fast to keep up. "And didn't you tell me last week that you recently had a date with a young woman named Miranda?"

Larry toed my carpet, shifted in his chair. "A minor coincidence."

I held the first chapter aloft and spoke in a raised and incredulous voice. "You wrote about a woman you've just gone out with into your—"

"Twice."

"You wrote her into the book *twice?*"

"No, we've been out twice. Once to dinner and once to a movie."

I eyed him closely, knowing how rarely Larry dated. "Dinner and a movie on the same day?"

Larry shifted again, ran a hand through his hair. "Yes."

"Then that's once, Larry. One solitary date. And you—"

"Okay then . . . once. But what do you think so far? Can you sell this?"

"Maybe. But I gotta read it all first. Did you also write your dog into the story?"

Larry winced, even recoiled in his chair. "Dillen? No way. I'd never embarrass my dog like that. Labradors don't like being in stories."

I kept thumbing the manuscript, as if this would hide my excitement about its potential. Surely the secular crowd would embrace it, although my wife, Angie—the devout Baptist who managed to drag me to church once a month—would likely object. I had not sold a project in eight weeks, however, and this one at least held the possibility of a paycheck. Plus, there was that intangible quality, the sheer gall Larry possessed to write this thing while living in the Bible Belt.

I tapped the title page. "You're sure about this title?"

Larry leaned back in his chair and put his hands behind his head. "It's perfecto. Absolute Southern-fried perfection."

"*A Pagan's Nightmare* is your idea of perfection?"

"It's da bomb, Ned. Now just go sell it."

"I'm gonna need to read more."

He got up and left with a simple little wave. And again, down the hall, that laugh—that zany, out-of-kilter laugh. "Been to Mickey D's yet, Ned?"

All my clients were boring compared to Larry.

When I launched my literary agency in 1991 with a second mortgage on our home, my wife insisted that I not represent any projects that might embarrass her in her church, where she co-led a women's ministry called C-Squared. It had something to do with spiritual growth, but I never asked for details.

On this night, at half past ten, she lay in bed with Larry's first five chapters on her lap, two pillows behind her head, and a glass of ginger ale on the nightstand. Angie was a youthful forty-four—she would say the same of me—and I'll admit that she looked hot in her lavender nightgown. But tonight was a Thursday and, well, Thursdays were not one of her preordained nights. On Thursdays she read and fell asleep, mostly because she worked until eight at her office, editing articles for a Baptist journal and an online webzine.

An hour earlier I'd brought home Chinese takeout, and we'd

shared sweet 'n sour chicken over steamed rice. Mid-meal she'd asked why I sounded so enthusiastic about work.

I swallowed quickly and gushed, "My friend and client, Larry, has an interesting idea that I may pitch to some film people."

"May I read a few pages?"

She asked so nicely, even cleaned up after we'd finished our meal. This was unusual, as Thursdays were one of my nights for clean-up duty. I tried to stave off her curiosity. "Honey, it has a bit of a comic tone, and I know you prefer heart-tugging dramas."

It was the way she ran her fingernail across my back that convinced me to let her read. Well, that and the nightgown that she usually wore only on Tuesdays.

So I handed her forty pages and jumped into the shower. I was thinking that—if I may mock the ad world here—Thursday was the new Tuesday.

When I emerged from the steam of the bathroom in my red robe, Angie was slapping pages down on the bed in rapid succession. She picked up the title page and, without taking her eyes off the paper, said, "Ned, I'm not sure what Larry means by this title . . . and I'm about to start chapter three and have yet to find one redeeming quality. Not one."

"Um, I need to floss my teeth."

She was finishing that chapter when I came out of the bathroom with a mouthful of mint-flavored Listerine. I sloshed it for five more seconds, went back into the bathroom to spit and rinse, then stood in the doorway in my best are-you-ready-for-me pose. I even fluffed my chest hair.

I had been standing there for nearly a full minute when Angie glanced up from the page. "It's Thursday, Ned."

And she began chapter four.

4

THE PLAQUE ON HIS OFFICE DOOR READ: "In appreciation for fifteen years of leading us to the big time. The staff at Fence-Straddler AM Radio thanks DJ Ned Neutral for helping to bring America together."

Sporting his favorite yellow Hawaiian shirt, Ned sat down in his booth and checked the weather monitor. He saw that Hurricane Gretchen continued to track toward Tampa and Orlando, though she was still some three hundred miles out in the Gulf. He wondered how he would conduct his show without his producer, who had strangely left in the middle of Monday's broadcast. So had the station's secretary, a former rock 'n' roll groupie who wore lots of black. Ned passed their absences off as a summer virus, perhaps food poisoning. He'd tried to call them both but could only get answering machines.

Ten minutes before his show began, Ned made a pot of coffee—the first time he had made the coffee himself in months. He took his mug and two packets of Splenda into his broadcast booth and decided he would do his show without a producer. A veteran of the airwaves, he could handle this alone.

DJ Ned was truly neutral, having voted for Reagan, then Dukakis, then Bush Sr., then Clinton for a second term, then Dubya, then Kerry. A caller had suggested that Ned change his handle to DJ Ned Flip-Flop, but he had gotten used to Neutral.

When the clock struck 11:00 a.m., Ned was aghast to see that all five lights on his phone were dim. He sipped his coffee and wondered if he was in for a slow day. Then, just as he was tearing open his second packet of Splenda, three of the five lights lit at once.

Ned set his mug on his desk and pressed line 1. "Morning, caller. Welcome to Fence-Straddler AM."

"Ned, Bill."

"Bill, Ned."

"Hi, Ned."

"Hello, Bill."

"Ned, I'm a factual, to-the-point, meat 'n potatoes, formal-on-Sundays kind of guy."

"You don't say . . ."

"And I have the hurricane solution. . . . We nuke 'em."

"Nuke the hurricanes?"

"That's right. We all know there are nuclear warheads in underground silos all over the country. Rumors abound that seven of them are buried behind condos in Ft. Lauderdale, and we all know that God helps those who help themselves."

Ned paused. "Haven't heard either of those rumors, Bill."

"Well, back to my point. We nuke 'em. It's the only way."

"Just shoot a warhead right into the storm. . . ."

"That's right. God wants us to maximize the benefit of our technology."

"But what if the hurricane eats the warhead, just sucks it down below the eye-wall, and the missile explodes a mile under the sea instead of above the surface?"

A pause on the line. "Hadn't thought of that, Ned."

"We must consider all possibilities, Bill."

"Well, I have my official Prophetic Decoder calculator handy. Can you give me a sec?"

"Why not? It's just valuable airtime." Ned paused, then whistled the first line of the *Mission Impossible* theme song. "Got your calculations yet, Bill?"

"How wide is the eye? And what is the speed of the hurricane?"

"Let's say the eye is forty miles wide, and the winds are 160 miles per hour . . . a Category 5."

Ned could hear calculator buttons being pushed in rapid succession. "Just one more sec, Ned."

Ned tapped his fingers on his desk. "No rush at all, Bill. Shall I put on some background music, perhaps some Sinatra?"

"The missing variable is the temperature of the Atlantic."

"Of course."

"But I can estimate. Here, I almost have the prophetic calculation. If the warhead were to plunge beneath the surface before detonation occurred, and the eye was forty miles wide and the hurricane's maximum sustained winds were 160 miles per hour, then the result would be—"

"Bill?"

"Yes?"

"The result would be that the little tropical fishies would somersault all the way to the Mediterranean. Next caller . . . *please!*"

Ned pressed line 2. "Who's my second caller?"

"Ned, this is Estella, from Tampa. I just left a breakfast meeting of Presbyterians for a Safer Coastline."

DJ Ned frowned into his mic. "That would be, um . . . the PFSC?"

"That's right. And at our meeting we were discussing these awful hurricanes and how the richest and godliest country on earth should be able to find a solution. So we're forming a lobby group to encourage Boeing to manufacture huge fans, like giant propellers, to be built along the coast, from Tampa down to Miami and all the way up to St. Augustine. These fans, hundreds of them, could be turned on all at once to blow the hurricanes back out to sea."

Ned rubbed his beard, gripped his microphone. "You're kidding, right?"

"Not at all. And for aesthetic purposes, the fans could be painted in beachy colors, say a pastel peach, like the new line of cookware at Bed, Bath and the Eternal Beyond."

The Eternal Beyond? Ned rolled his eyes. "Estella?"

"Yes?"

"That is without doubt the dumbest idea I've heard in my fifteen years of hosting this program. No, wait, it ranks second only to Bill's."

"Regardless of your opinion, Ned, the PFSC must put pressure on Boeing."

"And how might you go about that, Estella?"

"We'll boycott."

"Who'll boycott? You and your cohorts?"

"The fortunate ones. Now, what about helping us lobby for those fans?"

Now in the early stages of panic, Ned wiped the sweat from his forehead and wondered just how sick his coworkers really were. He was good friends with his producer—they had boated together on many a sunny weekend—though he held no particular affection for his gothic-dressing secretary. Still, Ned knew that even she had loved ones. "*Fans*, Estella?"

A long pause was all Estella could manage at first. Then, "The PFSC must do all we can to protect Florida from nature."

"Sorry, but I think you're just plain looney." DJ Ned cut Estella off as a weather update scrolled across his monitor. He immediately thought of his listeners. "Listen up, folks. Hurricane Gretchen has made a turn eastward, which is bad news for us. Its forward motion is now twelve miles per hour, with maximum sustained winds at one-thirty. Yes, you heard right, one-hundred thirty mile-per-hour winds."

To Ned's dismay, zealot winds seemed even stronger than tropical winds, and his palms were now sweatier than his forehead. He grabbed a paper towel from his desk drawer and dabbed himself. Yet he could not dab fast enough, so persistent was his sweat.

Finally he tossed the soaked paper towel into his wastebasket, took a deep breath, and addressed his audience. "Crackhead, if you and your trailer-park buddies are still around and haven't been accosted by Estella and her minions, you should be making plans to evacuate the trailer park within forty-eight hours. That goes for anyone in low-lying areas."

While a commercial played, Ned stood at his desk and scratched his head. *I thought PFSC stood for Pink Floyd Song Connoisseur.*

Lanny sped down a hazy interstate toward Augusta, Georgia. The time was 5:50 p.m., and the windshield of his sage green Xterra was by now coated with smashed moths and unfortunate flies. Lanny had tried Miranda's cell phone and her sister's home number a dozen times each, all to no avail.

"Just stay calm," he muttered to himself. "No one has spotted you yet, and there is surely some explanation for all this."

He whipped off of the interstate at the next exit, made a left, and pulled into the neighborhood and then the driveway of Miranda's sister, Carla. Carla's red Toyota Camry sat in plain sight, and mail protruded from the metal mailbox on the front porch. He knocked but found no one home. He ran around back but found it vacant.

Like a movie trailer on fast forward, Lanny saw his day pass before his eyes—the BP station and the golden crosses, the billboard and the school, the strange greeting from Detour Airlines, the radio broadcasting his name. And now his girlfriend missing. Maybe even her sister as well.

He felt safest in his truck, so he climbed in and backed out of the driveway. *Which way? Where to now?*

His mind scrambled to make sense of it all. He did not remember merging back onto the interstate, but minutes later he found himself circling Augusta, going nowhere and avoiding human contact. He drove with his chin on the steering wheel, staring straight ahead, refusing to look at other vehicles or even glance at a billboard.

By 6:30 p.m., the temperature had not dropped a degree, and Lanny was on his third loop around Augusta. He drove in the slow lane, and soon he reached for his cell and hit speed dial for the thirty-fifth time.

Miranda still did not answer.

He tried his golf and poker buddies again.

0 for 5.

Lanny's nature was to avoid trouble, and he wondered if trouble was running ahead of him toward Florida, if whole legions of zealots sought his capture. Perhaps he should spend the night in his truck. He slowed his speed to fifty miles per hour and pulled down both sun visors. He refused to turn on his radio.

He kept circling Augusta, thinking of Miranda and their fourth date, when they had walked barefoot on a golf course at sunset, hand-in-hand and hinting about the future. Peaceful green fairways were where Lanny had always found solace, his space to think.

Perhaps he wasn't thinking clearly, or perhaps he was deep in romantic reflection, or perhaps he saw the opportunity to live out a lifelong dream, but when Lanny saw a green sign that read HOME OF THE MASTERS, he took exit 199 off the interstate and onto Washington Road.

Maybe if I explain my plight, they'll let me hide here. Plus, if Georgian zealots are pursuing me in order to claim some big reward, this will be the last place they'll look.

A second green sign directed him to turn south. Excited just to be near Augusta National, he drove another mile until the right side of the road took on the look of a manicured fortress—green, private, and pristine. In the distance a majestic driveway sat behind a white-washed guard house. Lanny sat idling in the road, ogling at the even more majestic clubhouse that sat at the end of Magnolia Lane.

You shouldn't, said a voice in Lanny's head. *You'll get arrested.*

This is your big chance, countered a second voice. *So go for it. Plus, Miranda knows you love golf, and she could be hiding nearby and waiting for you.*

Lanny eased his truck up beside the guard house, which had an electronic barrier bar to prevent tourists and non-members from entering the stately compound. Tucking his hair behind his ears and lowering his window, he prepared to speak to whoever was in charge.

But to his shock and delight, Lanny found no guard at the gate. And yet the door to the guard house was open, and from inside the door a red button beckoned from atop a control panel. Had the staff disappeared as well? Or were they too out searching for him, wanting to claim the reward—whatever it was—for themselves?

Don't do it, said the first voice. *You'll surely get arrested.*

Go ahead, said the second voice. *Get out of your truck and push the red button.*

Lanny flung open his door, scrambled out of his truck, and pushed the red button.

The barrier bar raised in front of him.

Magnolia Lane stretched for four hundred yards, a shaded tunnel beneath stout limbs and waxed green leaves. Lanny drove the length of it in seconds. His was the kind of nervous glee found in children who suddenly discover themselves in an amusement park without adult supervision—the possibilities seemed endless.

He parked and glanced left at the empty practice range, where perfectly groomed grass hosted perfectly stacked mounds of white golf balls. Lanny grew even more excited when he saw no one on the property. Not even a policeman or a wandering guard on duty.

He got out and shouted "Miranda!" in his loudest voice. Her name echoed through the pine trees, though no one answered.

Alone at Augusta National, Lanny decided he would spend the night here. And since there was still over an hour of daylight left, he quickly pulled his golf bag from the rear of his truck. He hurried around the clubhouse to the first hole, unzipping a pocket of his bag to pull out a tee and a ball. Then he shouted again, "Miraaaaaaanda!"

Only echoes.

That's when Lanny noticed that he had forgotten to put on his golf shoes. In his excitement he had rushed to the course in brown, steel-toed work boots.

He paused on the tee box and removed his work boots and socks, stuffing them into his golf bag. He loved the way the grass felt soft and spongy beneath his bare feet. And it made him think again of Miranda and their fourth date.

He would play the course for her.

After three practice swings and a stretch, he imagined this was a Sunday afternoon in April, where a mass of twenty-thousand spectators all waited for him to hit his first shot. He imagined Miranda watching, cheering him on from beneath a white visor, wavy auburn hair spilling over her shoulders.

His swing was strong and fluid; his contact, pure.

The ball flew long and straight and came to rest two-hundred-fifty yards away, on an upslope of gorgeous green grass.

Funny what denial does to a man. Lanny thrust his arms in the air in triumph. He bowed to the crowd. He tossed them a ball. He blew a kiss to Miranda. He then lost his mind completely and began imitating every celebratory sports gesture in the history of television. He gave 'em the uppercut. He gave 'em the funky chicken. He gave 'em the break dance and attempted a back flip. He even moonwalked across the grass in his bare feet.

Finally the denial subsided, and he hoisted his bag over his shoulder and walked past the wrought iron sign beside the tee box.

Then he smelled the fresh paint.

Then he *saw* the fresh paint.

Panic set in even before he read its lettering. The sign had read—just like the larger one on the interstate—HOME OF THE MASTERS.

But someone had replaced the first two words and marked out the second "s," so that the sign now read OWNED BY THE MASTER.

"Hey you!" someone shouted. "Stay right there!"

The voice came from the ninth hole, far to Lanny's left. He turned and saw three men in white jumpsuits running toward him. They looked to be competing with each other, pushing one another out of the way to be the first to get to Lanny. They were nearly a golf hole away, however, so he knew he had time to scram. Behind them he saw the cans of paint they had dropped in order to pursue him.

What is it with these zealots and their signage?

He ran—as close to running as a man can manage with a forty-pound golf bag on his back—to the parking lot. Pebbles hurt his bare feet, so he ran on his toes to his truck. He tossed his bag in the rear, hurried to the driver's seat, and cranked the engine.

Around the corner of the clubhouse came the three men in white jumpsuits, yelling at him, pushing past each other, and waving their arms. The tall one shouted, "Stop! You're my Big Reward!"

Lanny fled those hallowed grounds. With no Miranda in sight and no lifelong dream fulfilled, he screeched his tires and fled. He now fully realized his situation—the religiosity had swept deeper across Georgia. His immediate thought was his only thought. *Maybe I can outrun it to Florida.*

The sun was setting over Georgia now, and he figured the smart thing to do would be to withdraw the remaining cash from his bank account. Across Washington Road he spotted a Wachovia sign, and fortunately, his teller card still worked. He withdrew the last two-hundred-and-forty dollars, stuffed one-hundred-sixty of it into his wallet, the other eighty under his floor mat. Just in case. Then he saw his likeness posted on the teller window. The bank was closed, but the poster showed him in frontal pose and profile, and below that, what he'd look like with a goatee, with a shaved head, and as a blonde. All of this under the heading "Have You Seen This Man? He Is Your Ticket!"

Frightened and confused, Lanny left skidmarks in the drive-thru and turned west on I-20. An hour later he was back on I-75, by-passing Macon and driving determinedly for the Sunshine State.

Determination quickly faded to drowsiness, however, so he decided that when he reached Florida he would stop and get some rest—being on the run takes its toll.

Mile after mile, Lanny fought sleep in the right lane. His only defenses against slumber were to roll down his windows and to keep trying Miranda on his cell phone. But every time he dialed, he only got her answering service.

He gnawed his lip in frustration and drove into the night.

Lanny woke early the next morning in a rest area outside of Jennings, Florida, just over the Georgia border. The sun was coming up, and he walked inside to use the facilities.

A copy of the WANTED poster from the teller window hung from the men's room door. Ditto for the women's.

Head down to avoid being recognized, he washed his hands, splashed some cold water on his face, and looked in the mirror. He rubbed his stubble and considered a shave, then thought better of it and hurried back to his Xterra.

Three hours later he could see the baked sprawl of Orlando in front of him, where he noted traffic moving the opposite way in a steady stream, as if they, too, were fleeing from something.

Rumbling along in the fast lane, Lanny tuned his radio to a local talk show and listened for a weather update.

5

DJ NED NEUTRAL spent the night at Fence-Straddler AM—
he felt safest there—and had stocked the station's kitchen with
food and double-bolted the front door.

It was now 7:45 a.m., and the female DJ who normally hosted
the morning show had been missing for nearly a day. So Ned decided that, with Hurricane Gretchen on the way, he should man the
broadcast booth from 6:00 until noon and keep his listeners informed of the storm.

A plate of Krispy Kremes and a black coffee sat to the right of his
microphone. Ned swallowed half of the first donut and gripped his
mic. "It's still early, folks, but if Gretchen continues on her easterly
path, we can expect her to make landfall below Tampa sometime
Wednesday night, and hit us by Thursday morning. For all you time-
challenged people, that means less than two days. Do you grasp the
magnitude of this? Today is Tuesday, the storm could hit as soon as
Wednesday night, and Gretchen's winds are up to one-hundred-
thirty-five miles per hour."

Ned paused and considered if he too should evacuate. His over-
riding instinct, however, was to try to sniff out any other unfortunate ones. "Folks, since we were deluged by calls from the religious
right yesterday, I'd like to ask for some of you non-religious types to
call in and share what you're doing in preparation for this hurricane. I'll leave all five lines open for you."

Commercials played as Ned stared at the bank of five dim
lights.

Thirty seconds ticked off the clock. All remained dim.

A full minute. Nothing.

Two minutes, then three. Still nothing.

When the last of six commercials finished playing, not one of the five lights was lit.

Ned gripped his mic and did his best to save face. "Alrighty, during the break I spoke with three atheists, and all were boarding up their windows and planning to leave Florida by nightfall. I would play their replies for you, but we seem to have a small problem with the playback feature today."

Four call lights immediately lit.

Ned stared at the shining bank of lights, hesitated, and pressed line two. "Welcome to Fence-Straddler AM, caller. What's your name and where're ya from?"

"Ned, I'm a disciple of Marvin the Apostle. We'd like to invite you to an accountability group for chronic liars. In fact, I can come pick you up at your station."

Ned panicked and hung up on this nameless fanatic. Then he addressed his audience in a measured tone of voice. "Um, folks, seems we have a new update from the National Hurricane Center. I'll go get it off the printer. Meanwhile, I'm going to switch you to our sister station in Tampa. I'll return in a few minutes, so just sit back and enjoy this oldie from the Bee Gees."

Ned switched to the sister station, and across the airwaves came a high-pitched voice, singing the chorus from *Stayin' Alive.* "See the city breakin' and ev'rybody shakin' and WE ARE ALIVE, WE ARE ALIVE."

Ned stood over his printer and glanced back at his DJ booth. He tilted his head and blinked as if he hadn't heard correctly. But then the chorus repeated. "See the city breakin' and ev'rybody shakin' and WE ARE ALIVE, WE ARE ALIVE. Ah, ah, ah, ah, WE ARE ALIVE!"

DJ Ned rushed back into his broadcast booth and switched off the sister station. He spoke rapidly into his mic. "Sorry 'bout that audio mix-up, folks. I'm a bit shorthanded at work today. But never fear, I have the latest update from the National Hurricane Center. Gretchen is now at one-hundred-forty miles per hour, slightly faster than yesterday and with no change in direction. That, of course, is bad news for us."

The bank of red lights went dim again. And then, just as he was about to ask for callers, line 1 lit.

"Welcome to Fence-Straddler AM radio," Ned said, "What's your name and how are you preparing for this hurricane?"

"Um, what hurricane?" There was a scratchy quality to the call, as if the caller was on a bad cell phone connection. "I just arrived in Florida from Atlanta. Been driving since sunrise. You said you wanted to hear from non-religious callers, so I called."

"And your name, sir?"

"My name is Lanny. Lanny Hooch . . . from Atlanta."

Ned smiled at hearing Lanny's innocence. "You know nothing about Gretchen?"

"Nope," said Lanny, "I'm in my truck. I spent the night at a rest area and haven't listened to the news."

"You're not aware that there is a major hurricane heading for the coast of Florida?"

"Nope. I'm just trying to find my girlfriend and flee the zealots."

Ned paused, shocked to hear someone else use the term *zealot*. "Hey, caller, do you mind if I switch you to a private line?"

"Not at all."

Ned replayed the newfangled Bee Gees song for his listeners and picked up his private phone to speak with Lanny. "Hey, man, you know about the zealots?" DJ Ned sounded anxious, desperate even.

"Yesterday in Atlanta they took over the schools and the BP stations." Lanny veered back into the slow lane so he could talk. "And the McDonald's too. The radio station even announced that some guy named Marvin has a reward out for my capture."

"Aw, man . . . don't tell me that." Ned then began an inquiry that seemed simplistic on the surface and yet was loaded with consequences. "You say your name is Lanny?"

"That's right."

"Mind if I ask you a couple personal questions?"

"Go ahead."

"You cuss?"

"Sometimes. 'Specially when I hit my thumb with my hammer."

"Drink?"

"On weekends."

"Go to church?"

"Never. You?"

Ned frowned at this boomeranged question. "Do I go to *church*? No way. I hang out at the beach on Sundays or take a trip somewhere."

Lanny remained just as suspicious as DJ Ned. "How 'bout the other stuff. . . . You cuss?"

"Not while I'm on the air. Hurts my ratings."

"Drink?"

"On the golf course."

Lanny managed a slight smile as he drove. "You chase the white ball?"

"Every chance I get. You?"

"Stopped in and played Augusta National on my way here."

"Yeah, right."

"I'm not kidding, Ned."

Ned looked at his phone incredulously. "Don't play me, man. Augusta National has people arrested just for peeking over the fence."

"That's just it. . . . There was no one guarding the place. The zealots left it open and I drove right up to the clubhouse."

"Just drove right up and teed off, eh?" Ned laughed at Lanny's boldly concocted story.

"All by myself . . . Okay, just for one hole. Then the wackos chased me off."

Ned paused, ran a hand through his hair, tried to blink away his shock. "So you're saying the zealots have now claimed Augusta National?"

"Looks that way."

"What about Pebble Beach?"

"How would I know that, Ned? Pebble is in northern California."

"True." Ned thought about the proliferation of religious callers and the odd dearth of secular callers. In fact, he was certain that

Lanny was the only non-zealot he had spoken with in two days. And yet he was cautious even of him. "Are you sure you cuss?"

"I'm sure, Ned."

"Gimme some examples."

"Examples? But I'm not in the mood right now."

"Then just pretend. I need to know that you're not a zealot posing as a non-zealot."

Lanny veered into the slow lane. "You mean just cuss on demand?"

"Just let it fly."

A long pause. "This is harder than I thought."

"See, you're one of them. A poser."

Lanny stared at his cell phone in disbelief. Then he recalled how he had drilled a small hole in his foot with his power drill back in 2002 while repairing some seats at Philips Arena. He let fly. "%*%$# and @#$%#$."

"Okay," Ned conceded. "Not bad."

"So, do ya now believe I'm not a zealot?"

"Yeah, I guess. Wanna meet for a burger or something? I gotta talk to somebody normal."

"And I've got to find my girlfriend. But I'll be passing right by Orlando if you want to meet up and go with me to Cocoa Beach."

"But there's a hurricane coming—"

"I've got to find Miranda."

Ned hesitated to reply. He wondered if he'd made a mistake by inviting Lanny to meet. And yet Ned could sense that an odd new world had enveloped Orlando, a world of which he did not feel a part. He figured it best to grab any normal friend he could find.

"I'm off the air in an hour."

Ned gave Lanny directions to a convenience store just off Highway 528 some forty miles east of Orlando, and Lanny agreed to meet him there.

The sky was deep blue and traffic was headed the opposite way as Lanny sped down the interstate. He turned off his radio, and for miles remained lost in his thoughts. *What if this DJ Ned is really one*

*of them? What if I've been fooled again? But then, what if DJ Ned can
help me locate Miranda? But then again, what if . . .*

He noted mile marker 31, then something much larger than a
mile marker. Frontlit by orange rays, this billboard stood tall on the
right side of I-75.

How Does It Feel to Be One of the Last Five?

(I was just kidding back in Atlanta)

~God

Lanny hoped beyond hope that if the billboard were factual, Miranda was the second of the last five. He already knew he was the
first.

6

AT A QUIK-STOP off Highway 528, Ned parked his yellow Mercedes and lowered the car's convertible top. He got out slowly and frowned as he inhaled the humidity seeping from a nearby marsh.

Lanny sat waiting in his Xterra, five parking spots to the left. Upon spotting the yellow SL, he climbed out and walked across the oil-stained lot to introduce himself.

Not so fast, Lanny thought.

At first the two men looked warily at one another. They stopped some ten feet apart, heads cocked to the side. Each then spat on the ground like a tough guy. Then, after sizing each other up in front of the store's glass door, they shook hands like a pair of G.I.'s who've found each other behind enemy lines.

"Ned Wallace, host of Fence-Straddler AM. Friends call me DJ Ned."

Lanny shook back hard. "Lanny Hooch, owner of Hooch Contracting."

Both men noted the traffic fleeing from the coast, and both peeked inside the store window at an idle cashier boy. "There has got to be some explanation," Ned offered, pointing at the slow parade of vehicles. "And I'm not talking about the hurricane. Maybe the rest of the normal folks are held hostage somewhere."

"I've thought of that, too," said Lanny. "I can't reach anybody."

Ned rubbed his beard and glanced suspiciously at Lanny. He decided to test this new acquaintance. "Ya know, Lanny, in the Middle Ages the Christians did some really bad things to people."

Lanny could not mask his confusion. "Was it the Middle Ages or the Dark Ages?"

This return question served to ruin Ned's test and put him on the defensive. "Don't ask me hard details like that, man. I was a communications major."

"I never went to college," Lanny confessed. He motioned Ned toward his Xterra. "You ready to roll? I need to get to Cocoa Beach and look for Miranda."

Ned shook his head and stepped toward the Quik-Stop's door. "After we get some refreshments. Let's think through this clearly and hope that our loved ones are somewhere safe."

Lanny followed behind and asked, "Do you even *have* loved ones? I mean you haven't mentioned—"

Ned cut him off with a single wave of his hand. "I have a best friend in the U.K., plus a few weekend party buddies here in Orlando—who are now missing. I got divorced twelve years ago. No kids. No siblings. Parents passed away."

And that was that.

Inside the store, they avoided eye contact with the cashier and moved quickly to the glassed refrigerators. Ned selected the last six-pack of Coors Light while Lanny grabbed two bags of barbeque-flavored Lays and some peanut butter crackers. The men toted their items to the counter, set them next to the register, and reached for their wallets.

Cashier Boy frowned at their selection. "Um, sir, I'm not supposed to sell you that." He pointed to the Coors Light. "The store owner is keeping that six-pack on display as a kind of souvenir."

DJ Ned put his hands on his hips and glared at the cashier boy. "Souvenir? One little six-pack is a souvenir?"

"Sir, it's from back before the—" Suddenly the cashier's eyes grew wide. He glanced behind him at a photocopy tacked to the wall. Two black-and-white photos adorned the paper. "You're . . . you're the two guys I heard about on the news."

"News?" asked Lanny, fighting his fears by playing innocent. He and DJ Ned immediately recognized their likenesses in the black-and-white photos, as if both men had made a Most Wanted list. "What news?"

"Yes," the clerk said, sizing up his customers. "You're, um, both in today's paper, too." He pointed to a stack of *USA Today*. The headline had nothing to do with war or politics or natural disasters. Today's headline, just like the traffic report on the radio, was of a more personal nature:

Reward Offered!
Marvin the Apostle is offering the Big Reward, a seat on his purple velvet sofa (you'll sit in eternity next to Marvin!) to anyone who captures and converts these two remaining rebels: Georgia native Lanny Hooch, and Florida native Ned Wallace, otherwise known as DJ Ned. **Hurry! Three-day time limit!!**

Below those words were pictures of Lanny and Ned, two shots each, frontal and profile. Pale and shaking, Lanny backed slowly away from the counter. Hot and fuming, Ned flipped the paper over to see what other news could agitate his day. He skimmed the latest rumors of his and Lanny's whereabouts, then noted a sidebar below the fold:

Religious Lotto:
Five lucky numbers will win tapes and DVDs of Marvin the Apostle's inspiring lecture, "Housing Assignments in the Everafter." Grand drawing this Sunday at noon!!

Still behind the cash register, the clerk backed against the wall, as if unsure what he should do. DJ Ned dropped a twenty on the counter and nudged Lanny toward the door.

"Who is this Marvin schmuck?" Ned muttered to himself. "I'll punch him in the nose."

"Get in line," Lanny said.

They had just pushed open the doors to leave when the cashier shouted, "Sir, your change—"

"Keep it," Ned muttered. He did not see the cashier pull two pairs of handcuffs from under the counter.

"Well then," the cashier shouted, "how 'bout accepting some free literature?" He held the handcuffs behind his back and came around the newspaper stand.

Ned was already out the door. Without turning around he shook his head no. The clerk followed.

At the car, Lanny glanced back and saw a flash of chrome cuffs. The cashier let the glass door slam shut behind him and strode toward them.

"Ned!" Lanny shouted. "Look out."

Ned had just opened his trunk to put the six-pack into his cooler. He reached in and brandished a tire iron, holding it high overhead.

"Just keep your distance, Zealot Boy."

The cashier paused near the hood before stepping back to the store's entrance, dangling the handcuffs in his right hand. "Someone *will* catch you two, ya know. You can't run far." He raised his empty left hand and flashed them a blue plastic wristband with WWMD on it.

"What is that?" Ned asked, still holding the tire iron.

"What Would Marvin Do," the cashier replied. He attached the handcuffs to his belt buckle and ran back inside the store and picked up the phone.

Ned insisted on driving, so he and Lanny sped away in the Mercedes, fearing they'd be followed.

"We leave the South *tonight*," Ned insisted, "maybe even the country."

Lanny kept watch behind them. "But . . . but I've got to find Miranda. She's the only thing that I really value."

"You saw that headline. They'll all be after us now."

For several miles both men remained silent, minds turning, grasping for answers. Finally certain that they weren't being followed, Lanny turned to face the front and said, "How can that Marvin guy know that there's a purple velvet sofa in the front row of heaven? I'm not even sure there *is* a heaven."

Ned chewed on the question for a moment. "Beats me. Maybe it's one of those prophecy things."

In forty minutes they'd driven past downtown Cocoa, then over a bridge and a marsh and to the entrance of Pelican's Harbor Retirement Homes. At the fifth house on the left—which looked exactly like all the other houses on the left—Lanny spotted Miranda's parents' car, a beige Buick. On the small front porch sat a black leather travel bag.

Lanny jumped out, hurried past the Buick, and ran to the front door. Ned remained standing beside his vehicle, unsure of how to help.

A note was taped above the doorknob of the house. It was written on a sheet of computer paper, and Lanny immediately recognized Miranda's handwriting. He pulled the paper from the door and, before reading the note, tried to turn the knob. Locked.

Monday, 8/17
Mom and Dad,

It's now 10:15. Didn't you remember that you were driving me to the airport at 10:30? When I came back from my jog I was thinking you'd be here. Also, Lanny has been trying to call me on my cell, but somehow all I get are the messages, not the actual call. Lanny is such a joker. He said that a BP station in Atlanta is charging non-Christians $6.66 per gallon for gas. Imagine that!

I've tried to call your cell but all I get is beeps. Same for Lanny's.

I can still make my 11:45 flight if we hurry. In case you return here and I'm not around, I'll be out looking for you down at the marina. That's the only place I figure you could be. Surely you didn't take off again for the Bahamas!

If I don't find you, I'll probably call a cab. Oh, Lanny left a second message that he would be willing to drive here to get me. With gas so high, I wish he would reconsider. But that is so sweet.

I'll find you two shortly.
Love,
M

When he finished the note, Lanny could barely think. He pounded on the door but got no answer. He peered in the windows but saw no lights. He opened the black leather travel bag, saw some clothes that looked like Miranda's, but nothing else. Finally he wrote on the back of Miranda's note:

8/18 2:35 p.m.
Gone to the marina to look for you.
Lanny

He taped the note back to the door, ran over to Ned's Mercedes, and climbed in.

"Head to Bluewater Marina," he said, anxious to get going.

"No sign of her?" Ned asked and backed out of the driveway.

"Just hurry, man."

My wife tried to burn Larry's manuscript.

On Friday morning I came downstairs to make toast and orange juice—and found Angie kneeling in front of our fireplace. Keep in mind that this was August, in Atlanta, and the woman had lit gas logs.

Our relationship had endured moments like this in the past. She had burned a copy of Larry's *Aliens Invade Billy Graham Crusade* manuscript the previous fall. Well, truth be told, I had offered her the matches for that one.

The previous fall, however, our finances were good. I had just sold several projects and put six months of living expenses in the bank. Now here we were, ten months later, depleting our savings to pay our mortgage and the college tuition for our son, Zach, a sophomore at Auburn.

Not today, Angie dear.

I crept up behind her and plucked the first three chapters from her hand just as she was about to insert them into the flames. Oddly, I found the whole thing comical—my wife kneeling on Berber carpet in her gym shorts and Braves T-shirt, about to torch Larry's work because it offended her.

"You know there are several copies of that, honey," I said, folding the papers and stuffing them in my bathrobe pocket. "Two have already been sent out to L.A."

Angie remained kneeling, facing the flames and nodding her head. "I know," she said softly. "But I'm worried about you, Ned."

I stood behind her with outstretched palms. "Don't you understand, honey? I can't sit around and hope that some famous screenwriter will just knock on the door and want me to go sell his stuff and earn a big advance from which I'll get fifteen percent. I have to pound the pavement and sell something."

She reached out and turned off the gas logs. "I could support us."

I knelt beside her and tried to explain my motivation. "Angie, your editing work brought in nine-thousand dollars last year. Six the year before that. If I don't sell something soon we'll have to live under an I-85 bridge with what's his name."

"Victor?"

"The guy we gave our chicken wings to after the Braves game."

"His name is Victor. Me and two other ladies from my women's group take him meals."

"Well, we'd be Victor's neighbor, complete with his 'n her cardboard bedrooms."

"Are you saying you want me to get a full-time job?"

My fragile male ego took her offer as an insult. "No, of course not. You want to balance part-time work and volunteering at the church, and you should stay with it." I tried to change the subject. "Ya know, I was just thinking that you and I haven't slow-danced in the kitchen in a long while."

Great timing, Ned.

Angie sat back and folded her arms around her knees. "What I'd really like is to talk to Larry in person about his story."

I stood and forced myself not to overreact. "But you were about to set flame to it."

"Oh, Ned, I knew you had other copies. You always have other copies. I just didn't want this in my house. Can you imagine what our friends at church will think if you agent this? If you attach our good name to 'believers kidnap pagans'? Not to mention my co-workers at the journal."

I glanced at my watch and tucked the papers under my arm. "Honey, um, I have to meet a client in a bit, and you know how traffic is. . . . I'd better scoot."

I leaned down and kissed her cheek—which was all she offered.

My meeting was actually a day's worth of phone calls. I just said what I did on instinct, to bow out gracefully and avoid argument. Truth was, not only had I sent two copies to L.A., I'd received an inquiry from a studio exec. Perhaps this would amount to nothing; he certainly was nowhere near the point of discussing numbers. In my business, "numbers" were all that mattered. When someone said they were going to send numbers, it meant that an offer was forthcoming, that their initial interest in a project was about to be, well, *monetized.*

In our bedroom I exchanged my bathrobe for a white buttondown, an orange Tennessee tie, and pleated khakis—my usual summer garb.

I left the house in a hurry and backed my Saab into the street. At the first stoplight I caught myself thinking like an amateur agent. My mind would not stop sifting through possible deal amounts. Five figures? Did I dare dream of *six?* Then I began calculating fifteen percent of various sums and comparing them to our debt.

Debt be gone?

Possibilities swarmed in my head, and I hardly remembered pulling into the second deck of the parking garage. It was there, while my car idled and the AC blew, that I called Larry.

He didn't even answer with a greeting. "The shoes fit now, Ned. Turns out I had swollen feet, due to all my pacing in the park, wondering about my future and hoping you were going to sell this thing."

I reclined my seat and said, "Things look . . . interesting."

"Whaddaya mean, 'interesting'?" He sounded like he was eating.

"What are ya munching on, Larry?"

"Bagels . . . from Atwanta Bwead Company."

"Plain, right?" Larry was even more anti-butter than he was anti-prude.

"Wight. Now what about 'interesting'?"

"I mean there's a possibility of interested parties."

A short pause. "You're serious?"

"Well, it's still very early."

"Ned, I really hope this works out. For both of us. And I hope I spelled all the words correctly. You know what a perfectionist I am."

What I said next was only to temper his enthusiasm. "Angie tried to burn your manuscript this morning. She doesn't think our Baptist roots jive with the content of your story."

Larry sighed into the phone. "I wish people would cut me some slack. This story may not be what she thinks."

"I'll give you slack. It's Angie I'm worried about." I glanced down at my tie and smoothed out a wrinkle. "Your story has got my wife in a tizzy, plus . . . I need to ask you a couple of questions."

This time the pause was longer, as if he was now leery of me. "Sure, go ahead."

"Are you still seated?"

"Yeah, why? You coming over to join me for breakfast? I eat alone way too often, ya know."

"No, I'm just getting to my office. But I need you to be honest and answer something."

"Um . . . I guess that would be okay."

"I need to ask you if you have recently been inside an evangelical church, and do you have any close friendships with people who are members of one?"

He sighed again. "Nope, haven't been. No real friends there, either. Just you, the gregarious Ned Neutral."

"And yet you're trying to write the next big thing for them?"

"For whom?"

"People of faith, Larry. Isn't that who you're writing for?"

"Well . . . other folks, as well. It's for everybody, Ned. Everybody who can appreciate good storytelling."

"But it's twilight zone, Larry. Your first six chapters are all twilight zone. And now . . . now our hero is on his way to a marina to search for Miranda?"

Larry paused again, and this time he seemed uncomfortable. "The shrink I've been seeing says the next chapters are some of my best, that I reached deep for these, all the way back to the Sunday school brainwashing, which I'm not going to discuss with you today."

"C'mon, Larry. I'm your friend. Just one anecdote . . . please?"

A long pause. "She made me stand in front of the class and hold an eraser in my teeth . . . for three consecutive Sundays. I was six years old and coughing up chalk dust."

I knew that Larry was receiving some sort of therapy for some sort of past misfortunes. But that was the extent of my knowledge. Our relationship was agent/client, and we both did a fine job of avoiding personal issues. Except, of course, for his dating shenanigans.

Not sure how to respond, I remained in my Saab and turned the AC on high. "So, what about the real Miranda? Have you seen her again?"

"Our second date begins in less than an hour."

"And I suppose you're going to take her to a golf course to walk barefoot on lush fairways at sunset?"

"Nope. We're touring the city on MARTA."

"Your second date is on public bus routes?"

"I have to see how she'll fit in with Atlanta's diversity. That stuff's important to me, ya know."

I shook my head and wondered if other agents had clients like this. "And Miranda actually agreed to go on this so-called date with you?"

"She's crazy 'bout me, Nedster. I can tell." He spoke quickly, like he wanted to end our call.

I got out of my car, locked the door, and walked across the second level of the parking deck, phone to my ear. "One last thing. Does Miranda know yet that she's the love interest in your story?"

Larry allowed this pause to linger before he whispered into the receiver. "Not a clue."

At the elevator I ended the call. Two minutes later I stepped out onto the 22nd floor and was met by gold chains, gold watch, and turbo cologne—all accessories to his pinstriped suit. Rocco-the-commercial-real-estate-salesman worked, and perhaps *lived,* across the hall from my office. We shared an administrative assistant, though he and I rarely visited.

But today he was right there, grinning with his hand extended. "How are ya, Nedster?"

"Good, Rocco. And you?"

Rocco was born to sell high-priced cars to stupid people. But somehow he had worked his way up to selling high-priced shopping centers to smart people. Or so he claimed.

His handshake was even stronger than his cologne, his teeth whiter than bleached rice. "Ned, I hear ya got something hotter than beach property. Something a good Catholic like myself might find entertaining?"

I moved past him, smiling. I pulled my office key from my pocket and unlocked my door.

"Yeah, Rock, you'd like the irreverent parts."

He was third into my office, right behind his cologne. "So, Ned-ster, mind if I take a look-see? I don't cut my next deal till 1:00. Got a little theatre sale up your way, in Buckhead. But I got some reading time now if you don't mind. . . ."

Each time we visited, Rocco would tell me what he was about to sell. Who knew if the deals ever got done? Who knew if Rocco could even *read?*

I decided to test that premise. Behind my desk, I pulled a copy of Larry's first six chapters and handed the stack to white-toothed, deal-cutting Rocco. "These pages don't leave the building, Rock. Got it? I want these back by the time you leave today."

He clutched them to his chest like a kid with a doll. "Guard it with my life, Nedster. Say, you want some coffee? I'm buyin' today."

"The coffee on our floor is free, Rocco."

"Still, I'll deliver. Black, right?"

"With one sugar. Thanks."

An hour later Rocco returned with a black coffee, four sugars, and three creams. He set them on my desk and stood there grinning. "Please, Ned, this had me giggling in the break room. I got twenty more minutes before I have to drive to Buckhead. Can I please read a little more?"

I dumped a pair of sugars in my coffee, nodded okay, and watched happy, grinning Rocco ease out of my office with chapter seven.

OYSTER SHELLS CRACKED and popped under the tires of DJ Ned's Mercedes. On the drive toward the coast Ned and Lanny had bonded like two survivors, determined to battle a common enemy. Lanny had shared his work debacles, the Atlanta traffic report, and how he feared for Miranda's life; Ned had recounted the strange new music, his lack of callers, and the renaming of Devil's food cake. Now Lanny gazed through the windshield at the moored vessels of Bluewater Marina, hoping that Miranda was near. He sniffed salt air, heard gulls caw overhead.

"See her car?" Ned asked. He cut the engine and unlatched his seatbelt.

Lanny said nothing.

Ned waited all of four seconds. "Well," Ned asked, "do ya see it?"

Lanny climbed out of the convertible, stood near the hood, and scanned the parking lot. He turned slowly, searching every spot. Finally, he stopped squinting and shook his head.

"She flew down, so she'd have driven her parents' Explorer. But I don't see an Explorer anywhere." Lanny strode toward the marina and motioned for Ned to follow. "C'mon, let's search the docks."

Ned tended to pamper his possessions, especially his car, so he secured the convertible top before hurrying across the oyster shells in his sneakers. He came up behind Lanny. "My neighbor kept a boat here once," he offered, not sure what to say but glad to be in the company of a fellow non-zealot.

They walked out onto the docks and turned left toward a row of impressive charter boats and pleasure craft. Lanny's equilibrium tottered when he approached the first four vessels and noted their names: the *I'm So Worthy,* the *I'm So Worthy 2,* followed by the *Formal on Sundays,* and the *Formal on Sundays 2.*

From the available evidence, a complete maritime conversion had taken place.

"Seein' a pattern here?" asked DJ Ned, trailing behind and making no effort to hide his sarcasm. "Ain't no more *Nina, Pinta,* or *Santa Maria.*"

"That's enough, Ned," Lanny said over his shoulder.

Ned would not shut up. A psychologist had once told him that he was one of those people who relied on empty chatter and humor to cope with stressful situations. "Looks to me like the zealots beat us to the marina. In fact, it looks like the zealots now *own* the marina. By now, they probably own the entire planet."

Ned struggled to keep up with Lanny, who surprised him by stopping and staring at the empty fifth slip. Below him were just docile waters and barnacled posts.

"What's the matter?" Ned inquired. "You were expecting an agnostic boat?"

Lanny stared out to sea and saw nothing but gentle whitecaps under a blue sky. "Slip number five was where Miranda's parents kept their charter."

"What was its name?" Ned inquired.

"They named it for their first child," Lanny said, on his toes and peering out to sea. "The boat is called *The Miranda.*"

Ned looked behind him at the boats they'd just passed. He glanced ahead at the sixth slip and noted its name. "Ya think the boat you're looking for in slip five was renamed the *Sanitized?*"

Lanny shrugged. He had no clue about this lingo. "How did you come up with that?"

Ned lacked confidence in his suggestion, but it was all he had. "I was just thinking, given that there's a boat called *Sanitized 2* in slip number six, and considering the pattern for slips one through four, then slip number five must be—"

"Hush, Ned."

DJ Ned was an optimist at heart. He'd been flirting with denial and was just now realizing the magnitude of the situation. His world suddenly felt smaller, pea-sized. Now, as he scanned the boats again, he even began to shake a bit.

A seagull swooped past, and Ned wondered if the bird might be only seconds away from turning into a dove. He watched it soar out over the ocean, and he was relieved, ecstatic even, to see that it remained a gull.

Lanny left Ned to birdwatch on the dock and jogged toward the marina office. "Be right back," he called over his shoulder.

Murals of palm trees and ocean adorned the outer walls of the building, but Lanny ran past them without a glance. He opened the front door and went inside.

Two minutes later he came running back down the dock, only to find Ned leaned over the stern of the *I'm So Worthy 2,* touching its name.

"Paint's still tacky on this one," Ned proclaimed, rubbing his fingers together like a detective checking blood.

Lanny stood panting from his run, hands on hips. "I got scared, didn't even talk to the manager. But a register listed the boat in slip number five as having left this morning. It wasn't in Miranda's handwriting."

Ned wiped his fingers on his shorts, glanced at the office. "You think she's on board?"

Lanny could not take his eyes off the empty fifth slip. "I think the manager could be a zealot. So Miranda and her parents probably fled when they found out what was happening. Mr. and Mrs. Timms own a time-share in Abaco. Plus, the hurricane is coming from the Gulf of Mexico, so Mr. Timms would have known the Atlantic was safe to navigate." Lanny stood on his toes and peered out to sea. "I have to get to Abaco. But get this, Ned—a sign on the counter said no one can charter a boat unless management checks your 'cleanliness status' on some Web site."

Ned glanced at the pocket of his shorts, where he'd just wiped the paint off his fingers, and realized that he wasn't very clean either. Then he peered past Lanny and saw the marina manager at the far end, holding a *USA Today*, talking excitedly into a cell phone, and pointing at Lanny and himself. In the distance a siren wailed.

"We gotta leave the mainland," Ned whispered to his new friend. "They're on to us."

Lanny turned and saw the manager staring at them and talking into his cell. When the manager ducked inside his office, Lanny and DJ Ned walked briskly off the dock and sprinted for the parking lot.

Ned again struggled to keep up with his leaner friend.

"Lanny, I wasn't gonna tell you this, but I have—" Ned was hesitant to finish his thought, caught as he was between fear, generosity, and gasps for breath.

"Have *what?*" Lanny demanded. "Spit it out, man."

"I have my pilot's license."

Lanny slowed to allow Ned to catch up. "No kiddin'?"

"No kiddin' . . . and a small plane, too."

Lanny's shock was exceeded only by his pleading. He stopped and grabbed DJ Ned by the shoulders. "I'll pay you, Ned. Anything you ask. Just name it."

Ned paused on the oyster shells, uncomfortable yet very aware of what was transpiring. Winded, he spoke between breaths. "You don't have to pay me, man. . . . I wanna get outta here, too. . . . Maybe the lunacy is limited to the continental U.S."

Lanny had no time to chew on such a premise. "Possibly. So, you'll fly us to Abaco?"

Ned considered the hurricane coming from the west, the zealots overrunning both Florida and his talk show, and now the growing sound of sirens. "Yeah . . . I'll fly us there. But do you even know where to look?"

Lanny cocked his head to the side as if a glimmer of hope had ridden in on Ned's offer. "I know that her parents' beach bungalow is near a lagoon on the east side of the island. Miranda wanted me to visit it this fall." Lanny jerked open the Mercedes' passenger door. "How far is the airport?"

Ned was still breathing heavily as he yanked his keys from his pocket. "My plane . . . It's in Melbourne . . . just ten minutes from here."

They were on the tarmac in eight.

DJ Ned's plane was a six-passenger Baron, and he revved its twin engines and waited for the runway to clear. Through his radio he made his first attempt at being a poser—he told Air Traffic Control he was flying a Reverend Hoocher to the Caribbean for revival services. Air Traffic Control spoke into Ned's headset, offering to play some special music for him and the Reverend before granting permission to take off.

Ned declined.

Strapped into the copilot seat, Lanny tried to imagine Abaco on a normal day, Miranda and her parents docking their boat, perhaps having a drink on the deck. He would not allow himself to think anything but positive thoughts, and he felt proud to have a girlfriend smart enough to flee zealots.

Ned felt proud of his plane, more proud of his ability to fly it, and prouder still of its sparkling clean interior. While they sat idling on the runway, he informed Lanny that no carbonated drinks were allowed in the front seats.

Lanny set his plastic bottle of Dr. Pepper in back and sat up straight. Confident that he could now fool zealots, Ned turned the Baron onto a long straightaway and checked his gauges. Lanny watched limber weeds swaying alongside the tarmac and wondered if he was doing the right thing. He fought his fear of flying by focusing on his desire to find Miranda.

"I hardly know you, Ned. You a good pilot?"

Ned adjusted his headset and grinned at his passenger. "Relax, man. Don't you know where the best place to be is when the zealots take over America?"

"Where?"

Ned pressed the throttle and shouted over the engine noise. "The Bahamas, mon."

Ned appeared to know what he was doing, and suddenly they were rolling very fast.

Lanny watched the weeds whiz by, then the airport terminal.

The Baron took off and soared over a thicket of palms. Ned banked right and motioned for Lanny to look down out his window.

Along the coastal highway a crew was installing a new billboard for a fast-food chain, one quite famous for its chicken.

KFP: We Do Pagans Right

Lanny's jaw dropped. "Ned! . . . They're wanting to fry us extra-crispy."

Ned shook his head. "Wrong, Lann-o. They don't wanna *cook* us. They wanna get us into their store so they can *capture* us."

Lanny peered down at blue waters for a long while. "Nah, I think they really wanna cook us."

BY THE TIME NED and Lanny arrived at the entrance to Abaco Marina, neither had spoken another word. They were as quiet and cautious as marines patrolling a Vietnamese delta.

Before leaving the sidewalk to descend the stairs to the docks, Lanny stepped up on a bench and borrowed Ned's binoculars. He scanned first for Miranda, second for *The Miranda.*

"I see a billboard advertising Red Stripe beer," he whispered "That means—"

"Means we're safe," Ned replied, stepping aside on the sidewalk to let two bicyclists pass. "But what about the boat you wanted to find?"

"Can't tell." Lanny jumped down from the bench and they hurried down the steps to the entrance.

A kind of calm overcame both men as they walked. Both knew this was largely due to location—the island breezes, no sign of zealots.

Still, Ned held to a measure of caution. Though he noted the sun stroking the palms, the clear aqua waters, and even a few teeming schools of fish, he kept turning and peering over his shoulder at any passerby, especially the ones coming and going from Abaco's sun-drenched marina.

This marina was circular and modest, holding maybe forty boats, total. Both Ned and Lanny felt relieved to see that the first two they passed—a white yacht and a pale blue sailboat—were dubbed *Sea Princess* and *Come Sail Away,* respectively.

"Free at last," Ned muttered to himself.

Lanny slung the binoculars over his shoulder. "There's no biblical character named *Sea Princess,* is there?"

Ned admired the yacht and said absentmindedly, "Nah, I'm pretty sure there's not."

Lanny walked ahead on the circular dock. "Guess we're safe, then."

Ned was still admiring the yacht when a small, caramel-colored hand reached out and tapped him on the arm. The boy appeared to be no more than twelve. He wore an Abaco Marina Staff T-shirt, and he smiled up at Ned.

"I wash your boat, mister. I'm dock boy. My job."

Ned took a step back and shook his head. "Um, son, I don't own this boat. But I do own an airplane."

The kid was not impressed with Ned's aeronautic possessions; he just wanted to earn a tip.

Lanny hurried back to speak to the boy. "Do you know this marina well?"

Dock Boy stood proud and smiled. "Yes, very well."

"Have you seen a charter called *The Miranda?*"

Dock Boy shook his head. "No. We have a famous fishing boat called *The Matador,* but no *Miranda.*"

Lanny pressed further. "What about a charter called the *Sanitized?*"

Dock Boy looked confused. "The *Sani what?*"

"The *Sanitized.* We think it could have been commandeered by religious freaks."

"Ahh," said the dock boy, cocking his head and pointing at the visitors. "You two are preachers, and you come to the islands to preach commandments."

"No, no, no," Ned replied with waves of his hands. "We are not preachers. We're not even religious."

Dock Boy nodded. "That's what many on island say."

Lanny grew impatient, and he moved in front of Ned in order to address Dock Boy. "So, are any zealots here on the island?"

"Zeelots?"

"You know—people wildly religious, offering rewards for capturing non-religious folks, and changing the names of boats to suit their agenda."

Dock Boy shook his head. "Ahh, no, no. Island as always. . . . Fishermen, tourists, sunbathers, and the flashy boaters like you." He held out his hand and grinned. "You have nice tip for dock boy?"

"I told you we don't own a boat," Ned said. But he peeled a ten from his wallet and handed it to the youngster. "You'll keep an eye out for *The Miranda?*"

"Yes, yes." The boy pointed south to the white sands. "You go enjoy beach and fruity drink."

Lanny also gave the youngster a ten. "And you'll keep an eye out for a thin, auburn-haired woman named Miranda?"

"Yes, yes. You enjoy fruity drink as well."

Lanny and Ned walked the rest of the circled dock back to the steps. He and Ned were already back on the sidewalk, striding in the shade of the palms, when Dock Boy yelled from the bow of a sailboat. "If you like movies, my cousin Manuel just opens Tiki Theatre. Just up street. Shows Americano classic every night."

Ned waved over his shoulder to dismiss him. "Okay, kid. Sure."

According to the maid Lanny spoke with in the Abaco rental office, no one had used the Timms's beach bungalow since early July. Undeterred, Lanny led Ned on a search of the shopping district—Lanny asking questions and showing pictures of Miranda, Ned listening closely to every music lyric that sounded from storefront or boombox. No one knew anything; the islanders seemed shy with all responses.

In front of a beachware store Ned caught up to Lanny and tugged on his shirt. "Aren't island people usually more friendly? Except for Dock Boy, everyone acts suspicious of us."

Lanny dismissed the theory. "It's just because *we're* suspicious. That makes everyone suspicious in return. It's a vicious cycle."

By 7:00 p.m. both men were exhausted from walking and decided their best course was to blend in and get something to eat. Ned could blend with the best of them, and in no time he'd convinced Lanny to join him in purchasing Bermuda shorts from a street vendor.

Lanny went for dark blue shorts, Ned for lemon yellow. They

changed in a public restroom and wore their wares to the local eatery next door.

After a dinner of grouper and boiled shrimp they walked out into the street at dusk, where Lanny stopped in mid-stride, eyes darting. *Not again!* Across the street, in the window of the post office, hung a WANTED poster—the same one they'd seen in the convenience store east of Orlando.

Both men ducked behind palm trees, scanning the street for bad guys.

Finally Ned whispered, "It's only one poster, Lann-o. No one suspects us yet. Just wear your sunglasses and follow me." Ned strode up the street as if he knew what he was doing.

Lanny walked briskly beside him, tugging his shades low on his nose to see in the twilight. "I say we leave the island."

"No, I say we duck into someplace dark, somewhere public. This is no time to panic."

Three minutes later they arrived late at Manuel's Tiki Theatre. In the vacant lobby—which was crafted of bamboo poles and affixed with posters of classic movies—Ned checked to see which film was featured. The Tiki Theatre had only one screen, and on the door hung a small chalkboard:

> Tonight our movie is the 1997 Academy
> Award Winner, TITANIC.
> Refreshments are BYOC (bring your own coconut).
> Bring whatever, except for blenders.
> Show starts at 6:45
> Donation: $5.00

Lanny checked his watch—8:17 p.m. "Maybe we shouldn't," he said to Ned. "It's too risky, plus the show will be halfway over at least."

"But it's BYOC, not BYOP," Ned countered. He motioned toward the entrance with his head, and Lanny reluctantly followed. Both men stuffed a five into the donation box, and Ned pulled open the door to the theatre.

It was small, as island theatres go. Most of the sixty seats were taken, but Ned and Lanny found two together in the third row. They settled in, and slouched a bit as the scent of coconut and strawberries filled their nostrils.

The two men looked up at the screen to see Jack at the rail of the *Titanic,* watching solemnly as Rose was lowered away in a lifeboat.

Lanny heard sniffles from the row behind him. He leaned over to Ned and whispered, "You've seen this before?"

"Twice," Ned whispered back. "You?"

"Four times. Miranda owns the DVD."

Sniffles grew louder in the Tiki Theatre as the great ship began to sink. Rose had scrambled out of the lifeboat to rejoin Jack, and now the two were together again on the teetering vessel, struggling past fellow passengers and sprinting for the railing. Soon the stern of the *Titanic* hung in the air. Jack and Rose clung desperately to the railing. The great ship foundered and went under, and in seconds the young lovers were flailing in the frigid Atlantic. Their only chance was to stay afloat in the ocean and hope someone found them.

Ned blinked back a tear as the tragedy unfolded—Rose lay on the chunk of wood as Jack clung freezing to its side. Soon Jack was frozen stiff. But as Rose was about to utter her famous line, "I'll never let go, Jack. I'll never let go," her words instead came out, "I'll never use a swear word, Jack. I'll never use a swear word."

No one else in the theatre even blinked at the edit. It was as if they all expected Rose to speak those very lines.

But not Ned and Lanny. Even before the lifeboat found Rose, and well before the ten-foot tall WANTED photos of Ned and Lanny appeared on the screen, both men crouched low in the aisle, bolted out of the theatre, and ran fear-struck into a balmy Bahama night.

Jack sank anyway.

9

T HE REALITY WAS INESCAPABLE—the zealots had come to the islands. With great stealth they had come. And so Ned and Lanny hid. With worry in their heads and sand in their underwear they hid within a cluster of palm trees and peeked out from behind the dunes on Abaco Beach. Both were afraid to go near the airport, and both wanted to get a hurricane damage report for Florida, although this too was a mystery, due mainly to lack of a radio and dead cell phones.

For sustenance, the two men had taken fruit and bottled juices and a cooler from the beach—while the owners were playing in the surf. They'd also taken two beach towels on which to nap. In an effort at a fair exchange, Ned had left a twenty under a sea shell.

"Any more fruit?" asked Lanny. It was late morning, and he kept lookout from behind a mound of white sand.

Behind him Ned opened the cooler and had a look. Sunlight shown down through the treetops and over his shoulder. "One more orange."

Lanny caught the orange Ned tossed him, then picked at its skin with fingernails too short for the task.

Already the beach was transformed. Already a zealot parasailing company—*We Fly You Closer*—had a line of people waiting to parasail from the surf. And already a drink stand was serving a concoction called a Pre-Glory Pizzazz.

"Probably just a glorified Slurpee," Lanny muttered from behind sea oats.

"And without rum," Ned whispered.

A lively, no-spiking-allowed beach volleyball game brought even more confusion—shirts identified the two teams as Dunkers versus Sprinklers.

"Those names mean anything to you, Ned?"

"Probably just their donut preferences."

Sprawled on his stomach and peering through Ned's binoculars, Lanny pressed his elbows into the sand and tried to pin blame anywhere but on his own inability to solve problems.

"Ned," he muttered, scanning the shoreline, "this island is the only place I know where Miranda and her parents would bring their boat. I think Dock Boy lied to us. He's really one of *them*."

Ned lay back on his stolen beach towel and stared up through the palm fronds. "The kid sure fooled me."

Lanny focused in on Dock Boy and watched the kid hurry around the circular dock. Lanny saw the youngster accept a tip and point three arriving boaters toward the beach and fruity drinks. "This is just like *Invasion of the Body Snatchers.* You never know until it's too late."

Ned briefly wondered if his buddy was right. He glanced at his own hands to see if any changes were sneaking up on him. After two minutes of staring at his fingers, and noticing no alteration in his skin tone or his mental health, Ned dismissed the idea. "Patience, Lann-o. We'll sneak back to the airport before sunset and head back to Florida. Then maybe we can disguise ourselves."

Tired of watching the marina, Lanny lay back on his towel and beat his fists into the sand. "I will not relax until I find Miranda."

DJ Ned opened their cooler and took the last banana. He had no comment.

"Why me?" Lanny asked the palm fronds. His voice broke into a fervent pleading. "Why would I be left? What good is a simple contractor to a world full of zealots?"

The emotion alone led Ned to respond. He peeled his banana and said, "I've been asking myself a similar question, but in your case they probably need your skills to change out a few million signs and billboards back in Atlanta."

"Don't joke, Ned," Lanny shot back, wiping a sleeve across his eyes. "They'll take over your radio station, as well."

This thought caused Ned to squeeze a bruise into his fruit. "Never."

"It could happen."

Ned remained defiant. "Then that's why you were left—to help me barricade the doors to my station."

This time Lanny had no comment; frustration had his tongue tied.

Through a gap in the dunes Ned watched the retreating tide cover the beach in creamy foam. He briefly considered the order of nature and the disorder of man but found the contrast overwhelming. "We both need to clear our heads so that we can think clearly," he said at last.

Lanny would have none of that. "My head hasn't been clear since I ate those McScriptures. Who knows, they probably put some sorta drug in the potatoes."

"Paranoia is bad for you," Ned replied. Though his warning sounded like wisdom, it was really just a poor attempt to hide his own worries. He finished his banana and considered the eastward thrust of the religiosity. "My best friend lives in London. So maybe we should try to get to . . . Hey, do ya think the zealots have taken over Europe by now?"

"I don't want to talk about it."

Ned tossed the peel over his shoulder and gazed eastward across the sea. "Think of it. . . . Empty pubs in Ireland, British zealots on the BBC, no kissing at the Eiffel Tower."

"Please stop. I do not want to talk about it."

"Then what *do* you want to talk about?"

Lanny scooped up a handful of sand and let the grains sift through his fingers. Again and again he sifted. "Think that hurricane made landfall yet?"

Ned stood and peered past the volleyball game at the ocean. "Probably. Unless the PFSC got those giant fans installed and blew the hurricane back toward the Yucatan."

Lanny beat his fists into the sand again. Though he knew Ned was only trying to cheer him up, his mind was too focused to be affected by humor. He folded his left arm across his eyes and recalled the past New Year's Eve, when he and Miranda had danced the night away to James Brown music. This reflection only served to make him miss her even more. He thought back to the revelry of that night, the slow dances, the fast dances. He recalled how Miranda had taken off her shoes for the fast ones and danced barefoot. He could even remember what songs were playing. . . .

Soon concern overcame nostalgia, and Lanny grew restless. He grabbed the binoculars again. Peering over the dune at the marina, he spotted a cruise ship approaching. *More zealots,* he figured, *perhaps a thousand of them. Seeking me . . . the Big stinkin' Reward.*

He handed the binoculars to Ned, who looked for only a few seconds before muttering, "We gotta get off this island. There's not enough real estate for us to stay hidden."

Lanny could watch no longer. He rose from his beach towel and brushed off his shorts. "C'mon, Ned. I have an idea."

"Where are you going now?"

"To disguise myself and find some Internet access."

Ned had no time to object; his buddy was already loping inland. He brushed the sand from his shorts and followed Lanny over the dunes and away from the ocean. They entered a bamboo forest and emerged on the shoulder of a two-lane road. Sporting their Bermuda shorts and sunglasses, they walked along the shoulder, looking just like two tourists out exploring.

Minutes later they entered town. They walked cautiously past the entrance to the Tiki Theatre and the beachware store, where they spotted two more posters of themselves. One block later they detoured around a street preacher shouting something unintelligible through a bullhorn.

Seconds later Lanny entered a tiny Internet café called Islandnet. Ned followed him inside, his pulse racing.

Unsure if the proprietor was a zealot, Lanny tossed three ones on the counter and offered his best poser greeting. "Religious howdy, religious howdy," he said, turning for the computers. "We just need a few minutes of Web time."

The startled clerk stared curiously at the duo for a moment before shrugging and placing the money in his cash drawer.

All six computers were set against the front window, a situation that only served to increase Lanny's stress. He sat down at the last of the six computers, logged on to the Internet, and went straight to the Google homepage.

Ned eased up behind Lanny's chair and peered over his shoulder. "Just what are you trying to find out?"

"Gimme a sec, Ned. I'm googling Miranda first, then us."

"I don't wanna be googled."

The name Miranda Timms came up blank. *No matches.*

Into the Google search bar Lanny typed, "Lanny Hooch, Atlanta, Georgia."

There was only one match: *One of the few remaining unfortunate ones left on the planet. Believed to have recently fled the coast of Florida for an island in the Bahamas.*

A stream of red words then ran across the screen: THOU SHALT NOT RESIST US! WE SHALL SUBDUE THEE ONE WAY OR ANOTHER.

Wide-eyed, Lanny pushed away from the computer and turned to Ned. Both men were ashen. They ducked as a pedestrian strolled by on the sidewalk.

"Let's head for the plane," said Lanny. "Right now. C'mon."

He scrambled from his chair and tried to flee but Ned caught him by the arm. "Not just yet."

Ned sat down at the computer, placed the cursor back on the search bar, and typed "DJ Ned Neutral, Orlando, Florida."

Again, Google offered only one match: *One of the few remaining unfortunate ones left on the planet. Believed to have recently fled the coast of Florida for an island in the Bahamas.*

Again the words streamed across. Ned tried to click on the "close" button, but that only increased the font. THOU SHALT NOT RESIST US!

That's when the clerk rose from behind the counter and said,

"Could you two gentlemen stick around a few minutes? I know someone who would, um, like to speak with you."

Small and thin, the clerk was no match for either Lanny or Ned. Lanny figured the guy had called for backup.

Ned nudged Lanny toward the door, his eyes on the clerk, who remained frozen behind the counter.

"Religious g'bye, religious g'bye," Lanny said with a wave.

Both men sprinted—pudgy Ned's gait was more like a jog—down the sidewalk and out of the shopping district and onto the road that led to the airport. This road curved past the Abaco Marina, however, and neither man noticed Dock Boy sitting on the sundeck with a dozen teenagers. The kid saw the duo running down the road and shouted, "Saw you in Tiki Theatre! I ran projector! You like my edits?!"

Ned wanted to go toss the kid in the drink, but Lanny insisted they keep running.

Out on the tarmac, twin propellers spun into a frenzy. Ned tested the Baron's flaps, adjusted his headset, and prepared for takeoff.

A sweaty Lanny tightened his seatbelt, anxious to leave Abaco and hoping Miranda was not on the island. *Was she captured? Forced to recite propaganda? Physically abused?* When his mind cleared he looked out over the wing and spotted their pursuers. Wide-eyed, Lanny pointed past Ned toward the terminal.

Ned glanced to his left and saw an official airport vehicle coming at them, lights flashing.

"Just go!" Lanny urged.

Ned shook in his seat. *What now? I could lose my license.* "Lanny, there are laws that we pilots have to obey and—"

Lanny grabbed his arm and put his hand on the throttle. "Those are now *zealot* laws, man. Just go!"

Ned glanced at the vehicle and the flashing lights, now only a hundred yards away and closing fast. He pressed the throttle and turned onto the runway.

Engines hummed. The cockpit vibrated. The car gave chase.

Ned didn't even ask for permission to take off.

Down the tarmac he went.

Faster. More throttle. Yes, we're pulling away. Now lift!

The plane climbed swiftly above the palm trees, then above Abaco itself. The loud hum of the twin engines drowned out Lanny's nervous chatter, and he exhaled as Ned banked over the coastline. Straight ahead in the distant west, the sun was an orange wafer, sinking on the horizon.

They were only a few miles out of Abaco, still climbing over blue water, when Lanny pulled Ned's headset from his right ear. Lanny leaned close to his pilot and shouted, "Is there any way you can circle back over the island and sky-write 'Lanny looking for Miranda' in big puffy letters?"

Ned pulled his headset back over his ear and checked his altitude. "Don't be ridiculous."

They didn't see me but I saw them. On a Midtown Atlanta sidewalk—Larry and a younger woman.

They walked side by side, not holding hands but nevertheless very together, each tuned to the other and striding with purpose, as if they were either late for a lunch reservation or out walking for their health. Complementing strides, you might say. I used to walk like that with Angie.

On this hot clear Thursday, the young woman with the long auburn hair wore a beige skirt just above her knees, and it swayed as she strode and it swayed when she paused and it swayed when she pointed skyward. Something had caught her eye, and Larry stopped beside her and gazed skyward too, as over-interested as any guy trying to impress a girl.

I was seated across the street at a meat 'n three, a diner that was the antithesis of hip cafés and coffeehouses, yet had become a gathering spot for artsy types, simply because the food was good. Baked chicken instead of fried. Tenderloin instead of meatloaf. Nine vegetables from which to choose, and mason jars filled with exquisite sweet tea.

Across the booth from me sat a client. Alec was a mystery writer whose mysteries weren't mysterious enough. At least not for me to be able to sell one. Though I wanted to end our meeting quickly, I tried to offer appropriate consolation as we discussed the rejections from the seven publishers to whom I had submitted his work.

"Perhaps it needs just one more thorough rewrite," I explained. "But keep working. My wife thinks you have talent." Angie, for reasons unknown to me, believed the guy was gifted.

Alec left frustrated and downcast, as so many wannabe authors are apt to do, and my parting words were of little consolation. Honesty was my strong suit. No way could I support my family by selling non-mysterious mysteries.

Alone in the booth now, I craned my neck to see Larry and the young woman in front of an office tower, both in date mode, both peering over the edge of a bricked fountain while trying to avoid the spray. One could not help but wonder how Larry managed the social life he did—if she was indeed his Miranda, he must have talked a good game.

I failed to see how a guy could take a girl riding on MARTA for a second date and then manage to arrange a third. But there he went, beside her in his pinstripe slacks and loud pink shirt, the two of them striding like an A-list couple en route to a Broadway premiere.

We had no appointment for today, but I did have Larry's cell number. And with Angie giving me the cold shoulder over my representing Larry's work, I needed to convince myself that I was doing the right thing. With no hesitation at all I dialed Larry's number and looked out the window. He stopped at the corner of 10th and Juniper, and took the woman by the hand. This time her skirt swayed more violently as she tried to tug him across the intersection. But Larry remained planted on the curb and pressed his phone to his ear.

"Larry?"

"That you, Ned?"

"Yeah. I got some news. You sitting down?"

"No, Ned. I'm with, you know . . . the girl." Larry turned and looked at the sign above the intersection. "We're, lemme see, we're at the corner of 10th and Juniper, on our way to dance lessons."

"Waltz or Samba?"

"Swing dance. It's the greatest. I get to wear 1940s gangster garb. Pinstripe slacks and my pink shirt. You should see me."

"Yeah," I said, peering at him from behind a napkin holder, "wish I could see you."

The young woman tried a gentler tug, but Larry remained planted, as if walking and talking were too difficult for him. "So, why ya calling? Hollywood sending numbers? Is that it? I'll cancel swing if I need to."

"No, don't cancel your dance lessons. I just heard from a studio guy in L.A. And while he hasn't committed to anything yet, he hinted at my coming out there to talk."

"No kiddin'?"

"No kidding." I watched him pump his fist in the air, then reach out and hug the young woman. I decided now was a good time to press Larry for answers. "So, Larry, when do I get to meet this girl? You told me she was a brunette and was kinda slender. Sounds like she'd look good in beige."

A short pause. Larry turned in a circle. "Ned, you're freaking me out here. She's wearing a beige skirt."

I leaned into the diner's window to get a better view of them. "Will ya tell me her name?"

"You already know her name."

I ducked back behind the napkin holder. "Have you told her yet that she's the love interest in your—"

"Ned?"

"What?"

"Don't mention that when I put her on the line."

"Why would you put her on the line?"

"She wants to ask you something."

I paused and slid down in the booth, afraid of being spotted. "What could she possibly—"

"Just talk to her, Ned."

"All right, put her on."

Traffic hummed in the phone as I peered over the window sill and watched Larry hand her his cell. Then a female voice came on the line. "Is this Agent Orange?"

"Hi, Miranda. This is Ned, er, Agent Orange."

"Pleased to meet you. Larry has told me about how the two heroes are running from some mean people, but he won't tell me if there's a romance in his story. So . . . is there some kind of romance?"

"I'm still reading it myself, but it looks like there is a male character who cares deeply about a female character."

"Yes!" she exclaimed. "Then I'm sure I'll like the movie. Will you need any extras during filming? I took an acting class once—"

"Actually, there's no deal yet. And hiring extras is not my job. My job is to sell the rights to the production company and its producers."

"Oh." A silent confusion took over. "Well, I hope you sell it. Do you swing dance, Agent Orange?"

"Nope. I used to slow dance in the kitchen with my wife, but that's stopped for now due to—"

"That's so sweet. Here's Larry again." Traffic noise whined in the phone. Then Larry's baritone voice. "Talk to me, boss."

"I won't know anything else for a few days, Larry, but I gotta ask you something."

"Ask away, Ned. Just hurry. Our dance lessons start in three minutes and we don't wanna be late."

"How did you come up with a volleyball game with Dunkers versus Sprinklers?"

"I googled it."

"Thought so."

"Call me when you have numbers. I gotta go jitterbug now; then I meet with my therapist again tonight. He's bringing out some heavy stuff, Ned."

And just as I was about to ask for more details that I had no right to know, Larry hung up.

I remained in the booth and rejected six more manuscripts. When I looked up from the last one, I noticed that the lunch crowd had dwindled to just me and my waiter, a strapping youngster who could not have been over twenty-one. He came over with a dish towel in one hand and a fresh mason jar of sweet tea in the other, which I accepted with a thumbs up.

"You a professor?" he asked, noticing the papers stacked as high as the salt and pepper shakers.

"Literary agent. Those are manuscripts."

He nodded and wiped off the other side of my booth, casting interested glances at the papers as he wiped. "Any of 'em a good read?"

I drank from my mason jar and nodded in the affirmative. "One has potential."

The kid kept staring at the papers and wiping invisible crumbs. "Oh, yeah?"

"Yeah. The one in the blue folder." I pushed the folder toward him.

The kid wiped the same spot three more times. "Yeah?"

I figured a youthful opinion could be valuable. "You like to read?"

"Yeah. Plus I'm a theatre major at Georgia College."

He smelled of dish detergent and sweat, just like I did when I waited tables at Pizza Hut in Duluth in '82. Perhaps it was this reminiscence, this flashback to Angie walking into that Pizza Hut on a slow Tuesday night, and my refilling her glass after every sip just so I could talk to her, that summoned my pushiness. Or perhaps I was just feeling insecure. Truth was, I craved some younger feedback. Plus I had calls to make, so I handed him Larry's first nine chapters. "Enjoy yourself, kid."

"You really don't mind? You're my last table and—"

"Enjoy yourself."

He hurried over to the bar and began reading. I sat there computing fifteen percent of various sums, going against my usual professionalism and letting my imagination once again run ahead of reality. Then I thought of the relational variables that could accompany a deal—or no deal, if I allowed Baptist ethics to stunt the opportunity.

I thought of four possibilities:

Good money but unhappy wife.

Good money but no wife.

Content wife but no money.

Wife living with me in a cardboard box under I-85, next to Victor, who eats all our chicken wings.

Thirty minutes later the kid was back beside me. "This is pretty wacked, man," he said, handing me the stack of paper and shaking his head. "But it's interesting."

"In some circles it's also controversial. So much so that my wife is upset with me."

"Too bad." He stood there awkwardly for a moment before flipping the dish towel over his shoulder. He went back behind the bar about the time I left my sixth phone message of the day on Angie's cell phone.

Alone in the booth with my conscience, I was convinced that whenever Angie and I next spoke, I would persuade her to see things my way.

Out of nowhere my young waiter returned, this time in street clothes. And this time he leaned down to within a foot of me and lowered his voice. "Sir, do ya mind if I read some more? I start school next week, so I won't be serving you in here again."

I handed the kid chapters ten and eleven, and he went and sat at the bar to read.

D J NED SAW LAND over the propellors. The coastline appeared washed and rinsed, though neither man could see enough detail to determine whether Hurricane Gretchen had air-kissed Cocoa Beach, or pummeled it.

In a steady descent toward the Florida coast, Ned grabbed his radio and morphed into a poser. "Request permission to land with Reverend Hoocher from the Caribbean. He's exhausted from pursuing those two rebels and leading all-night revivals."

An awkward pause lingered from Air Traffic Control. "Um, okay. Permission granted. But tell the Reverend that he owes Marvin half of any monies collected from passing the plate."

Lanny pulled out his wallet, thumbed the four twenties inside, and shook his head no. *Not this week, Marvin.*

Ned parked his plane at the far end of the airport. In the nearly empty Melbourne terminal he and Lanny ran past three more WANTED posters of themselves, dodging two flight attendants in the process and hurrying out to Ned's Mercedes.

"That one attendant stared at us like we're some kind of exhibit," Lanny said as he strapped on his seatbelt.

"That's because we're not great posers yet," Ned replied. "Maybe we should smile more . . . or shave our heads."

He dropped his keys as he tried to insert one into the ignition. His next attempt was successful, and he started the car and drove them along the coastal highway, swerving around debris and downed limbs.

Lanny lowered his window and allowed the wind to buffet his face. "I'd like to revisit the marina in Cocoa Beach," he said to his driver. "I have a feeling that Miranda is close by, looking for me."

Ned raised his voice above the engine noise. "I have a feeling that there is a giant purgatory with three billion people in line to use the restrooms. And your Miranda is one of them, and so are my golf buddies."

"Please?"

Ned thought about this request for the next mile. "You're not afraid of getting captured?"

Lanny shut his eyes and stuck his head out the window like a dog craving relief. "I am no longer afraid of anyone!" he shouted to the wind.

Ned wondered if his friend was losing his mind, but he agreed to his request. Five minutes later Ned parked among the oyster shells at Bluewater Marina. Both he and Lanny opened their doors and sniffed foul air. The receding waters had left a stench upon the coast—a mix of diesel fuel and tidal marsh.

Lanny got out, shut his door, and hurried across the parking lot to the edge of the marsh. What he saw from ground level was much worse than from the air.

As if all vessels had tried to crowd into the same spot at once, eight boats—including both versions of the *I'm So Worthy*—had pulled from their slips and plowed nose-to-nose into one another. Smoke eased from the engine compartment of the *Formal on Sundays*.

The main dock was still standing, but just barely. Twisted in some sections and folded like an accordion in others, it proved a challenge to negotiate. Lanny stepped carefully from board to board, and he winced each time one groaned louder than expected. Ahead of him, with no such worries, a crab crawled up between the boards.

"Checkin' out the damage, eh?" Lanny said to the critter. "Or are you missing someone, too?" He watched it for a moment before nudging it into the water with his shoe.

Lanny continued on toward the boats, board by board. When he reached the point on the dock where he could see the first dozen slips, he was stunned to see a boat docked in the fifth.

The Miranda! he thought to himself.

Lanny recognized its shape and took off running. "Ned!" he yelled over his shoulder. "Ned, hurry up. I see the boat."

DJ Ned was only a few feet onto the dock, still negotiating the most heavily damaged section. His extra weight proved a strain for the support posts, and the resulting ripples sloshed against the *Humbleness,* whose deck was covered in seaweed and driftwood.

Onto solid dock now, Ned jogged, *clomp clomp* in his size-twelve Adidas, down to where Lanny stood pointing at the rear of a three-level cabin cruiser.

The *Saniti* sat undamaged in the fifth slip, right next to the *Sanitized 2.*

Ned pulled up beside Lanny and stared at the name—*Saniti,* as if whoever was changing the moniker got interrupted by the storm and had no time to paint the *z, e,* and *d.* Or had someone stolen the boat before some zealot could finish the alteration? Or—and Lanny savored this thought—had Miranda recently docked the boat herself? Perhaps this very afternoon.

"I'm going aboard," said Lanny, talking to no one in particular. He stepped down onto the boat without inviting Ned.

"I'll, um . . . I'll just wait right here," Ned replied.

Lanny stood on the deck of the *Saniti* and turned slowly, observing details, searching for clues. After a full minute of tight-lipped deliberation, he pointed to the *Sanitized 2* in the next slip.

"See that, Ned?"

Ned turned and looked. "All the seaweed hanging off the side?"

Lanny turned and pointed the other way. "Now look at the *Humbleness.*"

Ned turned and stared. "She's covered in seaweed, too."

"Exactly. But this boat I'm standing on has no seaweed. Which means—"

"It wasn't docked here for the hurricane. It just arrived also."

Lanny descended into the cabin. He searched the stateroom, noting the familiar nautical pillows that Miranda's mother had cross-stitched with blue anchors. He checked the tiny bathroom and saw a bottle of Pantene—Miranda's favorite shampoo. He looked in the closet and saw nothing but a couple of T-shirts belonging to her father. No note anywhere. No sign of anyone. Yet the cabin had been left unlocked, as if whoever docked the boat had departed in a hurry.

Lanny emerged from the cabin and frowned into the sunset. The sky was clear in the way skies are on the day after a hurricane, as if Gretchen had sucked all the impurities from the air as she barreled north into Georgia and the Carolinas. Lanny's shoulders slumped in disappointment. "Nothing. No sign of her."

Ned was a silhouette above him. "I'm really sorry, man. But look what I found."

Lanny squinted up at Ned, who stood perspiring above him on the dock, holding a dead gull by the wings. "Nice bird, Ned."

"While you were below deck I found it on board the *Choir Girl.*" Ned held the wings wide so that the gull's head flopped to the side. "Think this is some kind of symbol—a dead bird on the *Choir Girl?*"

"It symbolizes that you should wash your hands before dinner."

After tossing the gull into the water, Ned pulled at his sweat-soaked shirt and noted with a frown how many feathers clung to its side. "Any clean shirts in there?" he asked, pointing at the cabin door.

Lanny ducked back into the cabin. In seconds he emerged back on deck and flung a balled T-shirt at Ned. "Put that on."

Ned pulled off his wet polo and slipped on the gray T-shirt, screen-printed with Pelican's Harbor Retirement Home's 2005 Shuffleboard Champion.

"It's a bit tight," Ned complained.

Lanny paid him no attention. He climbed back onto the dock and motioned for Ned to follow him. "Seen anyone lurking?"

Ned hurried to catch up. "This whole marina is empty except for us."

"That's just plain weird."

"We didn't see a soul on the road from the airport, and no one here either. You'd think we'd have seen *somebody.*"

Lanny glanced left and right as he walked toward land. "Think all the zealots evacuated?"

"Air Traffic Control didn't," Ned replied. "That guy was one-hundred percent zealot. A purebred. Well, a gullible purebred."

They left the dock and walked across the oyster shells to Ned's car. Lanny paused at the front wheel and ran a finger over a small crack in the windshield. "Good luck getting insurance to cover this."

Ned climbed back into his yellow convertible, nodding as if he'd noticed the crack earlier. "If it comes down to a choice between hurricane damage or religious damage, I'll risk the hurricane every time."

"Same here." Lanny opened the passenger door and sat on a CD casing, which snapped under his butt. He tossed it into the backseat without apology. "Make sure you drive with extreme caution. Zealots could appear anywhere, anytime."

Ned stuck his key in the ignition. "I know a way we can hide. We can go to my station."

"The radio station? But they'll have already staked out the place."

The Mercedes engine roared to life. "I'll announce that I'm doing my talk show from Jacksonville. I've broadcast from there many times."

Skeptical of this plan, Lanny didn't even offer a nod. *The world comes to an end, and I get paired with Mr. Optimist.*

Along the coastal highway, the blacktop was covered in sand and limbs. To the sides of the road sat beach houses in various states of destruction. Roofs missing. Windows blown out. A fishing boat impaled in someone's living room. And the shingles . . . Roof shingles lay everywhere, mixed with palm fronds, Mother Nature's tossed salad.

At Lanny's insistence, Ned drove him back to Pelican's Harbor Retirement Homes. They found only the beige Buick in the driveway, the black leather travel bag blown across the porch, wet and tipped onto its side. Frustrated, Lanny placed the bag back at the doorstep and left a new note for Miranda.

8/20 7:50 p.m.
Just back from the marina to look for you. Will resume search
in earnest tomorrow.
Lanny

Then he went over to the Buick and stuck a shiny penny in the tread of the passenger-side back tire. When he returned here again, he wanted to know if the car had moved.

Ned and Lanny drove swiftly on Highway 520, heading for Orlando. It was now 8:00 p.m., and the road was empty for the next several miles.

"Don't forget about my truck," Lanny said as a reminder.

At the next exit, Ned pulled into the convenience store to let Lanny pick up his Xterra. They both feared being spotted by hidden cameras, and each left skidmarks in his departure.

Lanny followed Ned out onto Highway 528, and proved himself a worthy tailgater. Soon he saw headlights in the distance, a long stream of headlights from a long stream of vehicles, headed right for them.

"There they are," Lanny said to himself. He honked to Ned and pointed. "I knew it. A whole platoon of 'em. Back to kidnap us and reclaim Florida for themselves."

Ned veered off the highway, squealing tires as he sped up the next exit ramp, Lanny right on his bumper.

THE FIRST THING that DJ Ned and Lanny saw upon arriving at Fence-Straddler AM was a handmade sign on the door:

No one found. Fled premises.

At first this produced in them great alarm, but they figured the smart move was to leave the sign for all to see—and to barricade themselves inside the station. To accomplish this feat, Lanny employed his construction skills and his Craftsman cordless drill. With great efficiency he installed two-inch wood screws through plywood and into the door frames. Then he crisscrossed two-by-fours behind the plywood and affixed them with even longer screws. Three inchers. Even a few fours. *Ah, safer now.*

Above him on the second floor, Ned simply locked the windows. He was not much for manual labor.

Secured inside, the men had food, drink, and access to the airwaves. They had been away from the mainland for three days, however, and had no idea what had occurred in the States since that balmy Bahama night when Rose promised Frozen Jack she'd never use a swear word.

The next morning Ned came out of the shower room wearing a Fence-Straddler AM T-shirt and blue jeans. Barefoot but clean, he stepped inside the broadcast booth and began pressing buttons and testing the sound equipment. "Ever been on the air, Lann-o?" he asked.

Lanny sat against the wall, a turkey-on-wheat in one hand and an IBC root beer in the other. "Nah, never had the chance."

Ned lifted his mic high over the Plexiglass to where Lanny could see it. "Wanna appeal to the country—or what *remains* of the country—about Miranda?"

Lanny let out a carbonation burp and said, "Absolutely." He knew he'd sound emotional in his pleas.

First, however, he had to sit through Ned's opening monologue.

Ned sat in his DJ chair and gripped his mic. "Mornin' to the fruited plain. I hesitate to use '*Good* morning,' just out of deference to all my friends along the central East Coast area. The aftermath of Gretchen is anything but good, and residents are just now beginning to filter back in from the evacuation. Most will have weeks of rebuilding work ahead. I'm DJ Ned Neutral, your eyes and ears for the aftermath, broadcasting from my secret booth here in Jacksonville."

Ned pressed a button to begin a commercial. Then he summoned Lanny to the booth. "Lann-o, can you do voices?" Ned spoke quickly and watched the clock. He had less than two minutes before he was back on the air.

Lanny stood in the doorway, gripping the frame. "I thought you were going to let me plead for information on Miranda's whereabouts—"

"You can. But first I need you to pose as two non-religious callers."

"Aw, man, I'm not sure if—"

"Just try."

"What kinds of voices?"

"Slices of Americana. You go get on the phone at the producer's desk, and I'll hold up a sign for which voice to use."

Lanny grew more hesitant. "I dunno, man."

Ned grew persuasive. "C'mon! First voice can be your own. We need to fool the zealots into thinking more of us are left."

Lanny slowly began to cave. "I just dunno if I can do voices that aren't southern or—"

"Hurry, I'm back on the air in fifteen seconds."

Lanny scrambled out of the broadcast booth and over to the producer's desk just as Ned picked up the phone.

Ned adjusted his headset and watched the seconds tick off. Three . . . two . . . one.

"Ladies and gentleman, I realize that the bulk of my audience is nowhere near the Florida coast, and so you must rely on me, DJ Ned, to fill in the blanks. I have two callers on hold, waiting to share their bird's-eye view of the destruction. Is the first caller there?"

Ned pointed to Lanny and mouthed "talk."

Lanny held the phone to his lips. "Um, yeah, Ned, this is Danny, and I was just down at Pelican Retirement Homes and the place is a mess. Roofs torn off, cars smashed, limbs everywhere. Saw a bunch of churches destroyed too, though I don't go to church myself."

Ned put his thumb and forefinger together and gave Lanny the okay signal. "Ladies and gentleman, that was Danny from Orlando, who is one of our non-religious listeners."

Ned stood in his broadcast booth and held up a note card to Lanny. The word *Boston* was scribbled on the card.

"We have on the line another victim of Hurricane Gretchen, this one a gentleman from Boston. He lost his boat in the storm. Are you there, sir?"

"Yes, mah name is Lawrence Hoochinski and this morning after I pahked mah cah at the marina, I saw that my sailboat, the *Drink, Smoke, Cuss,* had lost its mast in the storm. It was half sunk in the marina. I'm just distraught over the scope of this storm damage."

"And what are your immediate plans, Mr. Hoochinski?"

"What else? . . . I'll probably drink, smoke, cuss, and watch a Red Sox game. Got to relieve the pain somehow, Ned."

Ned gave an even more enthusiastic okay signal to Lanny before addressing the audience a third time. "Ladies and gentleman, good people like Boston Lawrence have taken huge losses, and we should keep them in our thoughts and in our, um . . . *thoughts.*"

Ned gave two thumbs up to Lanny before gripping the mic and resuming his ploy. "Ladies and gentleman, we've just heard from two callers who sustained losses from Hurricane Gretchen. I'm here in Jacksonville and am going to open up the lines now." Ned winced as he said this. "And I hope to hear from some compassionate folks who are willing to help, not from any more wackos who think they know how to turn hurricanes back out to sea."

All five lines lit up instantly. Ned hesitated, his finger hovering above line 1. At the last second he reconsidered and pushed line 4. "Welcome, caller! Who are ya and where are ya from?"

"Neutral, this is Estella, from Tampa, and I resent you calling me wacko. Those giant fans should be—"

Ned cut off the call and stared through the Plexiglass at Lanny, who could only shrug.

"What now?" mouthed Ned.

Lanny entered the booth and stood beside Ned. "I think it's time for my plea."

Ned rose from his broadcast chair and motioned for Lanny to sit. "Just don't expect much."

Lanny was nervous about talking to the nation, but DJ Ned promised to stay there beside him, a two-hundred-forty-pound pacifier. Ned pulled the mic to Lanny's lips.

Lanny took a deep breath and began.

"Hello, America. My name is Lanny Hooch, and I am searching for my girlfriend, Miranda Timms." All five lights went dim. "She was possibly last seen near the Bluewater Marina in Cocoa Beach. Her parents live at Pelican's Harbor Retirement Homes, where she was visiting from August fifteenth through the seventeenth. Miranda is twenty-nine and has long auburn hair and a slender build. She works as a news editor in Atlanta and was supposed to have caught a, um, Detour flight home this past Monday at 11:45."

Every call light remained dim.

Ned tried his best to help Lanny. He had once been in love himself, and now he pleaded with his audience. "Listeners, please. Surely someone knows something about Miranda Timms."

No responses.

"Then does anyone know anything about two golf pals of mine, Jonathan Duval and Josh Mickels? Or a DJ Lex in London? Can anyone confirm that this zealot invasion has gone international?"

Nothing.

After ten more minutes and no callers, a frustrated Lanny told Ned that he needed a break from all the entrapment. Besides the lack of help he'd received over the airwaves, the sandwiches he'd eaten were not filling. This was due primarily to DJ Ned having stocked the fridge with low-fat turkey meat and no cheese or condiments. A religious renaissance was a fine time to begin a diet, Ned had explained.

By now Lanny didn't care how many zealots he came across. "I'm sick and tired of it all, Ned. I'm going out disguised amongst them and will just deal with it as it comes. You want a burger?"

Ned settled back into his broadcast chair and considered his new diet. Like his time in Abaco, his diet was short-lived. "Sure, get me a big one." Ned pulled out his wallet and gave Lanny a five. "Just don't let yourself get persuaded," he added with a wink.

Lanny accepted the cash and stuffed it into his pocket. *Persuaded* seemed to echo inside the radio station. Ned had added extra emphasis to the word, and Lanny had caught the message. Deep down, DJ Ned feared being the only one left if Lanny himself were to cave to the religiosity.

Lanny almost laughed at the absurdity of the notion.

At the door of the radio station, Lanny used his cordless drill to remove the screws and take down the barrier boards. He wore a white T-shirt on which he'd written his poser greeting, the only disguise he knew. "Religious Howdy" was written on the front and back.

He ducked his chin and read his handwriting upside-down. "It'll have to do," he muttered to himself.

The disguise worked. Lanny was back to the radio station in ten minutes, and in the Fence-Straddler AM break room he unloaded the food and whistled to his buddy in the booth.

"Come and get it, Ned."

Ned's voice boomed from his booth. "No one tried to capture or convert you?"

"Nope," Lanny shot back, tearing open a ketchup packet. "Amazing how easy they are to fool. Just wear something religious and they smile and practically welcome you to the club."

Reclined in his cushy chair, Ned gobbled his SinnerWhopper. It was not a whole SinnerWhopper, however, because he'd first removed the top piece of bread, convincing himself that he was cutting calories. This bread Ned intended for the gulls, so he opened his second-story window and tossed it blindly into the night, unaware that it would land on the hood of the same black Lincoln that had followed Lanny home.

Behind my Buckhead home sat a large concrete patio surrounded by sandstone rocks and assorted daylilies. Angie had planted the daylilies earlier in the summer, and now the gold ones had bloomed and the burgundy ones had withered. The patio was where Angie and I held our talks, and this afternoon's debate had already stretched for over an hour.

Our patio chairs faced each other from ten feet apart, and the long shadows from a mature magnolia crept toward my feet. Angie and I used to sit out here and hold hands. But not today. Today the ice in our tea glasses had melted into slivers, and my customary offer to fetch refills had been forgotten in the midst of argument.

Angie shook the slivers in her glass and set it back on the concrete. "I've told you three times now, Ned—I just don't want our name attached to Larry's work. You simply should not be involved."

"How are we going to keep our house?" I asked, forcing myself to stay both seated and calm. "I haven't received any interest for any other work. And you should see the manuscripts I've been trying to sell—fantasy novels that aren't fantastic, chick-lit that isn't chicky. But Larry's story is just so, so—"

"Irreverent and offensive to people of faith?" Angie leaned forward and put her head between her hands. She stared at the ground. "What about Alec, the mystery writer? His stuff is good."

I had no idea what potential she saw in non-mysterious mysteries—and I didn't bother to ask. I just changed the subject and tried to bribe her to see things my way. "Remember that trip you wanted to take to Greece and Italy? Well, maybe one day soon we'll be able to go and—"

"Ned, I'm not sure I want to go anymore. And if I did go, I'd want to pay for it with legitimate dollars, not tainted dollars, and certainly not . . ." Here she paused. "Pagan dollars."

I looked at her clothes—likely made in Asia by non-Christians, and her shoes, which I knew were made in Asia because I'd bought them for her for her forty-third birthday. Then I wondered about her choice of words, why she had said, "If *I* go," instead of "If *we* go."

Perhaps an innocent slip in the midst of argument.

Regardless, I let it pass and returned to the subject at hand. "Angie, there's no such thing as pagan dollars. Are you trying to imply that there is such a thing as religious dollars?"

She considered her words and made an attempt at revision. "Honest dollars," she whispered finally.

I pressed my case. "These will *be* honest dollars, dear. I'll honestly sell this story and will honestly deposit the check in our bank account and honestly take you to Greece."

"That's not what I mean. You're going against your values."

In my head, competing images fought for control: credit-card debt, another agent selling Larry's story, our losing the house, more credit-card debt, life under an I-85 bridge, and explaining to our son, Zach, how we could not give him any more money for college.

I did my best to reason with my wife. "My values do not include dividing up U.S. dollars on a religious basis. Did you know those plates we ate off of last night were made by Shawnee Indians, who also don't believe as you do?"

Angie plucked her tea glass from the patio and turned and dumped the contents across a sandstone in our rock garden. "I still don't think we should pay our mortgage or son's education with pagan dollars. You just shouldn't be involved, Ned."

"I'm already involved."

She stood and folded her arms. "Ned, think! People of faith do not go around kidnapping pagans."

"But it's funny."

She stomped her foot. "My women's group will stone me."

All I could think to do was to stare up at her and repeat myself. "But . . . it's funny."

Angie stepped past me to the sliding glass door and reached for the handle. She stood there as if trying to find the words to bolster her position. She settled for argument based on strength in numbers. "Ned, my entire women's group is hoping that you will come to your senses and distance yourself from this, this . . . pagan junk-art."

"Pagan junk-art?" I parroted. "Did you say pagan junk-art?"

She pulled open the sliding glass door. Over her shoulder she said, "I'll be visiting at my mother's tonight." The door was nearly shut when she added one last comment. "And please get a haircut, honey. You're starting to look like Larry."

The glass door shut gently—Angie was not a door slammer—and I tilted my glass and sucked out the last sliver of ice. I crunched ice like I crunched deal numbers—quickly and with determination.

Minutes later I heard Angie start the engine of her Subaru.

I did not chase after my wife. I plucked my cell phone from my pocket, phoned my favorite client, and asked him to meet me at the barber shop.

Angie was wrong about the story, right about my hair.

The first words I heard upon entering the Freedom Ring Barber Shop were, "Leave the sideburns long."

Larry sat in the third of four chairs, reading *Coastal Living* magazine. His barber, Frank, a former Air Force helicopter pilot, tied the bib from behind. For contrast, my barber of twelve years was an ex-Marine. His real name was Ed Pellitini, and his nickname was the standard Big Ed. Back in 1998, when the two of them first opened the business, several customers began a discussion that culminated in naming the barbershop. Ed and Frank took the patriotic name in good humor and painted the moniker in the front window. All customers who sat still in their chair at Freedom Ring Barber Shop got a tiny American flag to wave on the way home.

After a handshake, I lied when Ed asked me about Angie. "The usual," I said, settling into the chair. "Busy with church stuff while I try to sell manuscripts."

"You don't say. . . ." Ed wiped his scissors with a cloth. Since the first day I had sat in his chair, Big Ed had always said, "You don't say," no matter what I commented upon. His way of concentrating on the work at hand.

Larry looked unusually sedate as he turned the pages of his magazine. "Don't talk to me about any deals, Ned, unless you have new info."

Ed pushed my head down so that I spoke to the floor. "I don't have any more info. I just needed some male companionship. Angie went to stay with her mother. She got pretty mad about—"

"I don't wanna talk about women, either," Larry said from behind the pages.

I blew a hair clipping from my lips. "Aw, c'mon, Larry. I was hoping to hear all about your swing-dance date with whatsername."

Larry raised his magazine as if to hide behind it. "The dating world is brutal, Ned. She came to the lessons with me but danced three dances with someone else."

I feigned shock. "The nerve of her. And you two were getting along so well. . . ."

"I just couldn't get those four little steps down."

I looked at Larry and tried to summon genuine sympathy. But my own relational mess muted my effort. "Can't believe she'd dance three dances with someone else, just because of your inability to learn four little—"

Big Ed wrenched my head straight again. "I'm gonna give you four little mohawks if you don't sit still, Ned."

Frank snipped his scissors high over Larry's head and muttered, "Likewise."

Larry stared at the tile floor. "Miranda met a guy at the swing dance who danced like, well, he was instructing the instructors. He's some up-and-coming news anchor, and he kept asking Miranda to dance. Women are all about stability, ya know."

"And all about maintaining a good name."

This comment went right over Larry's head.

He kept flipping the magazine pages and gawking at opulent beach homes. "Miranda started talking about careers, and when she asked if I had a deal yet for my story, all I could tell her was 'maybe.'"

Clip, snip, brush. "That's a good word, *maybe.*"

"She knows, Ned. She knows I'm living off credit cards. Women have this sixth sense . . . the stability sense."

Clip, brush, clip. "And a seventh sense," I offered. "The Baptist morality sense."

This, too, went right over Larry's noggin.

"I'm tellin' ya, the dating world is brutal. You're lucky to have a loyal wife."

Loyal wife? For several minutes I stared straight ahead and wondered about Angie's going to stay at her mother's. She'd so rarely done that. Plus, she'd never shown that much interest in anything I represented as an agent. Maybe her women's group had her brainwashed. I did not understand her sometimes, and to my credit I refused to drown it all with drink. But I would indeed drown it. Somehow.

Larry flipped to the middle of his magazine, pausing only to warn Frank not to touch his sideburns. "Ned, did you know that on the Outer Banks the new beach homes have teakwood bars? I would love a teakwood bar when I get my beach house."

Snip, snip, snip. "Can I rent a room? I may need it."

"Anytime. And this coastal décor . . . Just look at this kitchen and how the decorator blended nautical themes with the cookware. See? All great shades of blue." He stretched out the magazine for me to see but Ed held my head in place. I nearly ruptured an eyeball trying to look farther left than my socket would allow. "Nice, Larry. I'll take the room with the porthole window."

"That'll be my room." He turned a page and said, "Looks like this builder's from Atlanta. We should call him."

"Yes," I said, playing along. "Since both of us are having such struggles with our women and have yet to cut a deal for your story, we should build a beach house together. Go live at the coast and oversee the construction until we feel like dealing with females again." Sarcasm felt oddly therapeutic.

Larry turned another page and grew even more animated. "It

says here that the owners parked a camper on their second row lot and lived there while the house was being built."

Snip, brush, snip. "Me 'n' you . . . in a camper on the Outer Banks?"

Larry could not be stopped. "I can write on the beach, and you can set up a literary office in the camper until the house is completed. Then in a year we sell the place for a big profit. Real estate is huge now, ya know. And we're gonna need tax breaks."

Ed's scissors snipped behind my left ear, and the metallic sound brought me back to my senses. "We're way off the subject of our relational problems, aren't we?"

I wasn't sure what I had said wrong, but Larry got that uncomfortable look about him again. He appeared to be thinking deeply, as if trying to work something out in his mind. His gaze darted from the magazine to my feet and back again to the magazine.

"Therapy, Ned. My therapist is out of town this week, so this is my substitute therapy. I can smell the salt air now." Larry held up the magazine to Ed. "Can ya smell the salt air?"

"Salt air," Ed parrotted, now working on my right side. "You don't say."

Larry sat straight again. "And you, Frank?"

"Very salty. Now lean forward so I can shave your neck."

Larry kept his sideburns and I got the clean-cut look. Parted to the left, as always. I shut my eyes while Ed dusted hair clippings from my face with a towel.

I did not earn a tiny American flag.

He tossed the towel into a bin, and I paid and tipped him. Larry paid and tipped Frank. We said our good-byes to the barbers and were heading for the door when Ed spoke from behind his chair, which now sat empty. "All this talk of building a beach house, of investments and stuff . . . what's with that? You two inheriting some money or somethin'?"

Larry and I exchanged a glance. *You tell him. No, you tell 'im.*

Perhaps we were getting ahead of ourselves. In retrospect, what followed was likely my attempt to drown the problem with Angie.

Vocational success is a type of Kevlar; it makes men bulletproof to unreasonable wives.

I turned and addressed my curious barber. "Ed, Larry has created something unique. And I'm hoping to sell it to Hollywood."

Big Ed sat down in his barber chair and snickered. "Yeah, sure. Of course you are."

"No, really."

Larry nodded with enthusiasm.

Frank placed a bib around Ed and prepared to trim his coworker's already short hair. "You two go fool somebody else."

I left Larry standing there to defend himself and hurried out to open the hatch of my Saab. Moments later, I walked back into the barber shop and over to Ed, who was instructing Frank, via hand signals behind his head, what kind of cut he wanted.

I thrust some pages into Ed's lap. "Here, Ed. All I can spare is chapters twelve through fourteen."

"What's it about?"

"Last pagans on earth, running from religious zealots."

Ed snorted to the ceiling. "You guys are playin' with me."

"No, we're not," Larry offered. "Read 'em and let us know what ya think." Larry gave Ed the thumbs up. "You might find it interesting, Eddie. You, too, Frankie."

Frank smirked and switched on his shears.

Big Ed sat perfectly still, a tiny American flag protruding from his shirt pocket as he began chapter twelve in his very own barber chair.

EVEN AFTER A THIRTY-MINUTE phone conversation, Detour Airlines could not help Lanny locate Miranda. They claimed no record of her arrival or departure.

Lanny grew so frustrated with the representative that he hung up, rushed out of the radio station at 10:00 p.m., and drove himself to the Orlando airport, unaware that he'd been followed. He felt confident in his ability to deal with zealots. He simply gritted his teeth, wore his poser T-shirt, and moved among them, regardless of the corny signage that tainted his coming and going.

At Detour's check-in counter he waited for a family to finish their business before resuming his pleas. The counter girl greeted him with a blank expression, as if she had no experience dealing with disappointment. She read the wording on his T-shirt, smiled, and said, "Religious howdy to you, too."

Lanny tapped the top of her monitor. "Surely this computer of yours can track the boarding of Miranda Timms, who was supposed to be on Flight 1241 from here to Atlanta last Monday at 11:45."

She typed the information into her keyboard and stared at her screen. "We have no record of a Miranda Timms, sir. And besides, Flight 1241 was delayed, then rerouted."

"Because of weather?"

"No, to tour Israel."

Lanny leaned over the counter and cocked his head to view the monitor. "Delta Express, I mean *Detour* Express, reroutes Orlando to Atlanta flights to the Middle East?"

"We do now."

"But . . . why?"

She kept typing, talking to her space bar. "Well, the new guided tours by Marvin the Apostle are a big hit. He's especially knowledgeable about the garden of good and evil. Would you like to book a flight?"

"Um, no thank you." Lanny stared again at the flight board, dumbfounded as to his best move. All he could think to ask was, "Where would I find this Marvin fellow?"

"Oh, we're not allowed to follow his movements, sir. He's accountable to no one." Counter Girl eyed Lanny's choice of clothing again. "But ya know, sir, Marvin would likely appreciate one of your Religious Howdy T-shirts. If you have an extra you could mail it to national headquarters in D.C."

Lanny rubbed his eyes and re-read the flight board. *Miranda, where did they take you? Did you even make it to the airport?*

"Lemme think about it," he replied, stalling to gather his thoughts. "But just who all is in D.C. now?"

She typed something into her keyboard. "I heard on the news that there are thirty-seven U.S. Senators in office, busy unseparating all the churches from the states."

Lanny kept the conversation going even though he held little interest in politics. "Only thirty-seven, eh?"

She nodded and continued to monitor her screen. "Eighteen Republicans and nineteen Democrats, which is a bit surprising."

Lanny could no longer feign interest, and his agenda pressed forth. "I really just wanted information on Miranda Timms. Can't you help me?"

Counter Girl blinked at him, as if waiting for more. Finally she said, "Could she possibly be an unfortunate one?"

"Um, I'm not sure."

Counter Girl had been very matter-of-fact with her news summaries, and now Lanny was certain—as long as he continued to pose well—that she was the one person who could help him. What he didn't see was her typing a note to security that someone had asked for flight information on an unfortunate one, and had done so without giving the secret two-word code phrase. Oblivious to his oversight, and curious as to the inner workings of the zealot world, Lanny stayed put, scanning his surroundings for clues.

Counter Girl tried to delay Lanny by holding up a lime green brochure and waving it in his face. "Can I interest you in our First-Timer's Special, sir? Roundtrip tickets to visit the Offering Plate Museum in exchange for advertising Detour Airlines on your car for one year."

Lanny wanted only information on Miranda, so he shook his head no. Counter Girl tried again to delay him by offering more specials, but he was no longer interested in talking. Frustrated and alone, Lanny left the check-in counter and rode the escalator down to the parking garage. The smell of car exhaust hovered around him, but he paid it no attention. For a long while he just leaned against the front of his Xterra and stared blank-faced at the ground. He replayed in his head the past week—the running, the searching, the desperation. *What did I do to deserve this fate?*

He pulled an old photo of Miranda from his wallet and stared at it for a long while. She was peeking out from behind an oak tree, smiling. The wind had whipped some strands of hair across her eyes.

Lanny's sigh was one part nostalgia, two parts remorse. She had invited him to fly to Orlando with her, but he had stayed on in Atlanta to finish some jobs and earn some needed money. He could have been with her . . . wherever she was.

Lanny slid the photo back into his wallet, stuffed the wallet into his back pocket, and unlocked the door to his Xterra. He never even glanced to the far end of the parking deck, where the two men in the black Lincoln were calling in his license plate number, which of course belonged to a Camaro up on blocks in an Atlanta apartment complex.

Lanny paused and listened as a jet roared away. He considered driving back to Atlanta, but he was weary and feared he'd be pressing his luck. Tonight, sleeping on the floor at Fence-Straddler AM Radio sounded pretty good.

At least the building had a shower. And at least he could talk to Ned.

Maybe the DJ would let him plead over the airwaves again.

He backed out of his space and pulled forward toward an exit sign. Then he turned left onto the descending loop out of the parking garage.

The black Lincoln followed at a distance.

Outside the radio station's main entrance, Lanny stood in darkness and muggy air and pounded on the door. For two minutes he pounded.

From the opposing side, Ned's voice filled with fear and doubt. "Who is it?"

"It's me . . . Lanny."

"How do I know it's you?"

"It just is. Open up."

Ned reached for the knob but stopped short. "I'll need some proof."

"Man, I was just with you on your plane. We flew to Abaco."

"And?"

Lanny pounded on the door. "And the zealots changed the movie dialogue in *Titanic*, you moron. And then we googled ourselves and ran to the airport and flew back to Florida."

A long pause. "And?"

"And then we went to the Cocoa Beach marina, where you picked up a dead gull and thought it was some kind of spiritual symbol—which was ignorant of you 'cause it was only a dead bird."

Another long pause. "Okay, you can come in now." The door opened in a rush, then shut hard as Lanny entered. DJ Ned patted him on the back and muttered, "Sorry."

Lanny squinted beneath harsh florescent lights. "What got into you?"

"I wasn't sure your poser T-shirt would fool 'em again."

"Works great, Ned. The zealots don't suspect a thing as long as you have religious wording on you somewhere. You should try it."

Ned led the way down an empty hall and changed the subject.

"Man, it's just so freaky being here alone. That, and all the changes to music lyrics. I've been listening to that sister station for the past hour and tracking the edits."

Lanny followed him back to his office, where Ned sat back at his computer and pointed to the monitor. He had it all organized in an Excel spreadsheet: In the first column was the name of the group; in the second column the original title of the song; and in the third he put parentheses around the zealot title.

Ned pointed to rows 1 to 3 of his spreadsheet. "The zealots went hardest after disco. These first three are the ones that irk me the most."

Lanny leaned down to read over Ned's shoulder:

KC and the Sunshine Band	*Shake Your Booty*	*(Do Your Duty)*
ABBA	*Dancing Queen*	*(Dancing's Wrong)*
Sister Sledge	*We Are Family*	*(We're Still Family*—but some are estranged red-headed stepchildren)

Lanny saw this musical diversion as an opportunity to get his mind off Miranda, so he pulled up a chair beside Ned and offered to help. By 11:00 p.m., Ned and Lanny had compiled a list of every song that they held as sacred, from rock to disco to rap to pop and even a dozen movie soundtracks.

DJ Ned knew that he could never battle the zealots on every front. But he could defend music.

At least he could do that.

Lanny was dozing in his chair when Ned went back into the booth for an 11:30 p.m. weather update. Ned watched the text scroll onto his monitor and waited for a commercial to end.

Seconds later he pulled the mic to his lips. "Good evening, folks. This is DJ Ned Neutral, still broadcasting from my secret booth in Jacksonville and hoping that your cleanup from Hurricane

Gretchen is going well. Lots of homes and boats were trashed last week, and I remind you that anyone who wants to volunteer should contact the local Red Cross, which I figure is one of the few entities that has not changed its name."

Ned decided that some music without lyrics, like some Miles Davis jazz, would be a nice alternative for his listeners. He slipped the CD into a slot and pushed PLAY.

Across the street in the Lincoln, both men wore headsets tuned to Fence-Straddler AM. The driver even tapped his fingers to the jazzy beat.

"Tomorrow?" asked his cohort, typing information into a laptop.

"Tomorrow."

Two of five red call lights had been lit since he went on the air, and Ned checked to see if either caller was responding to Lanny's request for help. Both, however, were lobbyists for the PFSC, so Ned ended the calls and signed off for the night. He shook Lanny from slumber and urged him to lay down on one of two cots that Ned had stored away. They dragged the cots into the hallway and placed them on either side of the water cooler.

Before going to sleep, Lanny removed his shoes and glanced down the hall at Ned's silhouette. The weary DJ was brushing his teeth over the kitchen sink.

"Ned?"

Ned spit and rinsed. "Yeah?"

"I'm going to go searching for Miranda in the morning," Lanny said and settled into his makeshift bed. "And I want to go alone."

Ned made his way over to the second cot and sat on its edge, stretching his fleshy arms. "Fine with me. I'll be busy here."

Tomorrow DJ Ned would begin fighting for his sacred territory. Tomorrow would be Waterloo for the originality-challenged. Tomorrow Ned would play all his favorite songs in their original version. From his own CD collection he would play them, just to aggravate the zealots.

For the affable DJ, rock and pop hits from the past three decades were the closest thing he knew to religion. Music made him feel a part of something. He'd do anything to protect music and those who wrote it. He'd even once mailed fifty bucks to Vanilla Ice when Ice fell on hard times.

13

LANNY HAD BEEN SITTING on the beach since dawn, trying to turn his confusion into comprehension. The sun rose boldly over the Atlantic, and behind him lay battered beach houses, the destruction from Gretchen. Workers had arrived early at the houses, and soon the high-pitched buzz of skill saws sounded in the distance. Each time a saw cut off and whirred to a stop, it reminded Lanny of his regular life in Atlanta—arriving home covered in sawdust, taking a quick shower, and rushing over to Miranda's apartment to see her. It was so easy, so routine.

After a few more minutes of reflection, he took a sharp shell and wrote in damp sand all the possibilities he could imagine.

1) She's out looking for me, maybe back in Atlanta.
2) She's hiding on some other small island in the Caribbean.
3) She's held captive, but safe.
4) She's been captured and converted, and is now a zealot herself. (Is the condition reversible?)

All four possibilities fought for supremacy. One seemed just as likely as another. He refused to consider a fifth possibility—dead and gone—simply because he knew Miranda was a smart girl, too savvy to fall prey to zealots. He remembered the feel of her embrace and wondered if he'd taken it for granted. He remembered the photo album of their vacations together and wished he'd brought it with him. Now here he was, alone on a Florida beach, wearing a T-shirt that broadcast a religion to which he did not subscribe.

Just so I can roam freely. He felt ridiculous. He started to pull the shirt over his head. But instead he made a fist and punched the sand. *How free is anyone who has to wear such garb? Feels more like imprisonment.*

A hundred yards down the beach, perched behind a high dune, one of the men from the Lincoln watched Lanny through a small telescope. His own T-shirt read "Enforcer of the Movement," and he spoke to the driver of the car through a cell phone. "We'll need them to be together before we nab them."

"Ten-four, Corporal."

Lanny remained seated in the sand, watching small waves rise and crash. He heard power tools fire up again, and he wondered how many of those workers had missing loved ones. *Do those remaining really miss them? And who has it worse: Distraught parents? Distraught kids? Little League teams with only four players?*

Oddest of all to Lanny was the lack of sadness—really of any emotion at all—shown by zealots. As if the fact of their domination outweighed regret.

Lanny checked his watch. 8:46. With his toe he carved M I R A N D A above the four possibilities. Then he stood and almost managed a smile as he thought of DJ Ned back at the station, already two hours and forty-six minutes into his six-hour play list of original pop songs. Ned had started with the A's and was working through the list alphabetically.

Lanny turned from the ocean and brushed the sand from his behind. Ten minutes later he entered for a third time the main road into the Pelican's Harbor Retirement Homes community. The house was his best source for clues, and he wanted to search inside. He parked his Xterra on the street and approached the house.

The beige Buick still sat in the driveway. Lanny knelt beside the back tire and checked for the penny in the tread. Still there, still shiny.

On the front porch the black leather travel bag still sat against the front door, and the note Lanny had left days earlier fluttered above the knob, its ink fading.

He broke in through a back window. Lanny pulled the screen off and left it teetering atop a bush. Then he crawled through the window and landed headfirst in a spare bedroom. He knew this was the room where Miranda would have stayed. On his feet again, he saw the bed made; the closet, empty. Same for the chest of drawers.

Lanny moved to the next bedroom, used by Miranda's parents and reeking of old lady perfume. He searched their bureau but found only some senior citizen pills, loose change. A calendar of events for community residents. A tide chart for August.

The living room was similarly neat, and the light blue carpet looked recently vacuumed. Lanny spotted a stack of mail on the kitchen counter, yet his perusal of it yielded only a power bill, a cable bill, some AARP literature.

That's when he spotted the flashing "1" on the answering machine. He pushed the button and saw Monday, 10:22 a.m. on the LCD screen. He listened for the message to play, hoping to hear Miranda's voice.

Instead he heard her mother.

"Miranda, we're on our way to the marina to check on your dad's boat. It's 10:20 now, and we'll be back by 10:45 to take you to the airport. There's some turkey and Swiss cheese in the fridge if you'd like to make a sandwich to take on the plane."

Lanny saved the message and listened again, hoping to hear something, some background noise, anything, to gain insight. But it was just a normal phone message, one that could have been left by any mother looking out for her daughter.

Hungry, Lanny opened the refrigerator and saw the package of turkey meat. He opened it, sniffed the contents, and decided it had gone bad. He unwrapped a slice of Swiss cheese and ate that instead. He washed it down with a can of Diet Sprite. Four cans of the beverage remained on the bottom shelf. Beside them sat a single bottle of Killian's Red. Miranda's favorite.

What now? he wondered. *Where do I go next? What's the smart move?*

Lanny found a pen and notebook paper behind the answering machine. He took a sheet and began writing out a note, explaining all he knew. When he'd finished, he searched for Scotch tape and, finding none, retrieved a hammer and small nails from his truck. Before tacking the note to the front door, he added one additional line at the top:

(I want to make sure you get this, so my apologies for nailing this to your parents' door.)

Dear Miranda,

I have been searching for you for eight days now. As far as I can tell, the entire country, and possibly the Earth itself, has been taken over by religious zealots. I am holed up in Orlando at Fence-Straddler AM Radio. The DJ there, a guy named Ned, is the only other non-religious person I have met so far. We believe a reward is still being offered for our capture and conversion, so we're doing the best we can to stay hidden. Sometimes we pose as two of them, but this is difficult, as the rules keep changing. Plus there are WANTED posters all over with our pictures on them. I have looked everywhere I know to look for you. I even went to Abaco via plane but you weren't there. I found your parents' boat with the name "SANITI" freshly painted on the stern. There was no sign of you. So I went on the air live to ask people to help me find you. No one responded. If you get this message, drive into Orlando to the radio station and knock on the door. If we are reluctant to open the door, just say the code word: "ABBA." Ned or I will open the door.

Love,
Lanny

Two minutes after Lanny left the house, the black Lincoln pulled up in the driveway. The driver got out with a tiny camera and took a closeup picture of Lanny's note. He hurried back to the car, drove to Orlando, and parked across the street from the front door of Fence-Straddler AM.

14

LANNY DROVE ALONG the coastal highway toward Cocoa Beach. Trying again to get his mind off Miranda, he slowed further and tuned his radio to DJ Ned's radio show.

Ned's play list was by now to the R's, and R.E.M.'s "It's the End of the World As We Know It (And I Feel Fine)" pulsed through the speakers. Lanny was in no mood to hum along to the chorus, though he could identify with the lyric and could still appreciate original songwriting.

He turned off the radio, however, when he passed a particularly hard hit area. Hurricane Gretchen had pounded this neighborhood, and music seemed inappropriate amid calamity. He thought of the parallels between his own misfortune and natural disasters. *More people displaced. Someone else missing a loved one.*

Lanny pulled his truck to the shoulder and observed workers moving in and out of a peach-colored beach house. They wore prison uniforms and appeared reluctant, mad even, that they had to repair this wind-damaged residence.

Lanny lowered his window, and the sharp scent of sawdust invaded his truck. That familiar smell! He considered his Religious Howdy T-shirt and thought of posing as a volunteer worker, just to find out why zealots got punished within their own world. But as he watched apathetic workers tote boards across the porch, he noted a sheet of plywood propped against a wall. On it was painted the rule of entry:

Anyone who enters this site must recite to the foreman
the national two-word code phrase. No exceptions!

Lanny pulled his gear shift out of park and drove away. *Code phrase? They now have a secret code phrase?*

He arrived back at Fence-Straddler AM just before noon, parked in the producer's spot, climbed out, and pounded on the door. "Ned!" he shouted. "Ned, it's me. The zealots are punishing their own people now. They even make them recite a national code phrase!"

For a full minute he heard nothing.

He pounded again. "Ned, open up."

"What's our own code?"

"ABBA, you moron. Now let me in. We gotta leave this place."

The door opened, music blared, and without so much as a "hello," Ned scrambled back to his DJ booth.

"Nope, I gotta load the next batch of songs, Lann-o," he said over his shoulder.

Lanny practically yanked Ned from his booth—which was a difficult task, given that Ned weighed two-forty. "We need to leave, man. Right now. I just saw a black car parked across the street, and I'm sure I saw that same car following me into Pelican's Harbor Retirement Homes earlier this morning."

Ned tossed his headset into his chair and went to his window and peeked out. Then he turned and sized up Lanny as if he were the enemy. "You led them back here to capture me, didn't you? You're . . . you're now one of them, aren't you?"

Lanny frowned and shook his head. "You need me to curse again? Drink an alcoholic beverage? No, Ned, I am not one of them. But they know we're here. And they know you're not broadcasting from Jacksonville."

DJ Ned was still not convinced. He folded his arms, glared at Lanny, and came up with a test question. "What music genre did the zealots hit hardest?"

"Disco."

"Okay, but is dancing wrong?"

Lanny frowned in frustration. "No, man, I love to dance. But not right now. Right now we gotta flee this station. Is there a fire escape out the back?"

Ned peeked out again at the Lincoln two floors below. "No, but there's a first-floor window in the supply room that faces the opposite way. And my Mercedes is parked on that side, as well."

Lanny grabbed a couple of canned drinks from the fridge and stuffed them in a plastic grocery sack. "Where do we go . . . Miami? The Keys?"

Ned kicked off his loafers and quickly slipped his feet into sneakers. "What if we wear dark shades and get lost in the middle of a crowd?"

"What crowd? Where is there a big enough crowd? We should flee to Canada or Mexico."

"How 'bout a very large theme park?"

Ned must be deep in denial, Lanny thought. *Who else, when being pursued by zealots and having lost their friends, would think of visiting a theme park?*

Ned reached into his desk and waved two all-day passes at Lanny. "These were for a giveaway I was going to do on the air. But I figure now we should keep 'em for ourselves."

Lanny glanced blank-faced at the tickets. "I can just imagine what that place will be like."

Ned laced up his sneakers, insisting that his plan was the right plan, that to try to flee the country would be the worse mistake.

Across the street from the front door of Fence-Straddler AM, a second black Lincoln had joined the first. Both cars sat idling, and both drivers scanned the building with binoculars. The driver of the second car spoke into a two-way radio. "When the DJ announces the last song on his list, we rush the building."

"Ten-four."

Ned announced over the air that he needed extra time for the W's— who had lots of hits—and that he'd continue his show for another hour. This was of course a lie; his intention was to flee in the next sixty seconds. Ned pulled open a second desk drawer marked *Promotional Stuff,* and brought out two beige T-shirts, both still wrapped in plastic.

"These are blank, Lann-o. We can mark them up any way we like. You said all we have to do to move among them is to wear religious clothing. So, we'll pose in these." He tucked one under his arm and tossed the second shirt over his booth.

Lanny caught it, yanked off the plastic, and slipped the shirt over his head. "What if they ask us for that national code phrase?"

"You said that was for prisoners only. Anyway, we'll plead amnesia. Or we threaten someone until they tell us the phrase."

Lanny tucked his shirttail into his jeans. "I dunno, man. I have this feeling we should go to Canada or Mexico, anywhere but the South."

"We hide out in the theme park," Ned said, pulling his own shirt overhead and leaving the tail hanging over his shorts. "I'll drive."

And down to the first floor and out the supply window they went—Ned first, Lanny assisting from behind with a push and a grunt.

They drove away quietly, leaving the two black Lincolns on the other side of the buildling, still watching the front door and Lanny's Xterra, still tuned to Fence-Straddler AM and bobbing their heads to the Who's "Who Are You?"

15

EN ROUTE TO THE THEME PARK, Ned whipped his yellow Mercedes into a convenience store parking lot.

"Be right back," he exhaled. He climbed out before stooping to address Lanny, who had not unbuckled his seatbelt and had no plans to do so. "Just gonna grab a newspaper."

Still skeptical of Ned's plan, Lanny lowered his window to get some air. He pulled out his cell phone, called the marina, and asked if anyone had boarded the *Saniti*. He was told that the boat had not moved since the hurricane.

Lanny's heart sank. "Thank you," he said before ending the call.

Ned now had one foot propped on the newspaper stand and appeared to be searching the classified ads. Lanny honked the horn and motioned for him to get going, then he pulled down the sun visor and assessed his face and hair. *Wow, I'm haggard!* he thought. *Miranda wouldn't even recognize me! I need sleep, peace of mind. What I don't need is to be accosted by zealots at some theme park.*

Lanny honked a second time at Ned before turning his attention to the store next door—a Barnes and Noble. He scanned the store windows and read a poster advertising new books to be released in September:

COMING SOON!
Non-fiction for busy people: *Mondays with Marvin*
Re-release of Hemingway: *A Farewell to Pagans*

Lanny turned away in disgust, failing to note the foreboding in that second title. In his quest to find Miranda, he'd paid little attention to himself and his own safety. From the parking lot he saw only the signage that crowded his world. And signs—those stoic little persuaders—were on display everywhere.

"The entire country has become one giant cheeseball," he muttered to himself.

He watched a gull soar over the bookstore and swoop down to a grassy median. Lanny wished he had some bread to throw, if only because Miranda liked to feed birds.

Ned returned with his paper, sat behind the wheel, and continued searching the ads.

"What are you looking for now," Lanny asked, "more original music CDs?"

Ned shook his head. "Personal ads, Lann-o. I have a hunch that if any other non-religious people are left in Florida besides us, they might have placed an ad."

Ned's index finger slid slowly down the page, through dozens of he-zealots seeking she-zealots, and vice versa. Ned traced down a second column of ads and stopped near the bottom. "Ah, see here, I found one. It says, 'Handsome Nissan looking for a blue VW.' "

Lanny pointed to his brain, as if urging Ned to think. "That's *my* ad, you dufus. I already told you that Miranda drives a 2004 light blue Jetta, and that she and I kid each other that even our cars have a budding romance."

"No way. You told me that?"

"Sometimes when she drives over to my house in Atlanta she'll nudge her VW's bumper against my Xterra's."

Ned looked dumbfounded, and could only repeat himself. "No way . . ."

"Believe me, Ned—if Miranda sees that ad, she'll know it's me."

Ned scanned the rest of the personal ads but found none that weren't obviously posted by zealots. "So much for my great idea," he said and cranked the engine. "Let's go get lost in a crowd, maybe ride a rollercoaster."

Lanny gave no reply. He was watching the gull again and remembering the good times.

DJ Ned drove swiftly until traffic slowed near the theme park's entrance. He noticed Lanny's despondent air and tried to think of something to cheer him up.

"Ya think Señor Toad ever repented of his wild ride?"

Lanny failed to see any humor in the question.

Ned could not contain himself. He was determined to get his new friend out of his funk. "C'mon, Lann-o, it's not like they've changed the name of the place to Deity World."

"How do you know? It could be Deity World . . . or even Dooms-day World. I just have a feeling that it's not the world you think it is."

Ned honked at a slow-moving Audi and motioned for them to get going. "Just be thinking of what we should write on our T-shirts."

"This is a bad idea, Ned," Lanny replied. He slumped in his seat, sunglasses covering closed eyes. "Maybe we should turn around."

Ned would have none of that. He reached over and shook Lanny's shoulder. "Wake up, man. We'll just act like one of them, maybe get some inside info on how to survive under their rules."

Lanny sat up and removed his sunglasses. At first he saw noth-ing religious other than a few bumper stickers. *Perhaps theme parks are exempt,* he thought, not realizing that he, too, was edging toward denial. *Maybe Ned is right. Maybe this is okay. And what if Miranda is waiting for me at her all-time favorite ride? The one in the dark, in-side the mountain. Yeah, that's where she'd be.*

Traffic slowed further, stalled, and began rolling again. Ned and Lanny could see only trees to each side and the long line of vehicles in front and behind.

Yet the closer they rolled, the more nervous Lanny became. Like most people, he was doomed to repeat mistakes from which he failed to learn a lesson. And his mistake—both his *and* Ned's mistake, ac-tually—was to not heed the first subtle warning that this idea was a bad one.

The warning looked so innocent at first glance. Just a roadside vendor peddling trinkets and T-shirts. Stationed on Lanny's side of the road, the gentleman held up his wares for all to see. What Lanny didn't notice on the shirts was the tiny print under the larger print. Under the name of the theme park were the large words *FUN FOR*

ALL, and underneath that phrase were the teeny tiny words ALL WHO ARE FORTUNATE.

Ned pulled ahead a few feet and glanced right at the T-shirt display. He, too, missed the tiny lettering.

"Lotsa people working to make a buck any way they can," he muttered, easing past the peddler. Ned produced a magic marker from his shorts and handed it to Lanny. While traffic stalled again, the two wrote "Fun for All" on each other's blank beige T-shirt.

Lanny unbuckled his seatbelt and turned to check behind them. Nothing suspicious. He looked out both windows. Still nothing. But as Ned rolled forward again, Lanny began shaking. His complexion paled. His palms turned clammy.

"Turn around, Ned," Lanny demanded. "I'm getting the shakes."

Ned eased his Mercedes another twenty feet, then ten more, closing in on the parking ticket booth. "I can't. Traffic has us blocked in. Plus we're almost to the parking lot."

"Did you ever swap out your license plates like I told you to?"

"Nah, forgot."

Ned rolled forward to the booth and showed the ticket taker his two all-day passes.

The young man examined the tickets. "Sorry, sir, these are no longer valid."

Ned politely disagreed. "But they're not expired—they're still good. I checked."

"It's not the expiration date, sir," the youngster explained. "Ownership has changed, and Deity World is now invitation only. In fact, you're trespassing."

DJ Ned was so mad he could have spit, especially since he had correctly guessed the park's new name. He shook his head, threw his gearshift into park, and glared at the clerk. "What if I refuse to leave? What if I demand admittance?"

The youngster did not reply in kind. He did not reply at all. This struck Ned as odd, and he sat there staring out his windshield, a fuming customer. What he didn't see was the clerk pushing the red security button inside his booth.

Neither did Lanny. All Lanny did was lean across the console, meet the gaze of the clerk, and change the subject from park admittance to lost girlfriends. "Listen, man, can anyone here help me locate a Miranda Timms?"

"I'm sorry," he said, "but if she's an unfortunate one, then I have no specific information. Although I can offer a factual tidbit."

"Go ahead. Shoot," said Lanny, hoping for an important clue.

The ticket clerk cleared his throat, paused a moment, then spoke as if to a large gathering of geologists. "Only thirty percent of the earth's surface is covered with land; the other seventy percent is water."

Huh? Confused, stunned, and downright bewildered, Lanny wanted to ask the clerk to expound on his geographic factoid, but he was distracted by a marching sound from behind the car.

Ned was the first to see the guards in black fatigues. They marched up quickly, three to each side of his Mercedes. One reached to open the driver's door, and Ned saw the patch on his shirt: EOM: Enforcers of the Movement.

The door opened. "What?!"

A hand on Ned's arm. "Step out of the car, sir."

"But what have I done?"

A gentle tug to his arm. "That's just it. . . . You haven't done anything."

Ned now faced the side of his yellow hood—as they frisked him.

"But this makes no sense." He looked across his hood at Lanny, who was also enduring an embarrassing frisking.

Lanny and DJ Ned were led around to the front of the Mercedes, where the pair were instructed to stand with their backs against the grill. The six guards in black fatigues stood in front of them, arms crossed, faces sweaty and lacking expression. Park officials redirected traffic into other lanes.

One of the guards—the apparent leader, since he wore a large brass badge that read Marvin the Apostle—stepped forward and said, "Thou hast the right to an explanation."

Ned frowned his most sarcastic frown. "Do tell."

Lanny feared the worst. Out of the side of his mouth he whispered to his buddy, "They're gonna kill us, Ned. I just know it. They're either gonna cook us extra crispy or torture us like back in the Dark Ages."

Ned whispered back, "Stop panicking. They don't even have guns."

Which was true. But there were six of them, and they appeared strong, and they had billy clubs dangling from their belts.

Marvin the Apostle stepped closer and stopped, feet spread wide, eyes narrowed at the astonished trespassers. "Thy refusal to joineth the movement shall resulteth in steepest punishment . . . *eth*."

DJ Ned turned to Lanny and whispered, "Oh my gosh, this guy speaks King James English."

"Is that what that is?" Lanny asked. Suddenly he recalled googling his name—and the stream of words that ran across the computer.

Marvin raised a finger to halt their talk. "Thou hast been observed and followed and foundeth guilty. Now shall thy countenance be transformed forcefully, since thy deadline for voluntary surrender also hath pass . . . *eth*."

"What deadline?" Ned protested.

Lanny slowly made a fist.

"Shusheth thy mouth," Marvin cautioned. "Thou needest to listen. I speaketh on behalf of the United States of America. Thou hast been giveneth invites over the television, hints in our movies, clues in our newspapers and our fast-food restaurants; thou hast been reacheth out to in our songs and books, we've even lefteth dozens of pamphlets on your doorstep in order that thou could seeth things our way. And still thou declineth to join us?"

Rethinking a fist fight, Lanny propped one foot on the bumper and crossed his arms. "Not only do we, um, refuseth to join you, we don't even *know* you. All we see is, well, do ya mind if I use a construction term here?"

Marvin frowned and motioned for Lanny to get on with it. "Thou shalt continueth."

Lanny paused to gather his blue-collar thoughts. "All we see is your vinyl siding, either that or your paint. You all seem satisfied to slather religious latex over everything that's broadcast, everything that's printed, and everything that's visual. But who are *you*? I mean, even now you're urging us to join you while you hide behind your odd speech and your commando costume."

Neither the logic nor the insult did a thing to prevent Marvin and the guards from leading Ned and Lanny to the back door of a waiting black Lincoln. The car had just pulled up, a blue light flashing on its dash. Tinted windows prevented either man from seeing inside, and Marvin the Apostle opened the door himself. "Entereth the vehicle, please."

At first Ned refused. Then a guard shoved him in the back.

When Ned stooped to enter, he heard a quacking sound.

Waiting in the backseat was not another guard but a red-haired guy in a full duck outfit, minus the head.

"What'd *you* do?" Ned inquired.

"Don't ask."

Lanny slid in last, leaving Ned scrunched into the middle.

"Shusheth," said Marvin from outside the back door. "No talking."

The outer lane had cleared, and off toward the interstate sped the black Lincoln. Neither Lanny nor DJ Ned nor the guy in the duck suit knew where they were being taken, only that their horizon had shrunk immensely.

This was indeed a small, small world.

I had observed protest marches before, though never in front of my own home. And never a middle-aged-female protest organized by my own wife.

It was Friday at 11:40 a.m., and my plan had been to work at home until noon and then leave to play golf. Larry and I had a 1:10 tee time at a municipal course north of Buckhead. He was supposed to pick me up at noon, though now I wondered how he would get past the twenty-odd women marching circles in my otherwise quiet suburban street. Most of them, including Angie, hoisted signs that read, JUST SAY NO TO PAGAN JUNK-ART, and, STOP AGENT ORANGE FROM KILLING OUR VALUES!

I opened the front door and stood on the porch in my khaki pants and orange Nike golf shirt. After two seconds of gazing across my lawn at the circus, I shouted, "Angie, are you out of your mind?"

I shouted this as loud as possible, hoping to alert neighbors to my plight. I wanted a bit of sympathy. I wanted the protestors to leave quietly and allow me to enjoy the day with Larry. And I wanted to keep Larry from being upset by my wife's orchestrated hysteria. At that moment Larry was the only sane person I knew besides my barber and my son, Zach, who never called home from Auburn. Especially during summer semester. But last I checked, Zach was still sane.

Angie did not even acknowledge my question. Instead, she continued marching with the others, shouting a rhyming slogan—"We will not be denied; the pagan story must die!"—and pumping her cardboard sign up and down like some manic drum majorette.

I stood with crossed arms and observed them for another minute. Trying to appear unaffected, I went inside, found an orange cap to match my shirt, and came back out on the porch to observe them further. I even practiced a few golf swings. This must have made them mad, because they began shouting louder and louder. It wasn't long before their protest slogan grew monotonous: "We will not be denied; the pagan story must die! We will not be denied; the pagan story must die!"

Up, down, up, down went the signs, imperfectly timed to their shouting.

It wasn't even a very *good* slogan, what with that extra beat in the second clause. But what could you expect from a hastily assembled group of Southern Baptists?

I pulled out my cell phone and called Larry, hoping first to warn him and then to ask would he please park one street behind my house.

He answered on the second ring. "Almost there, Ned. Just waiting for the light to turn green."

"No, don't drive down my street!"

"Why not? You don't wanna play golf with me?"

"Of course I wanna play. But they're protesting."

"Who's protesting?"

Instinctively I pointed at my wife. "Angie and her minions. They're marching in front of my house because of your story, because of 'Dunkers versus Sprinklers' or 'Believers kidnapping pagans' or . . . who knows why."

A long pause. "I didn't mean to offend anyone, Ned."

I shifted into mediator mode. "They're just hypersensitive. Park one street behind mine and I'll escape through my backyard."

"But isn't there a fence back there?"

"I'll scale it. The street is called Nottingham. Wait for me, and I'll meet ya in five minutes."

"Whatever you say."

I went inside and pulled my golf bag from a closet. I slung the strap over my shoulder and hauled the bag to my living-room window. One last peek between the curtains.

The protest showed no sign of slowing—another car full of women pulled up. A Volvo. From its trunk they unloaded bar-b-que, potato salad, buns, and two-liter bottles of lemonade. At the edge of my driveway they set it all out on a card table draped with a red-and-white checkered tablecloth. All of the protesting women then locked arms and marched in circles around the table, still shouting their slogan, occasionally stepping out of line to grab a bite of sandwich, a spoonful of salad, or a sip of lemonade. Only in the South.

I knew I had to flee quickly. I flew through the kitchen, accidentally knocking a phone book off the counter with the golf bag. I grabbed my briefcase, pulled open the sliding glass door to the patio, and angled between daylilies and sandstone rocks. In a hurry to get away, I jogged the last twenty yards to our white picket fence. Golf bag over fence. Then briefcase. No way was I leaving any work papers in the house for Angie's army to pilfer and burn.

My breathing quickened and my head spun from the thrill of escape. I ran across a neighbor's back lawn—fortunately no one was home—and heard a horn honk. I stepped out onto Nottingham Street, looked to my right, and saw Larry two houses down, parallel parked under an oak. He waved out the window of his Bronco and pulled up to meet me.

After slinging my bag and briefcase in the back, I climbed in the passenger side. For a moment we just looked at each other and grinned stupidly.

"Alcatraz in Buckhead, eh?" Larry said as he pulled away.

"Just get me to the course."

I supposed that to Larry—to any casual observer really—Angie and I did look a tad dysfunctional. I even enjoyed a private moment of glee imagining her tromping inside the house with her sign and her cohorts and finding no one home.

Larry sped through a yellow light and laughed out loud. "Escaping over your backyard fence to avoid your wife's protest march. You're a very funny guy, Ned."

I didn't feel very funny. I didn't even feel like much of a *guy*. Like many men, I had bought into the theory that acceptance into the brotherhood of maleness is tied largely to financial and business success. Even if other men are unaware of our difficulties, we tend to feel shame when things go badly. We sulk. We avoid group settings. We bow out early from conversations. *Refills, anyone?*

In Larry I had a comrade in struggle—a somewhat warped com-rade, true, but a sojourner just the same. He was living off credit cards and hope. I was living off an IRA and fear. Fear that if I didn't sell his story, I would soon become a sulking, shamed, busi-ness failure.

Two stoplights from the course, I posed the question. "Tell the truth, Larry. Do you fear failure?"

"Honestly?"

"Honestly."

"All the time. I just hide it by being . . . well, you know how I am."

I nodded. Then he nodded back and said, "What about you?"

"I've got a son in college, a crazy wife, a mortgage, and no other good manuscripts. Of course I fear failure." That was about as deep as Larry and I had ever talked. And in an effort to not mess it up, I changed the subject. "You haven't updated me on the girl, the one from the swing dance."

He floored it as the light turned green. "And you haven't updated me on your efforts to make me financially fulfilled."

"First you update me on the girl."

He turned into the course's parking lot and parked facing the driving range. Before he even cut the engine a golf ball hit the pave-ment three feet from his door and bounced into the side of a Chevy. *Clunk.*

Larry backed up and parked on the far side. "The girl is like that golf ball, Ned. She's off course and not understanding her true di-rection."

That was way too philosophical for Larry. Something was up. "You okay?"

He pulled his keys from the ignition and stuffed them into his pocket. "I didn't think Miranda was like most women. . . . But she hasn't even returned the e-mail I sent yesterday. Probably because I couldn't swing dance." His mood had taken a swift turn downward.

This prompted an important question. "Larry, that prompts a question. Are you keeping her as the love interest in your story?"

"Of course."

"But still no appearance by Dillen?"

Larry frowned and reached for his door handle. "I told you, Labradors don't like being in stories."

"Have you even called Miranda again?"

"Nah, but I will." He opened his door and took a whiff of hot Georgia summer. "Let's play golf, pahdner."

Our standing rule was to not talk about business on the course—and on this day we did not. For over four hours we managed to honor our rule. We observed nature, told corny jokes, and searched the woods for each other's golf ball. At least until the last hole.

When we arrived at the par-five eighteenth hole, I admitted to him that decision-makers in L.A. were dragging their collective feet, and thus I did not have an update, and would not have an update until I flew out to L.A. for face-to-face discussions.

Larry became strangely quiet. He walked to the back of the cart and pulled a club from his bag. "Ned, another agent called me. Said he could have a deal done by tomorrow evening."

My heart sank. My knees shook. I dropped my golf ball on the cart path and watched it bounce three times and roll under a bush.

Larry gripped his club and took a practice swing, nonchalant as always.

I retrieved my ball and turned to face him from the far side of the cart. "But we had a deal."

"It was only a handshake." He let his words linger in the humidity. Then he broke into a wide grin and teed his ball. "Just kidding, pahdner," he said. "But another agent did call."

He smashed his ball deep down the fairway and picked up his tee.

I tried to act like he hadn't scared me. But I couldn't get my ball to balance on the tee. All day I'd been relaxed, and now this. I knew that in some L.A. circles, an acquiring producer might tip off an agent buddy in order to return a favor—or to simply gyp a no-name agent like me out of a commission.

My hand trembled as I teed my ball and watched it fall to the ground.

"Need some help, Ned?" Larry was leaning against the cart with his feet crossed and his club propped against his hip, mimicking the pose of a tour pro.

"You got me good."

"I told the other agent that I was loyal to you."

I stood over the ball and managed a weak practice swing. "Appreciate that . . . pahdner."

I swung wildly. My ball hit the cart path for a fourth time and bounced into a pond.

Larry was quick with the platitude. "Take a mulligan, Ned. After what you've been through today, you deserve a second chance."

After finishing the last hole—Larry won the match by seven strokes—I felt the need to play mediator, to explain the protest march to Larry. I truly suspected he did not grasp the reasoning behind it. I drove our cart around the practice putting green, stopped at the rear of his Bronco, and settled on a proper way to begin. "Larry, there's content in your story that turns normal churchgoers into raging protestors."

Larry was adding up his score and paying me only minimal attention. "I understand that." He wrote a figure on the scorecard. "Hey, did you know you shot a 92 today?"

"Sure, but do you understand *why* those women are enraged?"

"Not enough romance in the story? You know how women love lots of romance. . . ."

For ten minutes I sat in the golf cart with Larry and explained to him that some in the church community might think portions of his work a wee bit irreverent. He repeated that he understood. Thing is, I didn't think he understood at all. To Larry, the words *I understand* were much the same as my barber muttering "You don't say," as he trimmed my hair. They were meant to be dismissive, to avoid further conversation.

He handed me the scorecard, and I tucked it into my shirt pocket and considered my situation—a twenty-handicap golfer with a thirty-handicap job. The ramifications of this were too much to process, so I shifted back into mediator mode, hoping to glean some insight from Larry that would help me ease tensions with Angie when I arrived home. If she even *came* home; she'd stayed at her mother's the previous night.

"Ya know, Larry, I've been wondering what sparked your imagination."

"For the Abaco scene?" he asked, changing out his golf shoes for his loafers.

"No, the whole thing." I pulled my golf bag from the cart and shoved it inside the Bronco's hatch. "You say you never go to church or even have religious friends, and yet you've obviously been observing the evangelical world. At least the commercial aspects of it."

Larry brushed grass from his golf shoes and tossed them inside his vehicle. He seemed hesitant to answer. Finally he set his bag next to mine and shut the hatch. "You don't wanna know."

Thing is, I *did* want to know. Lots of agents don't ask, but I was truly curious. "You're not going to tell me?"

"Might hurt our relationship."

What could possibly do that?

A cart boy came up and drove away with the cart. I climbed into the passenger side of Larry's Bronco and acted as casual as possible. "Surely you can tell me what sparked your creation."

He sat behind the wheel and, as if this was going to be painful for him, spoke without looking at me. "The spooky pursuit aspects I got from my childhood, but the legalistic parts came just last year, Ned, from observing your wife. How she interacts with you . . . and with the world."

"Angie?" I asked, stunned at his directness.

"Today's protest thing didn't even surprise me. It was just—" and here he pointed to the eighteenth hole—"par for the course."

I sat bewildered, wanting to nod my agreement.

But I could not. Angie was, after all, my wife.

We hardly spoke on the drive back. I felt pulled in opposite directions. No, in three directions. Call it an obtuse triangle of puller-ization. Larry tugging me toward relativism; Angie tugging me toward legalism; and then there was money—*success!*—tugging me toward manhoodism. Maybe I needed a fourth direction, but that was too much to consider. My brain was scrambled.

Larry turned onto Nottingham Street. I almost got out and snuck in through the backyard again but reconsidered and asked him to pull around the corner. We both leaned into the windshield to peek down my street. No one in sight.

Larry drove slowly to the front of my house.

The protestors were gone, as was Angie's Subaru. I unloaded my golf bag and golf shoes from the back and lugged them around to Larry's window. "Looks safe here for now. I'll call ya from L.A."

He pulled a golf tee from behind his ear and pointed it at me. "I'm countin' on you, Ned."

"Just make sure you call the girl again. Write her a love note. You're a writer. . . . Play to your strengths."

His eyes widened and he drove away smiling. It was only then that I noticed the note taped to my front door.

Ned,

All I can figure is that you snuck out the back door, probably to meet Larry for golf. Just know that any birdies you two made will not make up for the double bogeys in his story. I'll be home late, after my women's group finishes our study on submission. You'll probably be hungry, so I put some barbeque and potato salad in the fridge.

I still love you, Ned. I just disagree with you.
Angie
Also, you squished two of my daylilies in your haste to escape.

Larry may have been blunt in his confession, but he was right in his observances. I was married to someone who did her best to live within the holy huddle, who saw the world in black and white: as Christianized (sanitized), and non-Christianized (everything else).

Still, his confession rattled me. I mean, what does it say about a marriage when the husband has to sneak out his patio door and scale a fence to avoid a protest led by his own wife?

I couldn't really argue with Larry, or even be mad at him.

Perhaps he was right.

Perhaps, if she were given the power, Angie would sew the crosses on McDonald's uniforms.

My flight to L.A. left Atlanta early the following Thursday. At takeoff I settled into seat 6F, next to a window, and was surprised to see the flight only half full. Vacant seats beside me, vacant seats behind me.

As we ascended through storm clouds, I thought about Angie's descent into legalism. Or was it really legalism? Did I, Ned Watson, even have the ability to discern what should or should not be sold as entertainment? *Nah, forget about it. I'm already in the air and on my way.*

We hit turbulence just as we leveled off. I heard a thud and a spill of cans in first class.

A minute later a flight attendant appeared through the curtain with her arm around a second attendant, this one taller by a good six inches. The taller one was limping badly.

"She tripped over someone's handbag and needs to sit down," said the short one. "Is anyone in that seat?"

She was looking right at me, and I shook my head no and reached over two seats to move the seatbelt out of her way.

"Is anyone here a doctor?" she asked of the economy class. "She twisted an ankle."

Everyone shook their heads no.

The injured woman stood on one leg, turned her back to me, and slowly settled back into 6D. She grimaced as she sat. Then someone handed two pillows over the seat to me. The shorter flight attendant took one of the pillows and tucked it under her fallen comrade's ankle.

I offered the second pillow.

"That's okay," said the injured woman, grimacing again. "Just leave it in the seat between us."

She was a slender woman with brown, curly hair, plain eyes, and a Midwestern accent. But those eyes kept squinting through her pain, and it was hard for me to just sit there and watch this casualty endure a flight with no professional care.

After some adjustments to the pillow on the floor, the other attendant left and then returned with a plastic bag of ice. She wrapped it around her coworker's ankle and asked me to look after her friend.

"Of course," I said. She left to attend to her first-class duties.

The injured woman didn't look like she wanted to talk, so all I offered was the lame, "I hope United has excellent insurance."

"They do," she said softly. Her discomfort level seemed to have hit a plateau, and now she seemed embarrassed at her situation. "But I really need this job."

After a few minutes she reached for the airline magazine and began reading, as if to distract herself. I gazed awkwardly out my window, unsure if I should say or do anything else.

She read for all of two minutes before stuffing the magazine back in its slot. "I've already read that six times," she said.

I nodded and wondered what to say; giving comfort to strangers was never one of my gifts. The best I could manage was, "You like to read?"

"Love to read."

I reached under my seat, opened my briefcase, and offered her the first sixty pages, which she declined with a shake of her head.

"Go ahead," I said, noting a certain pushiness rising in me again.

"What is it?" she asked.

"Just a little something to ease the pain."

After accepting the pages with a confused glance, she adjusted the ice pack on her ankle and sat back in her seat to read. I tried to get a nap.

A few minutes later I heard a small giggle. I opened my left eye. "What part?"

"The gas gouging at the BP station."

"Ah."

I settled back into my nap as the pilot announced clear skies over Alabama.

For two hours no one disturbed my slumber. Then, somewhere over New Mexico, the injured flight attendant tapped my shoulder. "Hey, mister, my ankle is really throbbing. Mind if I read some more?"

So I, the good doctor, handed her chapter sixteen.

16

LANNY AND DJ NED smelled jet fuel. They listened as the black Lincoln drove away and planes took off in the distance. Neither man could see the planes, however, because both were blindfolded.

Lanny felt a hand on his shoulder, pressing him forward on the tarmac. "This is for your own good," said the guard in black fatigues.

"That's what my mom always said," Ned whispered. He pictured the guard tall and strapping, not someone with whom to scuffle.

"Mine, too," Lanny agreed.

Two steps later Lanny's foot hit something and he heard ice shake. He had kicked an Igloo cooler.

The guard opened the cooler. "Orange or cherry TraitorAde?"

"Cherry," Lanny blurted.

"Got any Gatorade?" Ned asked.

"No, Gatorade went out of business after, well . . . it was for the good of the country."

"So," Ned continued, trying to wrap his mind around the fact that his favorite sports drink had become extinct—which was hard to do, since his mind was already wrapped around the fact that he was a prisoner, "there's only *TraitorAde* now?"

The guard still knelt over the cooler, hands digging in ice. "For your kind, there is."

They were both given an orange-flavored drink and told to finish it in two minutes.

Behind them, jet engines revved, drowning out Ned's burp and Lanny's speculation that his drink was drugged. The guard disposed of the empties and tied their hands behind their backs.

"What happened to Marvin and his King James English?" Ned asked.

"He won't be traveling with us. He always takes his private jet."

The guard led them across a tarmac that was nearly sizzling, being that this was Orlando in late August. *This is surely the hottest tarmac in the world,* Lanny thought before bumping into Ned.

When they reached the stairs to the jet, Ned stopped on the first step and refused to go farther. "This is totally unfair," he complained. "We did nothing to deserve confinement."

The guard chuckled. "Oh yeah? It's just like Marvin told you— we've left hints for you, played our songs for you, edited books for you, and even left billboards on the interstate for you. None of it did any good."

"Then why don't *you* speak in King James?"

"Only those who rise to the high level can speak it. I'm earning bonus points today for escorting you."

Ned felt his blindfold tighten. "Well, which of you guards gets the Big Reward for our capture?"

"None of us. That offer expired. But we're going to convert you anyway."

The guard poked his index finger into Ned's back. Ned thought it was a gun, so he hurried up the stairs as best he could, a difficult task, considering his hands were tied behind his back.

The guard brought Lanny up the stairs next, though he stopped him just as they were entering the plane. "Lanny Hooch"—the guard said his name like a mother scolding a child—"when you stopped at the beach house we have under repair, we thought you were on your way to joining the *big team.* But then you just left."

Lanny turned on the top step and said, "I didn't know the national two-word code phrase."

"Of course you didn't," the guard shot back, pushing him inside.

Lanny ducked and entered the plane and stood beside Ned, who had managed to pull his blindfold down with his teeth and was now frowning at the accommodations. The plane was mostly dark inside, outfitted in military style. All occupants had to sit on long hard benches, facing each other, as opposed to traditional cushy seats in rows of three and four. At the back of the plane, all by himself, sat the red-headed guy in the duck suit. He, too, was blindfolded.

"Welcome aboard," he said at the sound of others entering.

The guard pulled Ned's blindfold back over his eyes and tied it tight.

Lanny wondered how the guard knew so much, and before sitting he demanded an explanation. "Just how do you people follow our movements so well? You know about my stopping at that beach house, and that just seems, well, spy-like."

"Yeah," DJ Ned concurred, also refusing to sit. "Spy-like."

The guard put a hand on each man's shoulder and shoved them down. "Not spies. Blogs. Hundreds of Internet blogs are fascinated with the two of you. There are even hourly updates scrolling on EFOX News."

Ned thought on this. "That would be, um, En . . . Forcers . . . of—"

"We're not sure about the 'X' yet, but we're working on it."

The guard tightened their seatbelts and stepped back to observe his captives. Fearing for their future, Lanny and Ned sat in silence, black cloth over their eyes, sharing the same burden but thinking far different thoughts.

People are blogging updates about me? All I want is to find my girlfriend and live peacefully in Atlanta.

Who's protecting American pop music without me manning my booth at Fence-Straddler AM?

"Where are you taking us?" Ned demanded.

"Quiet now," said the guard. He stepped out the exit door and slammed it behind him.

Blindfolded on a plane, Lanny figured that as soon as he began talking, someone would make him be quiet. He knew Ned was directly to his left, so he moved his feet around the floor to the right and kicked the air in front of him. He hit nothing.

He then said "Boo" really loudly, but no one rebuked him. *If there are guards on the plane, they must not be seated back here.*

Jet engines whirred to a higher and higher pitch, so loud they were almost deafening. The plane rolled forward, turned, accelerated, and took off. Death was only a distant worry to Lanny; his main thought was whether he was now getting closer to Miranda, or farther away.

Turbulence rocked the men into each other, and Lanny felt his teeth clatter. Soon the plane leveled off, and Lanny figured it was time to speak again. He kicked Ned's foot. "Where do you think we are?"

"Since it's only been about thirty minutes, we're either still over Florida or out over the Atlantic. I'm thinking they'll take us to Africa."

"Don't say that." Lanny stood, trying unsuccessfully to free his hands.

"It's probably Africa, Lann-o. Gotta be somewhere with a desert. I think I heard once that the zealots have a thing about making people march around in the heat until they're too tired to resist."

Lanny sat dejected and sightless and all tied up. He was about to sneeze when an unfamiliar voice sounded from the back.

"Are you the two guys who were with me in the black Lincoln?"

"Yeah," said Ned, not too surprised to hear this question. "And just who are you?"

A short pause. "Up until a few hours ago I was . . . well, just call me the Former Donald."

Ned was not sure how to feel about being on the same flight with a captured duck-man. "You still haven't told us what you did."

The Former Donald gave them a quack. "Can't tell you yet. But I can assure you that they aren't taking us to Africa."

"Then where?" Lanny asked. "I gotta know."

"You'll see soon enough."

Soon enough was only another twenty minutes. The plane descended, slowed considerably, banked, accelerated again, and then there was the sudden bump and skid of landing gear meeting pavement.

By the time the plane stopped rolling, Lanny had wriggled his hands free. He removed his blindfold and looked around at the sparse metal confines and the long, hard benches arranged in parallel. But there were only three passengers—himself, DJ Ned, and the Former Donald.

He glanced first to his left at Ned, blindfolded and still tied, then to his far left, where the Former Donald sat by himself, also bound and blindfolded, still in three-quarter duck attire.

Before the guards opened the exit door, Lanny had Ned untied. From outside and below, they heard Spanish voices mixed with English—regular English.

Ned hurried to the back of the plane and untied the Former Donald. All three men gathered at the exit door, listening to chatter they could not understand.

Lanny whispered his concern to Ned. "We're not back in the Bahamas?"

"Hardly," Ned whispered back.

"Then where?"

The door creaked partially open. Sunlight streamed into the fuselage and across Ned's sneakers. "I can tell from the dialect," he said with disdain, "this ain't Bahamas."

The door swung open, and Lanny sniffed warm tropical air. "Then where are we?"

"Cuba," said the Former Donald. He stood behind Lanny, waiting to depart, his blindfold dangling from his neck. "They always take resistors and troublemakers to Cuba."

Ned and Lanny stood fearstruck as they stared out at eight security guards in black fatigues. The guards stood on the steps and motioned for the threesome to depart.

A creaking set of rolling stairs sat against the exit hatch, and Ned took the first, tentative step into Cuban territory. The guards stepped backward ahead of him, watching his every move. Lanny followed Ned down but turned on the stairs to the Former Donald.

"Are there lots of resistors kept here?" Lanny asked excitedly. He was hoping for information that might confirm that Miranda would be among their numbers.

The Former Donald nudged him forward. "There were ten last week. But Cuba, too, has been swept over by the zealots." Halfway down the stairs now, the Former Donald pointed across the runway. "See those?"

Lanny was distraught to see a pair of Detour Airlines jumbo jets parked at the terminal. Then he looked above the wings of the plane he'd just departed and saw that he'd ridden on that very airline. Past the jumbo jets sat a Lear, the name MARVIN in huge script across the tail section.

Two steps below, Ned began shaking as he faced a lifelong fear. "Is Castro still in power?"

"Nah," said the Former Donald, waddling down the stairs in his duck attire. "From what I heard during my prior trip here, he was first to disappear."

"You get sent here often?"

"My second time. I'm a poser."

Ned and Lanny were overcome with dueling emotions. Fear of being held by zealots, but relief that Cuba was likely no longer communist.

Out on the tarmac, the security guards lined up the captives shoulder to shoulder. Lanny sensed that the Former Donald was a possible ally, that somehow he was in the same predicament as DJ Ned and himself. The lean young man with the red hair stood next to Lanny, downcast and silent. The guards removed the blindfolds dangling from each of their necks. Then, a brief frisking.

The three were loaded into a red van and driven into downtown Havana. En route, the Former Donald complained of being hot in his costume, so the guards issued him a pair of khaki shorts, an old Miami Dolphins T-shirt, and a pair of orange sneakers one size too big. The Former Donald changed his clothes right in front of Ned, who snickered at the sight of boxer shorts screen-printed with little ducks.

"They made us wear these," the Former Donald explained.

In downtown Havana, the van screeched to a stop. The three prisoners were led into a large, one-story brick building and ushered down a hallway of cheap tiles. They were then taken into a long, dark, dank room. The guards left them there, slamming the door behind them.

Ned, Lanny, and the Former Donald touched cool bricks and sat on the floor, backs to the wall, in total darkness. Lanny kept thinking back to the parking clerk's factoid, the "seventy percent water, thirty percent land" comment. *Was he referring to Cuba, or to some other place?*

Ned's voice boomed into the darkness. "Who else is in here?" He was sure he'd seen other people sitting at the back of the room just before the guard slammed the door.

At first there was silence. Then a dripping sound from a far wall.

"What's that dripping?" Lanny asked.

"Just water from an old pipe," came the voice. The voice echoed against enormous, cavelike walls. And it wasn't the Former Donald's voice. He still sat directly to Lanny's right.

"Who are you?" Ned asked the stranger.

"Freddie from Oregon," was the emotionless reply.

A pause. "Are you a zealot?"

"No. I tried to teach evolution to some fourth graders in Eugene. I've been here for a week now."

More dripping. Lanny cleared his throat and asked, "Do they feed you here?"

"Depends. Yesterday we had blackened sea bass and some key lime pie, which was likely a bribe. They do that sometimes. For the next week it's locusts, maybe some wild honey. Oh, and they argue amongst each other a lot, mostly over whether to serve us real wine or grape juice with the locusts."

Lanny squirmed against the wall, too overwhelmed to speak again.

DJ Ned, in an effort at leadership, told everyone his name and what he did for a living. "Who else is in here?" he inquired.

Three more drips. "It's me, Nute. Crackhead . . . I used to call your talk show."

"You the guy from the trailer park?"

"You got it, man, and I still ain't never done no drugs. But I really miss online poker."

A hipper, baritone voice said, "I used to play some poker myself."

Lanny listened to the dripping for a moment and shivered from the cold wall. "Who was that who just spoke?"

"MC Deluxe, rapper from Harlem. Original gangsta. Rhymin' king of 128th Street. And I, um, I miss my momma."

The Former Donald spoke next. "And what's your story, MC?"

A sigh was followed by a curse, as if MC Deluxe was halfway between grief and outrage. "Man, I was doin' my thing, ya know? Out on the street with my neighbors, blasting my beats and spoutin' my rhymes. There's this part in my song when I scrunch my eyes shut and punch the air, you know, to show my strength and power. But when I opened my eyes all my homies was gone and my whole street was empty. Sooo, white dude, what's *yo* story? Tell us yo story. Don't everybody wanna hear white dude's story?"

"Yeah, uh-huh, tell it," came the chorus from the far end of the room.

The Former Donald elbowed Lanny, who elbowed Ned. "You go first."

"No, you go."

MC Deluxe grew impatient. "Will one of you white dudes please tell us yo story?"

Lanny volunteered. "I was on my knees, on hardwood floors, in a Baptist church, in northwest Atlanta. I was kneeling in front of a baptismal and—"

"Man, don't be tellin' us no conversion story. You ain't in here 'cause of no conversion."

"If you'd shut up a minute, I'll explain," Lanny replied.

"Then go ahead, temperamental white dude—tell us yo story."

Lanny sighed and began again. "I was on my knees, in front of a baptismal, with my cordless drill and my hammer, when I hit my thumb. I forgot where I was and so I cursed. Then I went to the men's room, and beside the sink there was—"

"Tell it, man! You done saw a sign, dintya? Yep, he saw a painted sign, too. I know it."

"You're correct, MC. The sign said 'Someone Always Hears.' The paint was still wet."

A fifth voice, this one deeper, came from the corner. "I got that sign, too."

"I saw one in a Denny's bathroom," said a younger man. "Right after I slapped my cousin for stealing my fries. Now he's gone, too . . . and I really don't miss 'im."

Lanny coughed loudly. "Do y'all want to hear the rest of my story or not?"

"Ain't like we goin' anywhere, man," MC said. "This here must be some kind of religious reform school."

"Hogwarts for pagans," said Crackhead.

The room went silent for a moment. Then MC spoke again. "Tell it, white dude. Tell us yo story."

Lanny almost quit talking, so frustrated was he by his circumstance. Yet, he had nothing better to do. Plus he'd always heard that prisoners can best keep their sanity by being social.

"After I left the church, I stopped for gas at a BP station because I had to get to south Atlanta to install a kiddie commode. So after I finished pumping the gas, I looked at the price and saw—"

"Six dollars and sixty-six cents per gallon," MC said. "They gouged Harlem, too."

"Same price in Eugene," Freddie offered. "Even for diesel."

Lanny continued. "So I left the BP station and stopped for lunch at a McDonald's. I walk in and see that they have—"

The teenage voice rang out. "Crosses on the uniforms! Same at Burger King, only they were on the hats."

Everyone in the room chimed in. "Same at Hardees."

"Jack in the Box, too."

"My waffles at Cracker Barrel were shaped like little angels."

That was the last thing anyone said for a long while. The sporadic dripping from the pipe continued, and soon Ned leaned over to whisper to Lanny. "I think we've made some new friends."

Lanny had a brain flash. Suddenly he did not want to tell any more of his story to the dark room. *What if Miranda is in Cuba too, blindfolded in some other dark room?*

"Is there a Miranda Timms in this room?"

Silence. *Surely she would have spoken if she were here.*

He asked again. "I need to know if a Miranda Timms from Atlanta is here in Cuba."

MC Deluxe spoke first. "Naw, man. Ain't no Miranda here. No one here has any loved ones. It's just us. Bunch o' strangers who stank bad."

The Former Donald spoke in his best duck voice: "But I don't stink, Mr. Rapper."

Everyone laughed. But just briefly.

Then there was only the dripping sound from the leaky pipe, followed by the door swinging open, light pouring in, and Marvin the Apostle entering triumphantly in a flowing gold robe.

"Thou shalt keepeth quiet in my presence," he announced, raising a finger to halt questions. "All thy need knoweth is that tomorrow, thy reform shall commence . . . *eth.*"

Marvin stepped out the door and slammed it behind him.

Then he opened it slightly to loose the trailing edge of his flowing gold robe.

The Former Donald laughed and pointed a finger. "Thy robeth got a runneth in its threadeth."

Marvin slammed the door, and the room went dark.

LOW-RANKING GUARDS entered the room the next morning and informed all prisoners that reform school included a work detail.

The prisoners were led out into the Cuban sunlight, right into the heart of downtown Havana. This was the bad side of the city—graffiti everywhere, spray-painted walls, and worn wooden doors.

"This will not be hard labor," said the burliest guard, flanked on each side by comrades in black fatigues. He squinted into the morning brightness. "Whitewashing this graffiti will allow you to develop feelings of teamwork before you join Marvin's *big team.* And we all want to join the *big team,* don't we?"

No one spoke. No one nodded.

DJ Ned let his mind wander to more attractive demographics. "Can you tell us if there are any female non-zealots left?"

The guard blushed and motioned with his head toward the rising sun. "If there are, they're in a, um, different place than Cuba."

"Could you expound on that?" Lanny asked.

"No. We will not talk about females. All we want you to do is take this white paint and cover up the graffiti. You can work on the shady side of the street first if you wish. Work in groups of four. I'll bring back more paint at the top of every hour. Oh, and we'll have TraitorAde, too. Who wants orange and who likes cherry flavor?"

Seven hands went up for orange, thirteen for cherry.

DJ Ned, Lanny, the Former Donald, and MC Deluxe quickly formed a work team and selected the shady side of a two-story brick building for their first project. Each was issued a roller, a brush, and a five-gallon bucket of white paint. MC complained of the heat, saying nothing like this ever hit Harlem. DJ Ned pulled the top off his paint bucket and explained that a Cuban sun was much like a Cuban cigar—both pack a wallop.

The four men spread out at ten-foot intervals and began slapping white latex over the graffiti. "This isn't right," said Ned, looking pained as he leaned down to re-dip his brush. "I did nothing wrong."

Lanny covered and slathered Spanish words he could not read. "I knew we should have gone to Canada or Mexico instead of Deity World. I felt spooked as soon as we got stuck in traffic."

"Did you just call someone a name?" asked MC Deluxe. He raised his roller in a threatening manner. Paint dripped and splattered on the sidewalk.

"Chill, man. I said Orlando had me spooked."

Everyone seemed on edge—twice they flung paint at each other—but by noon they had covered two sides of the building. Except for one small, three-foot square in the corner, where MC had written his own graffiti: *My rhymes rock Cuba.*

After five of the guards brought lunch, everyone sat on the curb to eat six chocolate-covered locusts, which Ned claimed tasted like bad calimari. The guards then surprised everyone by loading Freddie from Oregon into a van. One explained loudly that this man had had his sentence cut short due to good behavior and a 'transforming of his mind,' and was thus on the next flight back to the States. Freddie boarded the van with a big grin and waved out the back window to the rest of the captives, a blue plastic WWMD wristband fashioned to his wrist. Then the guards reminded everyone that there would be no more early outs for good behavior, that everyone could expect to be in Cuba for at least a month, and that there was to be no talking during work detail.

The van had just departed when the guard in the passenger seat looked out his window and saw MC's boastful scribble on the side of the building. He ordered MC to whitewash the entire wall again and added two days to his sentence.

MC complained of racial profiling and refused to eat his last locust. "That dude better not show his face in Harlem," he whispered to Lanny.

Lanny told MC that he doubted Harlem was nearly as dangerous as it was in the past, given how things had changed. Soon they were alone again, painting away, and with the tip of his brush Lanny rewrote on brick his four possibilities for Miranda's whereabouts:

1) She's still looking for me, maybe in Atlanta.
2) She's hiding somewhere in the Caribbean.
3) She's held captive, but she's safe.
4) She's already captured and converted, and is now a zealot. (Is there a potion to reverse this condition?)

By 4:00 p.m., one city block of Havana's graffiti had been covered. Well, almost. Though Lanny had whitewashed his possibilities, one of his team members had slacked off. With only one more wall to go, the Former Donald remained curiously quiet—and uncharacteristically slow. He stood on the sidewalk at the end of the building, a good ways down from the others, pretending to paint but repeatedly glancing around the corner.

DJ Ned saw the Former Donald's strange behavior and went over to paint beside him. "You okay, duck?"

"I've been here before, man. After they wear us down with work, they'll try to brainwash us. I lied last time so that I'd get sent back to Orlando."

Ned thought, *Great, now I have two guys to cheer up. One obsessed with finding his girlfriend, the other afraid of brainwashing.* Though his brush held no more paint, Ned kept stroking the brick wall, just to appear busy. "You still haven't told us what you did to get sent here."

The Former Donald dipped his brush in the paint bucket. "I'd rather not say."

"C'mon, I won't tell."

"Promise?"

"Promise."

The Former Donald painted slowly but spoke with haste. "I wrote my own proverb on a bathroom wall. I was just having a bit of fun. It starts out with 'Do not visit theme parks on a Sunday.' They said the meter is an exact copy of one of Marvin the Apostle's King James proverbs, and that to parody Marvin in such a manner is sacrilegious. Therefore I had to be punished. There, that's what happened."

Disappointed, Ned frowned and went back to painting. He told the Former Donald that he held little interest in a duck proverb, or any other kind of proverb, for that matter.

"Wanna hear the rest of it?" the Former Donald asked. He dipped his brush again and sloshed the excess on the wall.

"No," Ned replied. "I don't wanna get caught talking and have days added to my sentence."

He turned to check behind him and saw at the far end of the block Marvin the Apostle huddled with the guards. Marvin donned purple fatigues and matching armbands, and in his hands he held a glossy-covered book. He flipped its pages and was overheard instructing the guards on the subtleties of brainwashing. After observing this spectacle for another minute, the Former Donald stopped painting and began peeking the opposite way again, around the corner of the building.

DJ Ned stopped in mid-stroke and said, "Don't tell me you're gonna try to escape."

The Former Donald had his back to Ned, still peering around the corner and scanning the streets of Havana. "I can't take any more of the brainwashing, Ned. I'm just a poser, ya know."

Ned sloshed some more paint on the brick wall and spoke out of the side of his mouth. "Ease up, Big D. We'll think of something."

The Former Donald knelt beside the paint bucket and pretended to tie his sneakers, which were already tied. "That's why I'm nervous. I've just thought of something."

Ned saw three guards huddled far behind them, still listening to Marvin's instructions and nodding with regularity. Ned knelt beside the Former Donald and pretended to tie his own shoes. "What'd you think of?" he whispered. "Tell me."

"Last time I was here, I was working on the roof of the building across the street, cleaning off pigeon droppings. And from up there I saw his estate."

"Whose estate? The pigeon's or Marvin's?"

The Former Donald leaned close to Ned and whispered, "Castro's."

Ned untied and retied his left sneaker. "What's so important about that? I figured Castro would have an estate somewhere."

Their whispering grew louder, and from fifty feet down the sidewalk Lanny whistled at them and held a finger to his lips. *Quiet.*

The Former Donald could not restrain himself. He moved to within inches of Ned's ear. "The estate is on the waterfront, man."

"So?"

"So, the zealots haven't touched his boat yet."

Ned tied his right sneaker for the third time, and now a trace of a smile formed on his lips. "Castro left a boat?"

"A huge one." The Former Donald spread his arms wide. "It's actually more like a yacht."

Ned and the Former Donald picked up their paint buckets and toted them over beside Lanny and MC Deluxe. Quickly the foursome huddled together while the Former Donald explained his plan—to sneak into Castro's compound after dark, steal the yacht, and be back in the U.S. before the zealots woke the next morning.

"We'll rename it the *Cuban Conversion*," he continued, "just so the Coast Guard won't suspect us."

All nodded their approval.

One of the guards looked up from the curbside lecture, pointed at them, and said, "Shhh."

MC Deluxe, whose arms were by now polka-dotted with white droplets, lowered his voice and informed the others that he was hip to any escape plan. He then boasted that he'd be the perfect guy to drive the vessel, given that one of his rap songs was about a drug dealer who owned a big yacht.

This last point resulted in a brief argument from DJ Ned, who claimed his flight-school experience as justification for captaincy. After a push and a shove, MC and Ned agreed to split the duty.

"Aren't we getting a bit ahead of ourselves?" the Former Donald asked, kneeling to paint the bottom of the wall.

"Way ahead," Lanny replied.

He wiped the sweat from his eyes and checked over his shoulder for the guards. Across the street Marvin the Apostle now brandished a leather whip, and his face grew stern as he instructed the guards in how to properly make it crack. One by one, each guard practiced cracking the whip against a metal dumpster, and the sound of punishment echoed through Havana.

The Former Donald winced at each crack. "We gotta go for it, guys. Maybe even tonight."

MC snuck two more glances at the guards flailing away at the dumpster. "Man, I say we bolt the first chance we get. They look serious 'bout them whips."

Paint droplets dotted Lanny's face, but he ignored his appearance and sloshed more latex on Cuban brick. Around him the whisperings came frequently now—almost as frequently as the crack of whips that frightened them—and he listened as a plan came together.

By the time the sun dropped behind the buildings and the day's work detail was nearly complete, a tired DJ Ned and a sweaty MC Deluxe had resumed their argument. Still facing the wall, they whispered harshly back and forth about why each should be the one to captain Castro's yacht—one man anxious to return to Harlem and his street rhymes, the other itching to return to the airwaves and his Margaritaville contentment.

And then, of course, there was Lanny, a man bent on finding his own lost shaker of salt.

She had to be *somewhere.*

AT DUSK THE GUARDS ushered everyone back to the long, dark, dank room. Tired captives carried with them their makeshift beds—lawn chairs. During the work detail someone had discovered a stash of reclining lawn chairs in one of the graffiti-stained buildings, and these nylon chairs were doled out for each prisoner to sleep upon.

Arranging their chairs along the left wall were, in order, DJ Ned, the Former Donald, MC Deluxe, and Lanny. The guards then distributed burned fish sandwiches and TraitorAde, telling the captives that they had but five minutes to finish dinner. The door shut and the captives ate in darkness.

DJ Ned had just taken his second bite when the door pushed open again. This time Marvin's robe was purple, and he shined a flashlight around the cavelike walls and across imprisoned faces. "Tonight thou seeth only this beam . . . but soon thou shalt seeth light that thou not yet knowest thou crave." He pulled his beam across each face a second time. "Thou doth understandeth?"

MC Deluxe swigged his TraitorAde and said, "Dude, I'm from Harlem, and you talkin' religious smack."

Marvin raised his head high and peered down his nose at MC. "My smacketh shall overcometh thy stupidity."

"Oh yeah? Then why you wear a gold robe one day and purple the next?"

"Monday Wednesday Friday I weareth the gold; Tuesday Thursday Saturday I weareth the purple."

Crackhead spoke up from across the room. "What about Sunday?"

"Thou art not yet prepared to seeth me on that day."

"Try us," Lanny shot back. "Thou art psychedelic?"

MC snickered. DJ Ned spewed TraitorAde on the floor.

"Shusheth thy mouths, captives!" Marvin demanded, clearly of-fended. "Tomorrow shall be thy testing. So prepareth yourselves, oh ye of little brains, for absorbing wisdom from my soon-to-be best-seller." He pulled the glossy-covered book from inside his robe and held it high.

"The Dummies' Guide to Zealotism?" asked DJ Ned, unable to see the title for lack of light.

"The Marvinci Mode."

With a swoosh of his robe Marvin the Apostle left the dank room, and this time he tugged his purple train through the thresh-old before slamming the door.

Before anyone could swallow his next bite of fish sandwich, the burliest guard reopened the door and counted down dinnertime on his watch. All this coming and going was confusing to the captives, but Lanny and crew ate without complaint and tried to look as en-ergetic as possible. The guard counted off the last seconds and told Crackhead to collect the paper plates and dump them in a plastic bag, which he did.

Everyone settled back into their lawn chairs, and the guard stood in the doorway and gripped the frames. "Everyone comfy now? Everyone gonna sleep well before facing the next level of re-form?"

The Former Donald reclined the back of his lawn chair and tested it for squeaks. Then he stood again and addressed the guard. "Sir, I have a question."

"About the lawn chairs? These are the only beds you'll get." He swept his arm across the room like a furniture salesman.

"No, not about our accommodations," said the Former Donald.

"About Marvin's? He sleeps in his Lear Jet."

"Not that, either," said the Former Donald. "I was wondering, since there are so many buildings left to be whitewashed, if my team of four could be allowed to work a night shift and possibly earn points for initiative . . . or at least good attitudes."

Lanny and DJ Ned and MC Deluxe all nodded earnestly, as if they loved the idea.

The guard rubbed his chin and said, "Let me check on that." He shut the door, and the room plunged again into total darkness.

The men lay on their backs and put their hands behind their heads. "Think he fell for it?" Ned asked.

"Let's hope so," Lanny replied.

"Gullible religious dudes always fall for it." MC whispered.

Five minutes later the guard returned with four spotlights, extension cords, and a little red wagon filled with paint buckets and brushes.

The Former Donald rose from his lawn chair and thanked the guard in a manner that could only be described as overly enthusiastic. DJ Ned and MC Deluxe quickly volunteered to carry the extension cords and spotlights.

Lanny was last out the door—and was left with the duty of pulling the wagon of paint buckets and brushes. He felt embarrassed to be pulling a little red wagon through Cuba, though he'd do anything to assist with the escape plan and renew his search for Miranda.

Down the baked streets of Havana, the guard led the foursome past the building they had whitewashed earlier in the day, and on to an abandoned, four-story apartment building. A rusty fire escape ran from top to bottom on one side, and the grafitti of forty summers covered every brick and crevice.

"This one looks like it needs lots of work," the Former Donald said, first to remove the lid from his bucket and take up his brush.

The others hooked their extension cords to spotlights and lay the lights face up on the sidewalk, beaming up the side of the building.

Their initiative impressed the guard, and he stepped back into the street and crossed his arms, surveying their progress. For a good hour—it was now just after 10:00 p.m.—he stood and observed. Spaced in their usual ten-foot intervals, the foursome painted with diligence, very aware that they were being watched.

"What now?" whispered MC Deluxe, re-dipping his brush.

"Shhh," Lanny whispered back. "Maybe he'll get sleepy or visit the restroom and leave us out here alone."

The guard remained in the street, monitoring progress, occasionally moving one of the spotlights to adjust its beam. For a long time he sat on the curb with a flashlight and read the first chapter of *The Marvinci Mode.* Meanwhile DJ Ned tried to appear calm by whistling while he painted, though he remained stuck on the chorus of "It's the End of the World As We Know It (And I Feel Fine)."

MC Deluxe could not take much of that. "Don't you know any other songs?"

"Perhaps you'd like to rap for us while we paint?" Ned shot back.

The Former Donald moved between the two men. "Relax," he whispered, "each of you can have a turn at steering the yacht."

Sometime after midnight the guard told the men that he had eaten some bad fish and would thus be reading Marvin's next chapter in a Portalette. He said he would check back with them before quitting time, which he set at 2:00 a.m. He began to walk away but turned with one last comment. "I'm only allowing you captives to work five hours. This is because we want you fresh for Marvin's lecture on the long-term advantages of joining the *big team.* And we all want to know the advantages of joining the *big team,* don't we?"

He made a whipping motion with his right hand and walked away.

All four kept painting and did not reply, although MC did give a brief wave with his brush, if only to urge the guard to leave.

As soon as the guard was out of sight, the Former Donald hurried to the fire escape and climbed the metal stairs to the roof. Lanny peered up from the sidewalk. "Can ya see anything?"

"The yacht is still there," said the Former Donald. "And the lights are off at the estate." He hurried back down the metal stairs to find the others anxious, waiting to bolt.

"Which way do we run?" asked Ned, dropping his brush in a paint bucket.

The Former Donald pointed south. "We go down one block, then left at the next street, then it's about a mile to the water-front."

MC Deluxe wiped his hands on his shorts, flexed his leg muscles backward like a sprinter, and said, "Let's get goin', then."

Lanny said, "Wait, guys. There's something else we can do to help ourselves." He went over to the unpainted part of the apartment building and stood against it, nose to brick. "Someone come paint around me," he said. "Quick, do it."

"What?" asked Ned, incredulous at this stupid idea. "Let's get going, Lann-o."

The Former Donald was the first to catch on. He saw the spotlights casting Lanny's shadow against the wall. "Lanny's right. Grab a brush."

The three others painted white around Lanny as he faced the brick wall and raised his right arm as if it held a brush. When they finished and he stepped away, Ned and MC realized the effect—a guard peeking from down the street would see the silhouette of a man painting. And though it might only buy them a few minutes, those minutes could be critical.

"Do me next," whispered MC Deluxe. He faced the wall some ten feet farther down than Lanny, held his arm high in the brushing position, and watched the others paint around him.

The Former Donald was next to face the wall, followed by Ned, whose silhouette turned out extra pudgy due to everyone being in a hurry to finish.

With the spotlights shown at just the right angle, the result was startling. At night and from a distance, the effect was of four men of varying height in the midst of painting a wall. MC being the tallest at six-feet two, Ned and The Former Donald the shortest at five-nine, and Lanny somewhere in the middle.

They left the buckets, the brushes, and the little red wagon on the sidewalk and ran down the street, heading the opposite direction from the dark and dank room. Past a dilapidated school and more graffiti—"Cuba Libre!" spray-painted on three consecutive store fronts—then past a basketball court and two cats on a fence, the men ran sweating into the night.

"Left now," whispered the Former Donald, running in a three-some with Lanny and MC.

DJ Ned trailed behind, panting. The next street was even darker than the last, and though the men all listened for the sound of sirens, none blared.

Ahead lay Castro's compound. Beyond that was the bay. Nearly out of breath from the long run, the foursome was relieved to see that the fence bordering the estate, instead of being barbed wire, was stone and masonry, perhaps seven feet in height. They stood panting, hands on hips, surprised to see an auctioneer's sign propped against the wall. The top half was written in Spanish, the bottom in English:

Notice of auction: Mansion and yacht to be auctioned off on September 2. Bidders must register before bidding. Monies to go toward construction of one of Marvin the Apostle's language schools on Puerto Rico. Thou shalt bid high!

"Does this make anyone feel bad about stealing the yacht?" Lanny asked, one hand already atop the wall.

"Nah," Ned whispered, "They can still auction it off from the States when they find it. They'll get higher bids there anyway."

Lanny was first up the wall—with a boost from MC. He helped the others over, they pulled him by the arms, and together they ran across acres of manicured lawn.

"Castro must have a thing for Bermuda grass," said the Former Donald, as if anyone cared.

They stopped and knelt in the grass when they thought they heard a siren. But it was just an electronic keyboard, sounding from the area of the guard quarters.

On their bellies now, the foursome crawled across the lawn, past a cobblestone driveway and a military jeep, then to the low stone wall on the waterfront. A long wooden pier extended out to the yacht. Midway down the pier, a single yellow light shone from atop a pole, and a pair of gulls sat in slumber on the railing.

The bay appeared tepid and motionless, almost innocent. Nervously glancing over their shoulders, MC Deluxe and DJ Ned waited for the Former Donald to tell them what to do next.

Lanny, however, was already running down the pier.

~~~~~~~

Two blocks off Rodeo Drive, I entered the plush, long-windowed office of producer Mylan Weems. A very blonde and very polished secretary had just shown me in. "Mylan is a busy man," she whispered on her way out.

He was on the phone, so we exchanged nods. I sat in his guest chair—mahogany, I think. I glanced first out his windows at sun-drenched Los Angeles, then at his awards displayed prominently along a burgundy wall, gallery lighting to boot. He kept talking and smiling and switching the phone from ear to ear. For the next ten minutes I watched business being done the California way: Showy, classy, and with glimmers of attitude.

I felt out of place. On one side of that opulent desk sat this producer, a man of gray hair and handsome wrinkles etched from decades of big deals and big dollars. And on the other side, Ned Watson of Atlanta, a man of slight paunch, formed from too many donuts and Saturday afternoon bar-b-ques. For all of her strange ways, Angie made a killer bar-b-que.

I was intimidated, and I think Mylan knew it; even before he hung up and introduced himself, he knew it.

After he'd shaken my hand and we'd settled into our seats, he began with compliments. My previous experience with producers had led me to believe they usually began in this manner. "Great tie, Nick. I, too, love orange."

"It's Ned."

"Right, sorry." A slight blush. He picked up a stack of paper from his desk, Larry's title page on top. He thumped it in the center. "Ned, I was interested after the first chapter, very interested after six. Then last week, as I was reading the reform school thing, well—" he picked up a silver-framed picture from his desk and turned it so that I could have a look. It was the producer and his wife at the Oscars, posing with Jane Seymour and Kate Winslet. "Your manuscript may never capture this kind of attention, but someday there might be potential for something low-budget."

Nervous, I nodded at his prized picture. "Yessir. I don't expect for this to—" I was choking. "But I feel like it has at least *some* potential. My wife, however, she—"

"Protested, right?" He sat the picture back on his desk and smiled at it. "You told me about her over the phone. Is this going to be a problem?"

I figured that's why he began with compliments, so that he could ease into his concerns over Angie starting some kind of grassroots protest. "I doubt it. She's just a bit reactionary . . . a Southern Baptist."

"And yourself?"

"I'm not reactionary at all."

"I meant are you a Southern Baptist?"

Nerves and fear and guilt all assembled at once in my head. Would confessing this small detail make or break a deal? Nah, I'd play it straight. Perhaps a smidgen of vaguery, just to be safe. "Maybe once a month. You know, to keep the wife happy."

He nodded, smoothed his thick gray hair. "Ned, the last thing we'd want, if we were to commit to the project, would be some kind of grassroots protest forming out of the Bible Belt."

Maybe the guy is a mind reader. "I guess it might depend on the ending, Mr. Weems."

His eyes widened and he snapped his fingers. "That's the other thing I wanted to mention. This manuscript I read doesn't contain an ending to speak of. Am I missing some pages?"

"No, sir. Larry Hutch is writing the ending this week."

He sat up, tapped his fingers on his desk, adjusted his framed picture again. "I'd like to read that ending as soon as possible. But you do know that Hollywood likes to invent their own endings. . . ."

"Yes, but perhaps we should see what Larry comes up with."

He thumbed the pages, chewed his bottom lip. "Yes . . . perhaps." He had avoided all mention of monies and deal points, and I knew better than to push. And yet, he'd paid for my plane ticket to come out and meet with him, so I figured he was somewhat serious. Plus, he looked like he wanted to say something. "Before I get to required deal points, and what we might be able to offer, I'd first—"

His secretary buzzed in.

Mylan checked his caller I.D. and covered the receiver with his hand. "Ned, my medieval drama is about to start shooting in New Zealand. This one has me by the throat. A-list actors, big budget, the works. . . . I'm sure you understand." He gestured toward his door. "Mind waiting outside?"

"Of course." I rose from my chair and took two steps back. "I'll just, um, wait in the lobby."

He picked up his phone with his left hand, offered a brief wave with his right. No eye contact; he was staring out his middle window at L.A. in all its palm-treed splendor. I opened his door and glanced one last time. He was smiling at his fair city and switching his phone from ear to ear.

Out in the lobby I sat alone and checked my cell phone for messages. One from Angie, six from Larry. I knew what Larry wanted—an update. Angie, however, had left the kind of message that was a rarity for her—an apology. Of sorts. I listened to it a second time. *"Ned, perhaps I overreacted. Okay, I'm sure I did. But I have some news: I just found out that the church is under budget, so I thought I would humor you with what one of the ladies in my women's group suggested. She suggested that I urge you to get Larry to tone things down a bit so that you could cut a big deal for his work and we could tithe generously. Sixteen of twenty women—all of them protestors—thought this a great idea, but I hope you'll be pleased to know that I was not one of the sixteen. Is it possible that this women's group is my own double-bogey? A bad influence? Anyway, I'm a mess today. I'll pick you up outside the United terminal at 6:35 tomorrow evening."*

Tithe generously? I'd flown to California, only to discover that my wife was hanging out with fruitcakes.

I folded my phone and set it back in my briefcase. I had the briefcase open at my feet, digging for a pen, when I noticed that a pair of rather long legs were occupying the seat next to me. These legs were muscular and toned and covered in black fishnet stockings.

I sat back in my chair and felt the stranger staring at me.

I glanced to my right. She was taller than me, had bigger arms than me, and wore a tight yellow skirt and blouse. Her hair was large and platinum. Her eyelashes could have doubled as a broom.

She noticed that I'd noticed. Then she nodded and smiled.

I nodded and noticed her very broad shoulders. Too broad. Much too broad for a broad.

She batted those eyelashes, crossed her fishnet legs. "Your suspicions are correct, sir," she said, kicking her leg up and down.

Was everyone in Hollywood so perceptive and direct? I turned uncomfortably in my chair. "You're a—"

"Yes, that's correct." She fluffed her thick hair and glanced at her nails. "But don't worry, I'm harmless. Mylan just asked me to try out for a part."

"For the dark medieval movie being shot in New Zealand?"

"No, a sci-fi thriller in the wine country."

"Ah."

Small talk was over, and she picked up a pair of magazines from the coffee table.

Gender confusion rocked my brain. I had never sat beside, or spoken with, a cross-dresser. During the ensuing minutes, as I sat silently staring at the floor, I decided that I could do it—I could muster the energy to treat this person like anyone else. I was too reserved for a formal introduction, however, so I decided that I'd assign her some kind of neutral name in my mind, something like Lynn.

Lynn tossed a *Hollywood Insider* and the latest issue of *People* down on the coffee table.

I felt her staring.

"What is that?" she asked next. "Are you a screenwriter?"

"An agent."

Lynn leaned a few inches closer, looking at the papers in my lap. "Must be good stuff if Mylan Weems wanted to see it."

"I believe it's decent," I replied, trying my best to be humble. "Wacked but decent."

Lynn admired her nails for a long minute. She reached inside her blouse and adjusted something, then something else, then turned her attention back to me. I could feel her staring over my shoulder.

"Mind if I . . ."

"Read?"

She checked her watch. "Yes, if you don't mind. Looks like Mylan is going to be a while."

I didn't want anyone else to read; cutting a deal had me preoccupied. "I really don't think . . . well, Mylan could call me back any minute now."

"But I'm a speed reader."

"No kidding?"

She leaned closer—and her perfume almost blew me into Nevada. "Seriously. Mind if I read some? Won't take long."

I handed her the first six chapters.

Lynn frowned and held the papers out in front of her bosom, as if they were a pittance. "C'mon, you can give me more than that."

I handed her twelve more chapters.

"That's more like it."

Pages fell into her lap every ten to fifteen seconds—I timed her while I waited for Mylan. Nothing better to do.

Lynn seemed mildly interested, then mildly engrossed, and a couple minutes later she even managed a giggle. "This golf scene in Augusta . . . 'Owned by the Master.'"

"You play golf, too?"

She dropped that page into her lap. "A five handicap. Plus I'm a Tiger fan."

I watched fifteen more minutes tick off the clock while Lynn— the speed-reading cross-dressing golfer—devoured Larry's manuscript.

The message from Angie had me feeling a bit more confident about my marriage, though I knew better than to call her from here. So while I waited for Mylan to summon me back to his office, I decided to return a call to Larry. I was scrolling through my list of numbers when my phone rang.

Larry had beat me to it. His seventh call in two hours.

"Hello?"

"What's happenin', Ned? I gotta know."

I stood and walked over to the window. I turned my back to Lynn and whispered into my cell. "At the moment, Larry, a she-male with great big eyelashes and black fishnet stockings is reading your stuff."

"Don't joke with me, Ned."

"I'm not joking. And she could probably beat us both at golf."

Larry paused, as if shaken by unexpected news. "But what about the producer?"

"Patience, Larry. In the meantime, update me on the girl. . . ."

"Miranda? She only went out once with the news guy. Yesterday she asked *me* out."

"No kidding?"

"She packed a picnic and drove us to Stone Mountain. We even practiced our swing dance on a big rock. I'll never figure women out."

"Me, either." I returned to my seat and told Larry that the next time I saw him in Atlanta, I would give him all the details. I relished face-to-face meetings when giving clients good news—and I was praying for good news.

It was now 2:30, and from the lobby I could hear the muffled voice of Mylan yelling at someone on his phone. I set my cell back in my briefcase and looked up to see Lynn batting those great big eyelashes at me.

"Do ya mind?" she said, pointing at my open briefcase.

"Not at all."

She had just begun chapter nineteen when Mylan opened his door and waved me back in. When I stood, Lynn reached out and touched my sleeve. "Can I keep this to read while you're in with—"

"Sure. Knock yourself out."

19

LANNY THOUGHT HE SAW a body bag. At this late hour, behind Castro's unoccupied estate, he ran down the pier and past the yellow light and dropped to his knees. He opened the bundle—only to discover four life preservers rolled up in a black tarp.

Beyond him, some fifty feet ahead, seawater lapped against the yacht. Behind him, some two hundred feet away, the Former Donald, MC Deluxe, and DJ Ned ran hunched-over in the dark, across the back lawn and onto the pier. They had run only a few feet when they suddenly stopped and lay low, afraid they'd be spotted by guards.

From his kneeling position at the tarp, Lanny turned and waved the men onward. "C'mon, hurry," he whispered, though they couldn't hear him from such a distance. "There's no one around . . . yet."

The threesome hurried down the pier and arrived panting beside their friend. "Why did you run off and leave us?" Ned asked, hands on hips and gasping for breath.

"I thought I saw a body. And I feared it could be her."

MC kicked the tarp and life preservers. "Man, I seen plenty of body bags in my time, and that don't look like no body bag."

"Well, it did from behind that stone wall."

The Former Donald strode ahead. "Will you guys stop arguing what is and what isn't a body bag and help me steal this yacht?"

The four men walked quietly down the last section of pier and stopped at the first tie rope, which was at least two inches in diameter and very taut. It was tied to a spike near Ned's feet. Lanny looked up at the bow of the yacht, some twenty feet over his head.

"Man, this thing is huge."

"Told ya," said the Former Donald.

MC began tugging and untying the front rope. Ned's effort to assist lasted only a few seconds. "Maybe we should get a couple of us on board and get the engines running before we untie any ropes."

MC paused, let go of the rope. "Yeah, s'pose so." He followed the other three toward a set of chrome stairs leading up to the yacht's cabin. He muttered under his breath, "I don't need no pudgy DJ tellin' me how to steal a boat."

Lanny was first up the stairs and onto the second deck. Brass railings abounded, as did pictures of the owner. The captain's area was a living room all by itself—plush red sofas, wet bar, Cuban art on three walls.

From behind the captain's area a faux roof extended overhead, open-air at the rear and covering a red marble hot tub. From the hot tub, one could see out the back of the boat. On top of the roof were deck chairs and a shell-shaped pool.

In the dark shade of the second level, Lanny stared at the hot tub, remembering how much Miranda had wanted one. They had even talked once of installing one on Lanny's patio should they marry. *I'm coming for you, M. I'm on my way.*

The other three men quickly ascended the stairs and boarded. They, too, stood with mouths agape, stunned at the opulence.

"Man, look at the size of that hot tub."

"Yeah," said Lanny, still lost in reflection. "Not bad."

The Former Donald moved to the captain's chair and began opening and shutting drawers and cabinets.

MC came up behind him. "What're we lookin' for?"

"Keys, man. We aren't going anywhere without keys."

All four men spread out around the second level and began looking under vases, behind pictures, in the cupboard, anywhere, for a set of keys.

After ten minutes of searching, MC stepped behind the wet bar and pulled open a cabinet but found it empty. He tugged on a drawer but found it locked. Then he peeked up at the others from behind bottles of rum. "What do the Spanish words *llaves extras* mean?" he asked.

"They mean 'spare keys,'" Ned replied.

MC found a corkscrew and pried the drawer open. Inside it he found sets of many different keys, all tagged with Spanish notations.

"What does *caja de herramientas* mean?"

"Toolbox," said Ned, watching anxiously from the opposing side of the bar.

MC read the next tag. "What about *equipaje de pesca*?"

"Fishing gear locker."

"What about *camion militar*?"

"Castro's military Jeep."

"What about *yate muy grande*?"

DJ Ned smiled. "It means 'very large yacht.' "

MC tossed the keys to the Former Donald, who inserted them in the ignition, goosed the throttle a bit, and turned the key. The sweet low gurgling from the back of the yacht summoned a round of high-fives.

"Untie the ropes," the Former Donald whispered. "Hurry."

MC was first to reach the stairs, where he hesitated and changed his mind. "Nope, no way. I got first dibs on steering the yacht, so you guys all go untie them ropes."

Lanny wedged past him on the stairs, descended two at a time, and went at the knots with quiet tenacity.

Ned, too, stepped around MC and onto the first step. On his way down to help Lanny, he spoke over his shoulder. "MC, how many yachts have you ever backed out of a dock?"

"None, but I did row a canoe in the Hudson River once."

Ned waved him on. "Come help us with the ropes. Let Duck back the boat out, then you and I can drive."

Though he grumbled, MC followed them down the stairs. "As long as I can be first."

"You can be first."

In seconds they untied the ropes and climbed again the chrome stairs to the second level. All three looked on anxiously as the Former Donald backed the yacht away and swung the nose to the starboard side. This was slow going, and all feared that the deep gurgling sound would awaken the guards.

Lanny stood lookout on the bow, which was the end closest to the compound. Beyond the dark mansion he saw Havana in slumber—except for one distant, hazily lit section of downtown. This was where the four spotlights still shone on their silhouettes upon the brick wall.

The yacht had motored only a stone's throw from the dock when an impatient MC took over at the steering wheel. He liked the chrome wheel's hefty feel. "One day I'll have me one of these."

The Former Donald attempted to offer pointers, but MC said he could handle it. He increased the power and stood with feet spread wide. His years on the streets had taught him how to fake confidence, and he was faking it for all he was worth. The engine noise was louder than he preferred, however, and this caused him to contort his face into a worried wince. His expression never changed as the noise leveled off to a steady hum and the yacht lumbered out into the bay.

"Everybody cool?" he asked his mates.

"Yeah," Ned replied, watching the depth gauge drop from twelve feet to fifteen. "Just keep going."

Light from a quarter moon angled across the waters and across Lanny's sneakers, which were covered in paint droplets. He gripped the railing and squeezed, hoping his nerves would exit through his hands. He looked again in the direction of the spotlights and wondered if any guards had come to check on them. He glanced at his watch. 1:14 a.m.

Only twenty-eight minutes had passed since the foursome had bolted from work detail and ran down the streets toward Castro's estate. Ned and the Former Donald kept lookout on the port and starboard sides, respectively. Lanny, however, remained on the bow, where he found himself with a bad case of the shakes. He was still not used to being on the run from authorities. He wasn't even sure if his shakes were from the escape, or from the growing realization that he'd been looking for Miranda for two weeks and wasn't a bit closer than when he began.

Everything visible—the pier, the stone wall, the Castro estate—

shrank in the darkness behind him, and he tried his best to consider the positives:

A successful escape from the zealots.

An ocean that appeared vacant.

A quarter moon instead of full.

MC Deluxe doing an adequate job of steering the yacht.

So far, so good.

It was 3:00 a.m. when Lanny discovered the big-screen TV in the stateroom, 3:10 when the Former Donald discovered French soaps in the showers, 3:15 when Ned discovered that there was no food on board. Only a stash of Cuban cigars in a cabinet, a single Reese's peanut butter cup and a case of bottled water in the fridge, one frozen mullet in the freezer.

Fish bait, at best.

A toilet flushed. Then, up from the cabin came the Former Donald, gushing over his find. "Nine bedrooms, eight bathrooms, expensive soaps, a pool table. This baby is loaded."

He, DJ Ned, and Lanny peeked in each of the rooms—including a pink room set up for children—before claiming separate bedrooms. MC, without taking his hands from the wheel nor his eyes from the sea, claimed the stateroom. All that brass and hardwood was irresistible, and as captain MC felt entitled.

Also hard to resist for MC was the shiny silver horn mounted left of the steering wheel. He wanted so badly to sound the horn to celebrate their escape. But he knew this was not wise, so he just rubbed the horn's surface with his hand. He steered the yacht farther north—in the general direction of Miami—while his three passengers took showers and scrubbed the paint from their arms.

Lanny and the others emerged one by one from below. Each was clean, each had wet, uncombed hair, and each had a towel around his neck. Lanny was first to ease into the red marble hot tub. He was quickly joined by DJ Ned, in Florida Gator gym shorts, and the Former Donald, who sported the boxers with the little ducks smiling from every square inch.

The three exhaled a collective "Ahh" as the water jets hit their backs. Each man lay back with his head against the red marble, eyes shut, letting the pain of imprisonment bubble off while MC whistled at the helm. He loved being the skipper, though he was not a good whistler.

Ned centered himself over a water jet and said, "This is so much better than white-washing graffiti, ain't it, MC?"

MC gave a thumbs-up and increased the throttle.

Lanny got his mind off Miranda by thinking of the Cuban people. He wondered if they thought conditions were worse under communism or under Marvinism. He figured brainwashing was a large part of either doctrine, and deemed it a tie.

20

AFTER THE ESCAPEES had motored a safe distance from Havana—they had traveled ten nautical miles, and Cuba had just faded from sight—DJ Ned was the first to break the silence. He was sprawled in the hot tub as if he owned it. "What's everybody going to do when we dock back in the States?"

"Besides run?" asked the Former Donald. He and Lanny had just reentered the tub.

"Yeah . . . besides that."

The Former Donald put his hands behind his head, as if he had it all figured out. "I have two friends in Orlando who are also posers. We'll leave Florida and probably head for Montana in my truck. My uncle lives up there, says things aren't so bad, less crowded."

Ned lifted his hands from underwater, admired his wrinkled fingertips for a moment, and pointed at Lanny. "How 'bout you, Lann-o?"

"I'll just continue my search. I'll run from whomever I need to run from, and pose when I need to pose. I'll cash out my savings and won't stop searching until I find Miranda."

The others all gave a thumbs-up or an affirming nod to Lanny's resolve. MC Deluxe turned from the captain's chair and said, "I never met any woman I felt that strongly about. I'm a career man, and I'm gonna continue my career . . . somewhere."

Lanny lay his head back against the edge of the hot tub and sighed. He had nothing else to add except, "What about you, Ned?"

"I may try to get to England. I got a DJ buddy over there, so maybe I'll move and change my name and go incognito."

"DJ Incognito!" said MC Deluxe, staring out the windshield, one hand on the wheel. "'Bout time we had some music." He switched the yacht to auto-pilot and began pressing buttons on the CD player. The yacht's stereo was mounted in teakwood, and situated so that a captain could reach it without getting out of his chair.

MC opened the CD changer and found six CDs already in the system.

"Man," he said, shocked at what he'd discovered. "Castro listens to Mariah Carey."

Ned kept his eyes shut in the hot tub but shook his head in unbelief. "No Springsteen or Journey?"

"Naw, man, none of that white stuff. Just Mariah and J-Lo and, aw, you guys won't believe this!" He waved a shiny disc in the air.

"What is that?" Lanny asked.

"Castro got himself a Backstreet Boys CD."

Lanny woke early. At 6:55 a.m. he staggered out of his bedroom, came up on to the second level, and wandered over to the starboard side. He watched the sun rising over the Atlantic. Land was not visible in any direction, and he was shocked to see that their yacht was now adrift.

No one at the helm. No captain. No gurgling engine noise.

Lanny hurried below and found DJ Ned snoring in a blue bedroom, the Former Donald sleeping quietly in a green bedroom, and no sign at all of MC Deluxe. Lanny checked the stateroom and the other vacant bedrooms, finding nothing but some crumbs on the floor of the pink room. Someone's mess. He worried that MC had become shark food.

And Lanny was largely correct.

After an exhaustive search of the vessel, he found MC seated at the stern, hidden by a large ice cooler. MC's legs dangled over the side, dark shades over his eyes. Blood seaped from his upper right arm, clotting fast but still in a slow stream toward his elbow. In his hands he held a thick fishing pole.

Lanny rushed over to him. "Man, I thought you'd fallen overboard. How'd you cut your arm?"

"Nope, didn't fall. I read in a book once that certain fish can smell blood from a mile away, and so I cut myself and dripped it on our frozen mullet. Then I stuck a chunk of the mullet on my hook. Somebody gotta catch some food, ya know."

"Good thinking, MC," Lanny said, impressed with his resourcefulness but queasy over the bloody arm. He sat down beside his new friend. "Any bites?"

"Naw, but I just started five minutes ago. There's another pole in the locker." MC pointed to the closet beside the captain's quarters, where he had spent the night among red satin sheets below a framed painting of Castro himself.

Lanny retrieved the second pole and tied on a hook. He sat back down at the stern and baited his hook with a chunk of MC's mullet.

MC wiped some blood from his arm and spread it all over Lanny's bait. "Now you're ready. Throw it on out there."

Ten minutes later Lanny had not had a bite. Ten minutes and twenty seconds later, MC's pole began quivering. Then bending. Then quivering and bending some more.

Lanny's whoop was followed closely by MC's holler.

It was only 7:10 a.m., and they had forgotten their comrades were asleep. But as long as there was a fish on someone's line, there was going to be some whooping and hollering.

The Former Donald came running out of his bedroom and onto the back deck, his hair sticking up at odd angles. "What are you guys yelling about? Y'all see some zealots? Are they chasing us?" He turned and looked in all directions, saw nothing but blue sea. "And just where are we?"

"Catching a meal, man," MC said, grimacing as he pulled hard on his pole.

This was not a thorough enough answer for the Former Donald. He noted the lack of a captain. He noted the drift of the yacht. Then he licked his hand and pressed his hair flat, as if appearances mattered. "Are we outta fuel?"

Lanny shook his head and helped MC to his feet. "Nope, just pausing to get some breakfast."

"How 'bout we split the Reese's in the fridge?"

Though sweaty and preoccupied with his pole, MC used his head to point below deck. "I think our DJ buddy ate the Reese's last night. I heard someone sneaking around in the kitchen 'bout 4:00 a.m."

There was no more talking after that. MC had never fished in the ocean before, and he was stunned at the brute strength of whatever had bitten his chunk of O-positive mullet. He reared back and tugged on the pole. He tried to reel in the line but found its resistance staggering.

Lanny reeled his own line out of the way, set his pole aside, and grabbed a gaff from beside the ice cooler. "You making any progress?"

MC gritted his teeth and pulled. "Ain't no fish getting the best of MC."

The Former Donald looked on amazed, not at the fishing but the fact that anyone would be up before 7:00 a.m., especially after stealing Castro's yacht the previous night. The Former Donald was not much of a morning person. He worked the afternoon shift at the theme park, and never woke before 9:00 or 10:00.

In a tangle of line and arms, MC and Lanny shouted instructions to each other. Then they reached over the stern with pole and gaff and hauled up something that very much resembled a shark. It flopped violently on the deck—until MC grabbed a block of ice from the freezer and smashed it on the fish's head.

With pride glistening on his young face, MC glanced up at the Former Donald. "How big you think this fish is?"

The Former Donald estimated twenty pounds.

Lanny nudged it with his foot and guessed sixteen.

The fish flopped twice more. MC whopped it again with his ice brick.

All three stood staring at the stunned fish until DJ Ned came up yawning from below deck. He walked back to the stern, eyed the catch, and muttered, "Twenty-one pounds, tops."

With an exaggerated frown, MC dismissed all guesses. He put his

foot on the fish, posed like for a picture, and gave his personal estimate of ninety-seven pounds.

Lanny found some scales in the tool locker and weighed the
catch. "Eighteen and a half," he said, turning the scales toward MC.
"Enough for a few steaks, I'd say."

MC Deluxe, being from the inner city of Harlem, had little experience with Caribbean fish. "Um, what exactly is that thing I just
caught?"

Ned yawned again before stooping to get a better look at the
catch. "It's a dogfish," he said. "A type of shark . . . and it's edible."

"I ain't eatin' no dogfish," said MC. "My momma would never
allow it."

Lanny put his arm around MC and spoke into his ear. "If it's all
we catch, then you'll probably ask for seconds."

Three hours later, it was all they had caught.

MC pulled his cold and stiffened dogfish from the cooler and
held it up for all to see. "Don't nobody tell me how to cook this
fish. I can cook my own fish. And yes, I will share with everybody,
even those of us who slept late. Even whoever it was who ate the
Reese's in the fridge. This is 'cause I'm generous. And when I get
my recording contract, I'll still remember you little people. But
right now, I gotta go play chef." He gripped the tail of the dogfish
and motioned for the others to clear the way. "Don't nobody
crowd me in the kitchen either. I get to cook my own fish my own
way, not fried up and covered with onion rings like you southern
guys do."

A hungry DJ Ned pointed toward the kitchen. "We don't have
any onion rings, MC. I looked."

"Still, I cook my own fish my own way." With a firm grip on the
tail, MC dragged the dogfish across the deck and hauled it to the
yacht's kitchen, which he was pleased to see contained a Jenn-Air
range, a spice rack, and a set of expensive German cutlery.

For two days they paralleled the Florida Coast, out of sight of land
but not far from Boca Raton. Meals retrenched into sameness. At a

rationed pace in the South Atlantic, they ate small portions of dog-fish steak for breakfast, lunch, and dinner.

"I'm sick of dogfish," said the Former Donald at the dinner table. "Can't one of you guys catch a mangrove snapper? Perhaps a pompano?"

He was strongly urged to hush—MC even pointed a fillet knife at him—and the men finished their meal in silence.

After the meal, Lanny finally got his turn in the captain's chair. He sat at the wheel alone, his mind solely on Miranda. He wanted her to be on this boat with him. Just the two of them, cruising the Caribbean and planning for happily-ever-after. For five hours he sat at the wheel and thought such thoughts. *I'd be happy if we could just share a rowboat.*

It was only the cooler air of evening that awakened Lanny from his daydream. He summoned MC Deluxe to take over at the helm, and MC was more than happy to oblige.

The gregarious rapper settled in to the chair, and the others gathered around him to discuss strategy. Land was still not visible, and soon a heated argument broke out over where to go ashore. They were now due east of Fort Pierce, Florida, some thirty miles off the coast.

DJ Ned had insisted that Miami was the wrong choice—the first place authorities would be waiting. Ditto for the Keys. The Former Donald suggested they turn around and dock in Fort Lauderdale, reasoning that most of the rich folk were gone and so the city would be largely vacant. Plus, a yacht docking in Fort Lauderdale was quite common.

"That's still too close to Cuba," Ned explained.

Lanny said anywhere on Florida's East Coast was fine with him. He just wanted to resume his search, to go look for clues among the retirement home and Bluewater Marina, maybe even return to Atlanta and look there.

MC Deluxe turned from his captain's chair. "But I wanna go all the way up the East Coast to Long Island. I can get to Harlem from there."

The disagreement continued into the red marble hot tub. Situated some twenty feet behind the captain's chair, it was a nightly luxury for all aboard. To be able to peer out the back of the yacht while under the cover of an extended roof, to enjoy the smooth ride at sea along with soft ballads by a boy band, made for quite the memorable escape. Not a man on board had ever owned a hot tub. Not even DJ Ned, who could afford his own airplane.

The calm seas put MC Deluxe in a better mood than his cohorts. While they sprawled in heated waters and defended their choices of where to go ashore, he turned from his captain duties and addressed them as one. "Do you guys realize that I've done almost everything for you since we escaped? Think about it. MC found the spare keys; MC bled on your mullet; MC caught you a dogfish; MC kilt the dogfish with a chunk of ice; MC cooked your dogfish steaks; MC even salt and peppered your dogfish. And now MC skippers you up the East Coast in his yacht. All this while you three Gilligans chill out in MC's hot tub."

DJ Ned and the Former Donald kept their eyes shut and gave no reply.

Lanny raised a hand from the tub and offered a thumbs-up. "You da man, MC."

Off and on for the next half hour the men argued about where to go ashore and what to do when they got there. One thing they all agreed upon—zealot-infested America was preferable to zealot-infested Cuba.

More room to roam.

So the foursome continued north, maintaining their distance at thirty miles offshore. They were soon due east of Daytona.

Sometime after midnight, DJ Ned suggested Fernandina Beach, reminding all that the town was surrounded with rivers and estuaries and lots of marsh. "Plenty of waterways from which to sneak in and dock. Anybody got a problem with Fernandina Beach?" he asked the crew.

Hungry again and tired of eating the same thing, everyone shook his head.

Fernandina Beach it was.

Around 2:00 a.m., Lanny went into the kitchen, opened the fridge, and noticed they were down to just one small chunk of steak. He returned to the hot tub and told the others of their situation. No one would admit to having eaten. Each man accused the other of eating more than his fair share, and so yet another argument broke out.

The Former Donald was the worst. "Why can't you guys catch anything?"

Since the first morning at sea, no one had been able to nab another fish.

Beyond them in the captain's chair, MC Deluxe kept both hands on the chrome wheel, steering the vessel north through the warm Atlantic. After another hour at the helm he felt so comfortable in his role that he invented a new rap. He called it "I'm Da Skippuh," and he rapped it to the stars, to the western Caribbean, anyone who cared to listen.

"Back in the hood my homies stay proud.

Their brother rock Cuba and he rock 'em real loud.

Nobody juke Harlem with the story I got—

The night Young Deluxe stole Castro's yacht."

For the chorus he turned and pointed at each man, his left hand still on the wheel, his knees bobbing to the beat. "I'm da Skippuh, yeah, yeah. I'm da Skippuh with my three Gilligans."

Lanny and the Former Donald clapped in mock approval. Then MC, back in his element, began the chorus again.

And again.

Oh, the repetition.

At the fourth recital, Lanny and the Former Donald joined in.

After the sixth, DJ Ned muttered he couldn't take anymore and submerged himself in the hot tub.

That's when Lanny heard a siren echoing across the water.

He scrambled out of the hot tub and stood at the railing and stared into the night.

They were being chased.

Dripping and scared and struggling to think, Lanny found a scope in the captain's station. He peered behind the yacht and across dark seas.

In the faint light from the quarter moon he saw them: Guards in black fatigues, ten of them perched on the bow of a Coast Guard cutter.

And this time they had guns.

21

IN THEIR EXCITEMENT to steal the yacht, none of the four had remembered to change the name on the stern to the *Cuban Conversion*. Perhaps this would have changed the outcome. Perhaps not. After all, hiding a one-hundred ten-foot yacht that's decorated primarily in Castro's favorite color—red—is not as easy as one thinks.

Although the Former Donald had conceived of the plan while white-washing Havana graffiti for the guards, he had failed to account for armed pursuers at sea. And behind them now, shouting through a bullhorn and brandishing rifles, were armed pursuers at sea.

The Former Donald crouched with Lanny and DJ Ned behind the hot tub, afraid that shots would be fired any moment. Still at the helm, MC Deluxe pressed the throttle to full—which was no easy task, considering his body position. He too had dropped to his knees. He was now unable to see where he was steering but was nevertheless able to hold the wheel with his left hand and reach up for the throttle with his right. His shoulders began to cramp. It was like being on your knees on your kitchen floor and trying to wash dishes in the sink.

"What now?" he shouted to the others.

"Just go as fast as you can," Lanny shouted back.

"I'm at full throttle."

"Is there a fuller than full?"

MC was about to reply when the bullhorn sounded.

"BRINGETH THY VESSEL TO A STOP!" The words echoed across the ocean. "NOW!"

MC glanced at Lanny, who turned to DJ Ned, who glared at the

Former Donald and said, "What do we do now, O great planner of escapes?"

The Former Donald appeared shocked that Ned could manage sarcasm at such a time, what with guards in black fatigues chasing them in a Coast Guard cutter, and Marvin the Apostle shouting through a bullhorn in the King James English.

One thing was for sure—Fernandina Beach was out. While on a normal day it made for a fine place to sneak back into the continental U.S., it was not so good a port while being hotly pursued.

At 4:05 a.m., MC Deluxe made a calculated decision not to stop. He turned the wheel slightly to the right and changed their bearings to north toward the coast of Georgia.

That's when the first bullet zipped overhead and into the night.

"Just a warning shot over the stern," said DJ Ned, trying to crouch his portly frame ever lower behind the hot tub.

"I thought warning shots were always fired over the *bow*," Lanny replied. His face was pressed against red marble, just above the Former Donald's feet.

Ned thought about this for a moment. "No, in Cuba, I think they fire over the stern."

The Former Donald, huddled between Ned and Lanny, his forehead on the floor, confirmed that in Cuba, warning shots were usually fired over the stern.

But why was their vessel teetering to and fro? MC fought with the wheel, which all of a sudden had a mind of its own. The yacht rose high upon a wave and dropped heavily over the crest, causing Lanny to bite his lip. He spat saliva and blood. Wave after wave pounded the front and starboard sides. Rain began to fall. Then bigger rain. Then sheets of rain.

Panic set in among the crew.

Besides not accounting for the possibility of armed pursuers at sea, the Former Donald had also not considered the possibility of another August hurricane. "Didn't anyone check the weather forecast before we left?" he asked the others.

MC turned and frowned at the question. "Man, how could we

check weather while locked in that dark room with all them prisoners who stank?"

A huge wave slammed the starboard side and rocked the yacht. "Hurricane Hellacious," said DJ Ned.

"Actually," said the Former Donald, "it would be named Hurricane Howard, although I'll admit that it feels more like—"

A second bullet split the air above the yacht. *Ziiiing.*

Lanny was the only one who kept his senses. On his stomach he crawled around the hot tub and behind the captain's quarters, to the stairs leading down to the stateroom. He disappeared below, then came back up two minutes later, still on his stomach.

"Where'd you go?" DJ Ned whispered.

Breathing hard, Lanny crawled back behind the hot tub. "To check the weather on Castro's big-screen TV."

"And?"

"And there's a tropical storm, or maybe a tropical depression—I wasn't clear on that part—east of Savannah, Georgia."

"And?"

"And I heard the weather girl say 'convection,' 'sub-tropical moisture,' and 'northwesterly movement.' "

"That means we're heading right into it," said the Former Donald, who, prior to his stint at the theme park, had flunked out of meteorology school.

MC reached up and turned the wheel slightly to the right, then cut back on the throttle. The yacht rose high upon a wave and dropped hard. "Aw, man," MC muttered to no one in particular. "We never had no hurricanes in Harlem. No warning shots neither." The next wave lifted them higher than the last. "Where I come from, people shoot for real or they don't shoot at all."

DJ Ned raised his bearded face from behind the hot tub to peer back at the Coast Guard cutter. The large waves and heavy rain had caused the cutter to fall farther behind, some two hundred yards perhaps. In addition, those same waves played havoc with the guards' ability to aim their warning shots over the stern. The next shot wasn't even close.

While the waves pounded and the guards pursued, a third argument broke out aboard the yacht.

"We gotta outrun 'em," Ned suggested.

"But we're down to our last eighth of a tank of fuel," Lanny noted.

"Just run us aground anywhere," shouted the Former Donald, who feared drowning as much as bullets.

MC felt seasick from all the ups and downs and lurching of the yacht. He rose from the floor for a moment and checked the electronic map above the steering wheel. "How about Tybee Island, Georgia?"

The crack of gunfire forced him back to the floor, hands covering his head.

"Tybee Island sounds just fine," said a young voice. But his was not the voice of any of the four.

Lanny, the Former Donald, DJ Ned, and MC Deluxe all turned from behind the hot tub and the captain's chair and glanced to the stairs leading up from below.

DJ Ned was the first to recognize the young man. "Crackhead?"

"It's me, Ned."

"How did you—"

Confused and frightened by the gunfire, the stringy haired Crackhead dropped to the floor. "While you guys were whitewashing graffiti the other night, I told the guards I was sick to my stomach. So when they told me to go relieve myself in an alley, I just started running toward the water. I dove in the ocean and swam down to the yacht. I must've climbed on board just before you guys did."

"Then you're . . . a stowaway?"

The resourceful Crackhead came crawling toward them. "I've been stowed away in the pink bedroom. In the closet with all the toys."

Ned nodded. He had rejected that room solely on the color scheme and had slept in the blue room instead. Then Ned thought back to the missing chunks of dogfish steak. "Did you eat those chunks of fish?"

A fifth bullet zipped overhead, and everyone dove to the floor again. Crackhead crouched low behind the hot tub with the others. "Just three little pieces, Ned. I was starving."

DJ Ned tried to wrap himself in a ball. "The Reese's?"

"Ate that too . . . last night, I think."

"Man, you need a bath," said Lanny.

Crackhead sniffed his own underarm. "I was afraid that if I used the shower, someone would hear me. I didn't know who was piloting the boat . . . until I heard someone rapping."

"That would be me," MC said proudly, reaching up again for the wheel and throttle. "What you heard was my new single, titled 'I'm Da Skippuh.'"

A bullet pinged off the antennae above the captain's quarters. MC immediately turned the yacht toward land. Through the rain and over the bow he saw a distant lighthouse.

Through the rain and over the stern, Lanny saw a spotlight beaming back and forth. The light shone from the Coast Guard cutter as it powered through the waves, closing the gap.

A frightened Lanny crawled over to help MC navigate.

MC pressed the throttle to full power and glanced behind at their pursuers. "They're gaining on us, man."

"Just stay calm and don't stop till we hit the beach," Lanny said. They were a quarter mile from land now, and Lanny noted the depth gauge to the left of the throttle. For a couple seconds it showed twenty-nine feet. Then it rose to twenty feet. Then to thirteen. Then nine, then six, then four.

The yacht lurched to a stop. The men went tumbling.

In their anxiousness to reach shore and flee, none of the crew had considered the possibility of sandbars.

Angie's effort at "I'm sorry" was Braves tickets. My own effort was imported chocolate from Rodeo Drive. She had reconsidered her southern belle protest movement, and now our shared desire was to mend the relationship. We exchanged gifts in her Subaru, moments after she picked me up from the Atlanta airport.

We sat idling at the United drop-off area, holding hands across the console. "Perhaps I overreacted, Neddie," Angie said, leaning toward me.

"I'm sure you did, pumpkin." Our foreheads met. "And perhaps I think too often of money."

"I'm sure you do. But I shouldn't have protested. The day you flew out to L.A. I read in Proverbs that a quarreling wife is like a constant dripping from a faucet. Am I like a faucet that constantly drips, honey?"

Nose to nose now, I replied with soft-spoken honesty. "Actually, you were more like an eruptive fire hose at full blast . . . but it's, um, water under the bridge now?"

Her eyelashes brushed mine. "Pristine aqua waters like our honeymoon on St. Croix?"

"Just like those waters, dear."

Now, before you go thinking that we sped home, kissed on the porch and in the foyer and down the hall, then spent a romantic evening making up and making out, just put the brakes on your lust-mobile. That ain't how it happened.

You see, the Braves tickets were for that night's game; we drove straight from the airport to the ballpark. On the way there—she'd asked me to drive, and I was weaving through Friday evening traffic—she ate my apology chocolate, licking her lips and pronouncing it delicious.

I glanced down at the console and noticed four tickets instead of two. It was like they had multiplied. A paperclip held them tightly together. All I could figure was that when Angie had given them to me, I had kept my eyes on her instead of the tickets. I had just assumed there were two.

She wiped her mouth with a napkin as we idled in traffic at the Turner Field exit. I used this moment to pick up the four tickets and spread them like a poker hand in my fingers. "Angie, honey, ordinarily when a couple attempts to make up, they prefer to be one on one."

Angie reached over and patted my hand. "Ordinarily, Ned. Yes."

We rolled forward at maybe two miles per hour. A flashing sign over the sidewalk broadcasted BRAVES—MARLINS, 7:35 TONIGHT!

I glanced at my watch. 7:02. "So, Ang, you're not going to tell me who we're meeting here at the ballpark?"

I suspected some relational counselors, perhaps from the Baptist church.

She patted my hand a second time. "While you were in L.A., I e-mailed Larry and invited him to the game."

"You contacted *Larry?*"

"Yes."

"And he replied?"

"He's bringing a date. They're meeting us at the ticket office."

Perplexed, I turned right into stadium parking. "He'll probably be with Miranda."

Angie immediately grabbed my right arm.

"*Miranda?*" she asked. "How can his date be named Miranda when the girl in his story is named Miranda?" Suddenly Angie had her hands over her mouth, eyes wide and unblinking, her gaze fixed over the hood. "Oh . . . oh my. Does she know?"

I parked between two minivans and cut the engine. "Last time Larry and I spoke, he had not informed the young lady of that slight coincidence."

No way was I wearing long sleeves to the ballpark. I pulled my white buttondown over my head and reached into the backseat for my orange polo. When my head poked through the opening, I noticed that Angie's hands remained over her mouth, and that her eyes had taken on a cool, calculating look.

I felt the need—even the obligation—to intervene. "Angie, you cannot initiate any confrontation with Larry tonight. This is supposed to be our make-up date . . . right? Didn't we just exchange gifts?"

She opened her door to climb out. "Can't I just ask him a few little questions between innings?"

I got out of the driver's side and shook a finger at her over the roof. "This is our make-up date. So tonight we're both limited to baseball, small talk, and hot dogs all the way."

She slung her purse over her shoulder and grinned in a manner that bordered on devious.

I went around the hood and took her by the hand. Together we walked toward the ticket office. "Promise me, Ang?"

"Okay."

"Say it with me. . . ."

She frowned and mocked the movement of my lips. "Baseball, small talk, and hot dogs all the way. Baseball, small talk, and hot dogs all the way."

Ahead stood Larry, waving at us along with his auburn-haired date. He appeared anxious for an L.A. update. She appeared so innocent for a muse.

Perhaps it was the crack of bat meeting ball that caused me to forget about Hollywood's disappointing offer. Or it could have been the reconciliation with my wife. Or perhaps it was the smell of hot dogs in the air and the boiled peanuts I'd shared with Larry. In row thirty-two on the first base side of Turner Field, he and I occupied seats one and four, respectively. Larry needed the aisle seat, what with his long legs. In seat three, to my left, sat Angie, and to her left, in seat two, was Miss Miranda Simms.

"Thank you so much for the seats, Agent Orange," she said after the next pitch. I thought it was cute the way she called me Agent Orange, as if that were my given name.

I caught her glance and pointed to Angie's head. *It was her idea.*

Between pitches, the four of us shared our backgrounds, and soon I discovered that Miranda had grown up in Florida, in a suburb of Orlando. I also learned that her parents owned an offshore boat and that she had a younger sister.

By the second inning, Angie had befriended both of our guests and was intermittently yelling at the umpires and making girl-talk with Miranda. "Isn't the night air wonderful?" she asked.

Miranda nodded. "I just love summer. I even drove Larry here tonight with my sunroof open."

"Oh?" Angie replied. "And what kind of car do you own?"

"A VW Jetta. I bought it new last year. It's blue."

The Braves had their fastest runner on first and nobody out when both women announced that they needed to visit the ladies room. I whispered to Angie as she stood. "Not a word to her about . . . you know."

Angie made the zip motion across her lips and followed Miranda into the aisle.

The Marlins' pitcher kept throwing over to first to hold the runner close to the base. After the third throw over, Larry turned and spoke across the empty seats between us. "Ned, I know you said you didn't want to talk business at the ballpark, but I can't wait any longer. I've got to know what that producer said or I'm gonna start pacing around the stadium."

I knew this was coming.

I could not look Larry in the eye. I just kept staring at the infield, not really focused on anything—until the Marlins' pitcher beaned the batter. The home crowd groaned at the sound of ball hitting flesh. Fastball to the shoulder muscle. Ouch.

The batter staggered to first, and I used this moment to try to level with Larry. "Angie and I promised each other that tonight would be a make-up date. We limited our topics to small talk and flirting. This means that you and I can't talk business."

Larry sat silent for a minute—until the pitcher walked the next batter to load the bases. "Did you and the producer talk numbers?"

"I told you—I can't talk business. Let's just enjoy the game."

Larry drew his legs in from the aisle and leaned over to pick something up from under his seat. He brought up an unopened packet of ketchup, tore off the corner, and squirted the contents into his right palm. Then he extended his arm across the empty seats. "Go ahead, dip your finger in it."

"For what?" I asked, wondering if he had gone mad.

"So you can write the number on your palm."

"With ketchup?"

"Of course. This way you can keep your promise to Angie, and I can find out what the producer offered."

The next batter strode to the plate, and I reached across seat 3 to dip my left index finger in Larry's handful of ketchup. Sufficiently dipped, this finger found its way to my right hand and drew a large red eight in the palm. I held this red palm up for Larry's inspection.

His reaction stretched over several seconds. He read my palm, blinked in disbelief, grinned stupidly, read my palm a second time. Then his grin grew into something beyond stupid.

He moved his lips in slow motion, "Eight *hundred thousand*?" he asked in a whisper.

I shook my head no before thrusting my palm across the seat at him again. Ketchup oozed down my wrist.

His eyes widened and his mouth dropped open. He gathered himself and whispered, "Eight *million*?"

I shook my head again, this time harder.

The crowd booed as the Marlins' manager removed the starting pitcher and brought in a lefty. Over the chorus of jeers, Larry shouted at me. "I don't understand . . . eight *what*?"

I momentarily forgot my pledge to Angie and shouted back. "Just eight. Eight thousand!"

I'd seen ruptured balloons deflate more slowly. Larry's very breath left him; his arms flopped over the armrests, and his legs slid back out into the aisle. He remained in this posture while the lefty warmed up and the crowd continued to boo.

"That's all?" Larry asked.

I nodded and wiped the ketchup from my palm with a napkin. "It's an offer to option the movie rights. A two-year option for eight grand."

"You declined his offer, didn't you? I mean, surely my stuff is worth more than that. . . . Isn't it?"

"I told Mylan that I'd talk to you about the ending, then get back to him."

Neither of us was watching when Atlanta's oldest player smashed his bat into the next pitch. Both of us, however, followed the ball's trajectory until it slammed into the right-center field wall. The first of three runners crossed the plate, then the second and third runners slid into home, one behind the other. The umpire signaled safe, hesitated as the ball got past the catcher, and signaled safe again. A three-run triple.

That's when Angie and Miranda returned with soft drinks and pretzels.

"Did we miss anything?" Angie asked as she settled back into her seat.

"Just a few runs, dear. Nothing major."

The small talk resumed and, thanks to a few deft questions from Angie, it was revealed that Miranda worked as a news editor, enjoyed the occasional Killian's Red, and preferred Pantene shampoo.

After the win, the four of us left Turner Field with thousands of other happy fans. Larry and Miranda strode ahead of Angie and myself, and it was then that Angie asked me a question with a tad too much volume. Her question was, "Can I ask Larry a little something about the yacht-stealing part?"

Miranda turned in mid-stride, eyebrows raised. "A stealing part to what?" she asked with a smile and great innocence, like people do when they interrupt at cocktail parties.

I butted in before Angie could answer. "Oh, just a term paper that our son, Zach, has to write for an ethics class at Auburn."

Miranda seemed content with my answer. Soon she strode ahead with Angie, the two of them on to some topic involving Underground Atlanta.

I walked along with Larry and spoke out the side of my mouth. "She still doesn't know that she's the main character in your—"

Larry smiled and waved to the Braves mascot, who had attracted a crowd in the parking lot and was handing out free plastic bats to kids. "Not a clue."

"Have you even shown her the first chapter?"

Larry applauded loudly as the mascot led the crowd in orchestrated cheers. "Nope," he said. "All things in their proper time."

I walked along wondering how this young lady would receive Larry's tomahawk chop of confession.

A quick scalping, perhaps?

At the exit gate we said good-bye to Miranda and Larry, then made a right and walked up a sidewalk toward our car. We passed a street vendor on the way, and before I could object, Angie was digging in her purse for money and ordering a hamburger all the way and a large Coke.

"You know how caffeine keeps you awake at night," I said as she paid the man. "And didn't you eat two hot dogs at the game?" Suddenly I was very concerned with my wife's figure.

She handed me her purchase. "Carry this, honey. It's not for me."

Five minutes later we were north of the stadium and beneath an I-85 bridge, standing on the curb and peering up into dark, angled crevices. "Victorrrr?" Angie shouted.

I felt the need to intercede. "Honey, this could be dangerous. This side of town is—"

"Victorrrrr!"

The raspy voice waited for a break in the traffic before speaking. The voice came from the fourth dark crevice. He had an old sleeping bag wrapped around him. "That you, Mizz Watson?"

"And Mr. Watson," I offered out of sheer instinct.

Angie stepped around me and scaled the first few feet of concrete. "It's me, Victor. I brought you a burger."

He shuffled down and accepted the meal and sniffed its warmth. "With pickles and ketchup and everything?"

"All the way. Just like you prefer. And a drink, too."

He climbed back up toward his condo before turning to me with one last comment. "If you're Mistuh Watson, then you should be proud to have a woman like *Mizz* Watson."

What could I do but agree?

Saturday morning I woke to the smell of pancakes. Blueberry, medium well.

Since Angie was still sleeping soundly in the center of our king-sized bed, this scent could mean only one thing.

Robed and barefoot and not very surprised, I descended the stairs and found our son, Zach, sitting at our breakfast table, chewing with gusto. His eating was intense; his clothes, wrinkly. Everything about him looked disheveled, from his Dave Mathews Band T-shirt to his khaki shorts to his leather sandals with the broken straps. A small duffel sat on the floor at his feet.

He chewed a huge bite, wiped syrup from the corners of his mouth, and grinned up at me. "Had a free weekend, Pop. Hope you and Mom still have room for me."

Since he was busy eating, my greeting was a simple squeeze of his shoulders. "You been up all night?"

"Yep, but it's not what you think. I've been reading."

"Of course you have," I said, not believing he would be studying on a weekend. "And did you make enough pancakes for all of us?"

"Plenty," he said, nodding at the stove top. "And by the way, great story."

"What story?"

"The one you left spread out on the sofa in the den. That's what I've been reading." He swallowed half a pancake in one gulp. "I just finished the part about the guys stealing the yacht. This the same story Mom warned me about?"

I opened a cabinet and withdrew a glass. "What did your mother tell you?"

Zach poured syrup on his next bite and let the morsel dangle on his fork. "Well, Dad, just before you went to L.A., Mom called and told me that you're representing a story that promotes atheism, foul language, petty crime, and very little respect for personal property." He counted off each of these shortcomings on his fingertips. Finally he glanced at me as if searching for confirmation. "So, is that the same story I found on the sofa?"

I tried to think of a worthy comeback, but the morning was too new so I exercised my parental right to change the subject. "What time did you get in?"

"'Bout 3:30 a.m."

I shook my head slowly and with great exaggeration. "Son, we've always been able to talk. So if you need to tell me that you were at your frat party, had a bit too much fun, and—"

Zach dropped his fork and waved his hands in front of my face. "Earth to Dad! I'm in a *service* fraternity. We work with foreign-exchange students, tutor people in English, hold car washes . . . that sorta thing."

"Oh." I opened the fridge and removed a carton of milk. "But still, you haven't even been to bed yet?"

"Nah, but I'll sleep today . . . after you let me read the ending. You do have it, don't you?"

Angie came up behind me and thrust an empty glass around my waist, shaking it to encourage me to pour. "Yes, Ned, we all want to see the ending."

I poured us both a glass, and we toasted our Friday night make-up date. She filled two plates with the remaining pancakes and set them on the table before hugging Zach from behind.

"Glad you're home, precious," she said, and dipped a finger in his plate of syrup. "Mmm, and you even cooked for us." Then she hugged him again.

"Mom . . . don't smother. Just one normal hug is fine."

After devouring my breakfast, I wiped my milk mustache and pointed into the den at my computer. "Clan, the ending is supposed to arrive this morning."

They pointed me toward the den, where I logged onto the Web and found an e-mail from Larry.

*   *   *

Ned, find attached the first part of the ending.

Call me later.

Larry-who-is-surely-worth-more-than-eight-grand

While pages printed, Zach and Angie held a brief argument over who should read first. They even pointed their forks at each other from across our breakfast table.

"I'm only home for a day and a half, Mom," Zach explained in desperation, threatening to shake syrup on her.

Angie conceded to her son. But then I printed out a second copy.

Zach took his pages from the printer and went outside to sit in the white rocker on our front porch. Pages in hand and rocking slowly, he had no idea that he sat just feet from where a protest had been held a week earlier, organized by his own mother.

The Watsons . . . just a normal suburban family.

22

A QUARTER MILE FROM SHORE, Castro's yacht had imbedded its nose deep in a sandbar. MC Deluxe caused the imbedding, yet no one was left on board to complain. At 4:35 a.m. the stolen vessel sat vacant, already abandoned, its crew having fled over the starboard side—via rope ladder. Lanny, DJ Ned Neutral, MC, the Former Donald, and the ever-surprising Crackhead were swimming hard for the shore.

A beam of light swept across the water, then jerked out of control like a bad home movie. Some two hundred yards behind the escapees, the Coast Guard cutter slid to a sudden halt, stranding itself on the same sandbar. This event—at least from the escapees' perspective—served to even things up.

By the time the guards in black fatigues realized what had befallen them, and Marvin had reclaimed his bullhorn, the fleet five were halfway to shore. Battling waves, rain, darkness, and some annoying seaweed that wrapped around their wrists and ankles, they swam hard and squinted through the downpour.

They proved unequal in swimming skills, however. The order had not changed since they first left the yacht: Crackhead was the best swimmer and remained several body lengths out front, MC Deluxe was in a tie for second with Lanny, the Former Donald held onto fourth, and DJ Ned was fifth, far off the pace.

Behind them the bullhorn sounded. "THOU SWIMMETH TO THY DOOM!"

Lanny turned in the water to check on Ned. Beyond the DJ he saw guards on the side of the cutter, lowering an inflated raft into the sea, Marvin behind them with the bullhorn. Through the rain Lanny saw seven guards pile into the raft, one of them revving an outboard motor.

Lanny heard the motor accelerate. A beam from a spotlight passed beside him, then behind him. Back and forth over the water went the beam. Lanny dove under, then rose to check on Ned. Still a long ways from shore, Ned trailed even farther behind, trying his best to propel his large frame through the sea.

"Ned, hurry!"

Ned was by now winded and struggling. "I'll make it, Lann-o. . . . Just go!"

Lanny tried to touch bottom with his feet but could not. His survival instincts screamed at him to keep going. He swam harder, harder still, and soon was only a few yards behind Crackhead and MC, who remained out front.

To his right Lanny saw marsh grass, only the tips of the blades showing. The tide had risen, and if there was any beach, it was hidden by the marsh.

Far to his left, the guards in the inflatable raft angled across breakers and bounced over waves. Their spotlight shown firmly on the Former Donald, who had turned left in an attempt to outmaneuver—but had unknowingly swam right into the path of the guards.

"Split up!" yelled MC Deluxe, whose toes had just touched bottom. He and Crackhead moved along as best they could in neck-deep surf, pulling against the current, feet bouncing on sand.

Again the spotlight swept across the water. This time Lanny dove deep and swam for the marsh. Only then did he notice how warm was the seawater. He surfaced and glanced behind him to look for Ned. No sign of him. The saltwater stung Lanny's eyes, and all he could make out in the distance was the inflatable climbing the next wave, on a beeline for the Former Donald.

Unable to spot Ned and fearing for his own safety, Lanny hid in the marsh. He parted thick blades and pulled himself into the middle. There he crouched, making sure his head was below the top of the grass. Soon he heard yelling, a struggle . . . but no gunshots.

He had just caught his breath when the spotlight beam came sweeping toward him. Lanny had once seen an escapee in a movie breathe through a hollow reed, using it like a snorkel, but he had neither the time nor the light to search for hollow reeds. He simply submerged himself in seawater and marsh grass, gripping roots on the bottom to hold himself under. The spotlight passed overhead.

Buried under a foot of water, Lanny heard only an outboard engine some distance away. Then the motor shut off. Lanny waited as long as he could, but he needed air. Finally he emerged between grass blades, inhaling in one continuous gulp. He could not see the shore for the marsh, but he could hear the muffled shouts.

The spotlight swept toward him again. He feared for his own capture and went under. Seconds later he rose to get a breath, and now the shouts were loud, and sirens sounded from the beach.

Lanny stood on his toes and peered over the top of the marsh. Two vehicles.

Now four! He saw the Former Donald being led into the back of a Jeep.

Again the spotlight swept across the marsh, and Lanny quickly went under. When he resurfaced, his heart sank.

Down the beach he heard MC Deluxe yell, "Loose me, man!"

From somewhere beyond MC, Crackhead shouted at his captors. "I never done no drugs. I never done nothin' to nobody!"

The spotlight ceased its searching, and Lanny stood on his toes again. He saw only headlights from the Jeeps, and a steady drizzle reflecting in the beams. No sign of DJ Ned. Then he heard doors slam, engines start. He didn't know if Ned had been captured or drowned—or both.

Lanny remained in the marsh grass for over an hour, until the first light of dawn crept upon Tybee Island. The shore was vacant now. The Jeeps and the guards and his friends were gone, and Lanny struggled to free his feet from roots and mud. He pulled away and waded out of the marsh, black mud in his sneakers, sharp cuts on his ankles. He sloshed through warm surf onto an empty beach, where the many footprints gave evidence of a struggle.

He stood there dripping like a castaway, his head spinning from the sheer speed at which his circumstances had changed. *One minute you're on a yacht with your buddies in a red marble hot tub, the next you're alone in wet clothes on an empty beach.*

Lanny turned and gazed out to sea. Some four hundred yards away, the yacht and the Coast Guard cutter sat at odd angles to each other. Small waves bumped against their port sides.

The sun had yet to emerge and the landscape was still murky when Lanny tromped across the beach and entered a sparse wood. A few palms, some scrub brush, a picnic table. In the distance he heard traffic on a road. He waited in the woods until the traffic passed, then he ran across the road and into a more manicured wood. All the leaves and sticks had been removed, and the dirt had been raked. He found himself running across a mammoth lawn.

No, not a lawn, he thought as he jogged. *I've stumbled upon another golf course.*

Here in the early morning light, wet and tired and hungry, Lanny was welcomed by his old nemesis—*signage.* This one was small and square and wooden. It had a golf landscape painted in the middle, green and straight, with a pair of white sandtraps etched on opposing sides of the fairway.

Hole #14, 527 yards
Par 7 for the Fortunate.
Par 2 for everyone else.

As was his desire, Lanny had arrived safely back in America. And though he missed his friends and hated that they'd been recaptured, he had made up his mind as to his proper course of action. He would find some dry clothes, get something to eat, and resume his search for Miranda.

Home, sweet home.

23

(a short little chapter dedicated to
the capture of DJ Ned Neutral)

DJ NED WAS NOT CAPTURED in the surf with the others. Nor was he caught on the beach or in the marsh. The portly music lover had fooled the zealots—at least for a little while. As the guards sped through the waves during their wee-hour pursuit, Ned knew that he could never out-swim their inflatable to shore. So he took the largest gulp of air he could hold, dove under, and began swimming along the bottom—and out to sea.

At that moment, the guards had their spotlight fixed on the Former Donald. Beyond him, MC and Crackhead were spotted running along the beach, and so the inflatable had passed right over Ned. He had heard the propeller buzz over his scalp.

Ned surfaced well behind the raft and back near the sandbar. He dove again and swam along the bottom until the tide pushed him around the sandbar and to the starboard side of the yacht. He hid on the far side of the bow, just beneath the anchor. He peeked around the bow and saw the Coast Guard cutter stranded on the port side, where two remaining guards waited for the inflatable to return and pick them up.

Pressed against the yacht's side, his feet sinking in wet sand, Ned heard the two guards board the yacht at the rear. Ned looked up some twenty feet and saw the tops of their heads as they searched the bow. Finding nothing, the guards departed and hitched a ride on the inflatable. The raft sped toward shore, where all the action was taking place.

Ned had witnessed part of all three captures. First the Former Donald, who was plucked from the surf; then Crackhead, who was halfway up a palm tree when the spotlight found him; and then MC Deluxe, tackled in the sand as he sprinted for the woods. Not that anyone caught MC from behind; the guards had the benefit of the Tybee Island Beach Police in bright yellow Jeeps. These officers had shone their headlights into MC, blinding him as to where to run.

Alone then and wondering what had happened to Lanny, Ned climbed the rope ladder to hide out in the yacht. For the next few minutes he toyed with the idea of starting the engines and trying to back the yacht out of the sand. But he knew the noise would give him away.

Perhaps wait for sunrise, he thought. *Wait till the beach is clear.*

Ned went to the captain's chair and peered out over the steering wheel. Over the bow he saw the first police vehicle leave the beach. Then a second and a third.

Ned held a Cuban cigar, about to light it and celebrate his clever escape, when the guard who had hid in the supply closet came out and slapped the handcuffs on him.

Ned dropped the cigar to the floor and mumbled a curse.

The guard led Ned to the bow, then spoke into a walkie-talkie and told his comrades on shore to come pick up a fourth escapee. Ned saw the inflatable raft turn from the beach and motor toward them.

"Back to Cuba?" he asked the guard.

The guard nudged him to the railing, just above the rope ladder. "You got it."

By now the rain had ceased, and the sky morphed from murky gray to murky pink. The pair stood there on the bow of Castro's yacht and watched the raft bounce toward them on the waves. While they waited, the guard checked Ned's handcuffs for proper tightness and asked, "Wasn't there a fifth escapee with you all? Some construction guy by the last name of Hooch?"

"He drowned two days ago," Ned said, looking as solemn as possible. "Tried to swim ashore near Boca Raton."

"Oh . . . I'm sorry."

DJ Ned may have been a slow swimmer, but he was an excellent liar. And he was certain that Lanny would have done the same for him.

24

I T TOOK THREE DAYS, umpteen lies, and the charity of a long-haul trucker, but Lanny managed to hitchhike back to Orlando, where in the dead of night he found his sage green Xterra undisturbed, still parked in the producer's spot outside of Fence-Straddler AM Radio.

Only this time there was no one inside the station to answer the code word.

The lights were off, and Lanny did not even try the door. He simply waved good-bye to the charitable trucker and unlocked his Xterra. All he had with him were the clothes he'd been given to wear—a *Got Religion?* T-shirt—plus his wallet and yesterday's Savannah newspaper.

Atop the fold in the religion section—which made for practically the entire paper—was the headline: *Marvin and Friends Capture Four on Tybee Island!!*

Lanny turned on his dome light and read for a second time how his four friends had been returned to Cuba. He was particularly interested in the last sentence of the article: *One of the five escapees, Lanny Hooch from Atlanta, drowned in an attempt to swim to the mainland near Boca Raton.*

Being a man without a country was bad enough—and being a man with a lost girlfriend was even worse—now Lanny was a man without a life, at least according to the *Savannah Register.*

Lanny slept in his Xterra for over two hours. But it wasn't normal sleep. For the first time since the zealot invasion, he slept hard enough to dream. . . .

Lanny had just driven to Miranda's apartment to pick her up for a date. She came walking out of her door, smiling in a red dress, her hair

pulled over one shoulder. He met her halfway up the sidewalk and
they embraced. Then he walked her to the passenger door of his Xterra
and gently held her hand as she climbed in. Blissful, Lanny hurried
around the truck and eased behind the wheel, wanting to kiss her. But
when he leaned across the console to meet Miranda's lips, she pulled
up short and spoke in a voice of doom: "THOU SHALT NOT KISS
BEFORE MARRIAGE, SAYETH MY TRUE LOVE!"

Stunned, Lanny retreated, wedging himself against his door.
"But . . . but aren't *I* your true love?"

"NEVER! MY HEART BELONGETH TO MARVIN!"

Lanny woke shivering in his Xterra, sweat dripping from his
brow.

Dream over. Back to the nightmare.

After sunrise he drove once again out to Cocoa Beach and to Pelican's Harbor Retirement Homes. His previous note still dangled
from the nails in the front door; the black leather travel bag still sat
on the doorstep; and the penny, that shiny copper penny, was still
lodged in the tire tread of the beige Buick.

Beside the car Lanny picked up a rock. With great frustration he
hurled it into the street. Then he shouted to the sky, "Miranda,
where are you?!"

Like a hungry bird returning again to an empty feeder, Lanny
drove next to the Bluewater Marina. *If Miranda isn't there, I'll go look
for her in Atlanta.*

Skies were clear when he arrived in the parking lot, and he hurried across the oyster shells and down to the docks.

She wasn't there, of course.

Neither were most of the boats. All but three had sailed away to
parts unknown. Other than the *Saniti,* only *The Humbleness* and the
Formal on Sundays 2 remained in port.

Lanny gritted his teeth and stepped down onto the *Saniti.* From
what he could tell, the cabin had not been touched, neither had the
deck. This lack of additional clues forced on him a new kind of
anger, a resentment of his own life: He cursed the takeover; he

yelled again for Miranda; he spat into the water and kicked a bench. Finally he reached above both ears and pulled his hair.

Lanny sat on the dock for hours, his mind spinning further into turmoil. But by early afternoon too many memories plus too many disappointments added up and caused him to flee. Off the dock he ran, yelling things unintelligible. He had become a crazed man, and before he left the parking lot and hit the highways for Atlanta, he did something that befit the crazed.

From a neighboring Mazda, Lanny stole both a license plate and a bumper sticker. The car was covered with a rainproof tarp—which made it a logical target. Lanny figured the owner was out to sea, hopefully for several weeks.

The license plate he took read CU N HVN; the bumper sticker read simply, *Repent of Bingo*. It tore at the edges as he pulled it off. He had some glue in his toolbox, however, and that was enough to secure the sticker to his right rear bumper. Satisfied, Lanny stepped back and admired his new accessories. He figured these items were all the disguise he'd need.

And he was proved right.

At the Cocoa Beach BP station, an attendant came out and inspected the rear of Lanny's truck. He then shook Lanny's hand and said, "Thanks for stoppin' by, brother. Today our low low price is only twelve cents per gallon."

Lanny nodded in faux appreciation and pumped fifteen gallons into his tank. He wanted to punch the guy for calling him "brother," but Lanny was now a full-fledged poser, so he kept his cool and went inside to pay.

He felt no joy from being charged only a dollar and eighty cents for fifteen gallons—he'd become numb to any stimuli not directly related to Miranda. In fact, he failed to notice that this was the first positive thing to happen to him since he and MC Deluxe caught the dogfish.

A long journey to Atlanta lay ahead, so Lanny added a grape soda to his purchase. Fidgety and anxious to resume his quest, he thrust a five-dollar bill at the cashier.

The young cashier boy rang up the total, glanced at Lanny's five, and said, "Sir, I need to remind you that you only have three more days to exchange your old currency for the new."

Nerves aflutter, Lanny dropped his can of soda on the counter. He quickly picked it up, saying, "Yeah, sure . . . I know."

The cashier took his five and handed him his change. "Your change is two dollars and sixty-seven cents."

"Whose face is on the new—" Lanny glanced down at the ones in his palm. "Oh, never mind."

"Looks very authentic, doesn't he?" the clerk said, smiling.

Lanny stepped backward to the door, his eyes still on the bills in his palm. "Yeah . . . just like, um, the real thing."

Outside in the heat again, Lanny took deep breaths and tried to stop shaking. He didn't want to stuff the new bills into his pocket, yet he knew he needed to continue to pose or risk getting sent back to Havana and the paint brigade. And somewhere in the back of his mind, Lanny knew that those fifteen gallons purchased under disguise had saved him nearly a hundred bucks.

He drove quickly to the interstate and sped north. As Orlando became Ocala, and Ocala became Gainesville, and Gainesville, Valdosta, he fought sleep. He stayed awake by lowering his windows and letting the air slap his face. Miles later he began wondering if DJ Ned, MC, and Crackhead were again whitewashing graffiti, and if so, were they listening to the Former Donald whisper yet another daring escape plan? Lanny hoped so; he missed his friends.

Just after 10:30 p.m. he reached Atlanta, where he merged onto I-85 north and took exit 99 past Pappadeaux Seafood Kitchen. A mile down the road he turned into Miranda's apartment complex.

In front of building G sat her light blue VW Jetta. A light came on inside her first-floor apartment.

Lanny didn't even make it all the way to a parking space. He threw his gear shift into park and ripped off his seatbelt.

No way! How did she get . . . ?

Lanny leaped out of his Xterra and sprinted toward the door.

Right after I turned down the 8K option offer from Mylan Weems and submitted Larry's story to three other studios, something unexpected happened, something akin to the final minutes of an Ebay auction. A 12K offer came in. Then a 17.5K offer—which I almost urged Larry to take, just so I could make a few shekels in commission. But my phone kept ringing—independent film people, a start-up firm, and Mylan himself. The conversations were sometimes so short that I'd forget who I'd spoken with last.

"Hi, Ned, what about 26K?"

"Um, we're weighing options. But thank you."

"Ned, my main man! How's 35K look?"

"Can I think about it overnight?"

"West Coast greetings, Nedster! Mylan here. Take a swat at 54K?"

I adapted quickly to the lingo. "Nice, Myle-baby. Lemme talk to Larry."

"Me again, Ned. We can go 72K."

"That's *very* generous of you."

In the life of a literary agent, there is no sweeter phrase than *bidding war.*

I asked Producer Number Four what had suddenly gotten his interest up. He said that a clean-but-irreverent story might have wider appeal than he'd originally thought.

I said, "hmmm," and thanked him for his next offer.

Mylan called me a third time and expressed his growing interest in the project, complete with compliments and the fact that he was holding all calls so that he and I could talk.

I told him I had two other producers on hold, and that I would get back to him.

I'll never forget Mylan's parting compliment. He said, "Ned-baby, today I'm an Israelite, and Larry's story is a golden calf."

My job as Agent Orange was threefold: to shine the calf, to arbitrate the bidding war, and to bring maximum benefit to my client. To my delight, all this shining and arbitrating and benefit-maxing was taking place even before any of us had received the balance of Larry's ending.

Not that we had to wait much longer. While I sat in my 22nd-floor office, phone to ear, Larry wandered in. He'd come by every day for the past week, asking questions, hoping for good news. Today was a Tuesday, and he stood over my desk, arms spread wide, eyebrows raised. *Well?*

I covered the receiver with my hand. "Larry, you'll have to wait outside in the break room. I'm on the phone with L.A. This second producer has me on hold for a minute—we're in discussions."

Larry remained planted. "Numbers?"

I nodded. "Yep." Then I pointed to the door.

Larry's mouth dropped and his eyes nearly burst with excitement. "Then I have to stay, Ned."

"No, you'll mess this up."

"I have to know."

Again I pointed to the door. "Please."

"But I have the rest of the ending with me." He pulled a bunch of folded pages from his rear pocket and dangled them overhead. "Lemme stay or else you don't get the ending."

I put my ear to the phone, heard nothing, and covered the receiver again with my hand. "You're bribing me? While I'm on the phone trying to sell your story?"

He shook the pages, waved them in front of my face, teased me with their contents. Then he pulled a CD from his other pocket. "I saved it on CD for ya too. Please, Ned, I have to know what's happening. I'm almost out of money, and Miranda is asking all kinds of questions about my vocational future. Plus I only have twelve dollars of credit left on my VISA card." He dropped the pages and the CD on my desk and took a step back. "Please?"

I ceased pointing at my door and gestured instead across the office to my potted plants. "Sit against the far wall between those two ferns, tie a handkerchief over your mouth, and don't make a sound."

"You're kidding."

"I'm not. This is too important for interruptions and emotional outbursts. If you want to stay, you have to sit, tie, and remain silent."

Larry lumbered over between the potted plants and sat. "Ned?"

"What now?"

"Can I borrow a handkerchief?"

I pulled one from my desk drawer, wadded it into a ball, and tossed it over-handed to him.

Larry caught it in mid-air and sniffed hard. "Is it clean?"

"Yes. Now . . . shhh." I put my ear to the phone again but heard nothing. I glanced amused at Larry as he struggled to tie the handkerchief behind his neck. "By the way, Lar, I can't believe you let DJ Ned get recaptured and sent back to Cuba."

Larry pulled the handkerchief down, his excited expression fading to a frown. "Ya know, I really had a hard time with that . . . what with you being my friend and all."

"I'm touched." I set the phone in my lap and reached over to pull a couple sheets off the printer. "Larry, I have something for you to read while you wait."

He rose to his feet and came loping back to my desk. "What's this?"

"Other possible endings," I explained, and handed him the papers. "Several people whom I've let read your story so far—including my barber, my wife, and that flight attendant I met en route to L.A.—have e-mailed me their version of how the story should end."

"But how did they get—"

"I've been e-mailing them the chapter files as you gave them to me. They've bugged me to death. Plus, I thought one of them might come up with something that would inspire you."

Producer Number Two came back on the phone and apologized for the wait.

"Quite all right," I said to him, motioning for Larry to stay quiet.

He returned to the ferns, retied his hankie, sat on the floor, and began reading.

The producer informed me that his script doctor had just had a brainflash. The two of them were reading the theme park scene where the parking clerk gives Lanny the clue about "seventy percent of the earth being covered in water." The script guy then got hold of a Bible and read the first two verses of the book of Genesis. He set the book aside, thought about it for a while, and came up with what they thought was the perfect ending.

"I'm tellin' ya, Ned," said the producer into my phone, "this could work."

"I'm all ears."

He then explained that in the second verse of Genesis, it says, "God's Spirit hovered *over* the deep." The producer and his script guy concluded that all spirits—good or evil—must therefore lose their powers *beneath* the deep. So Miranda could be discovered hiding out in a submarine with a crew from the United States Navy, who did not touch her because they were good and proper sailors under the command of a Christian commander. This ending would satisfy a wide and diverse audience, the producer explained. It would offer a dash of patriotism and a dash of biblical accuracy, together with the reunion of the lovers. He said these three points were what the studio wanted to convey—an ending that has something for everyone.

I put my finger in my mouth and made the *gag me* face to Larry.

But Larry wasn't looking at me. He was busy reading the endings e-mailed in from the readers, including the one from Zach, who had returned to Auburn for the start of college football season. This may or may not have swayed his attempt at a proper conclusion.

Oddest to me was the fact that only one of these readers thought Miranda would be in the apartment.

Big Ed turned in the shortest rendition. He thought no way would Miranda be in her apartment. Instead, she had time-traveled to 1944 and was shivering and lost on the beach at Normandy, where a burly sergeant named Big Ed rescued her in the middle of a cold, dark night. After reuniting Miranda with her long lost boyfriend, Big Ed was presented the medal for bravery from President Roosevelt.

Rocco—who, along with his turbo cologne, stopped by my office at least twice a week—said Miranda could not be in the apartment, simply because a dashing commercial real estate agent named Rocco had just sold the complex for big bucks. He was turning it into high-priced condos, which he would sell to yuppie Atlantans who were willing to take out interest-only mortgages in order to feed their materialism. Miranda would eventually turn up at the marina aboard the *Sanitized 2,* wearing gold chains and diamonds she'd found while on a deep-sea dive. Lanny would mooch off of her and they would settle into a high-priced condo in West Palm Beach, which would be sold to them by—you guessed it—a dashing realtor named Rocco.

Zach also thought Miranda would not be in the apartment. She would be found working as a roadie for the Dave Mathews Band, who incidentally had come out with a hit song called *Zealots Marching.* In a surprise twist, Dave himself fell for Miranda, but Lanny rushed behind the stage after a sold-out concert, dropped to one knee, professed his love for Miranda, and won her back. They got married in the chapel at Auburn, the day after Auburn beat Alabama 56 to 3 in the Sugar Bowl. My son, the romantic.

The young waiter who was studying theatre at Georgia College also e-mailed me. He said no way would Miranda be in the apartment. He thought Lanny and DJ Ned and MC Deluxe would first need to reunite. They would develop their newly acquired acting skills and form an acting troupe comprised solely of posers. These posers would come up with a hit Broadway show that featured amplified sounds of the noises people make while eating. The name of this production would be *Chomp.* The threesome would tour the world and earn millions from the royalties off *Chomp;* then they would use these monies to bribe Marvin's guards into revealing where Miranda was hidden—in an abandoned theatre in Taos, New Mexico.

Angie was the only person who thought Miranda would be inside the apartment. Angie said the perfect ending would be if Lanny discovered Miranda sitting on the carpeted floor and reading *Mere Christianity,* by C.S. Lewis. Miranda would give the book to Lanny, who would immediately pronounce C.S. brilliant, convert, and become the maintenance manager of Charles Stanley's mega-church in Atlanta. Lanny and Miranda would eventually have four kids, two of them identical twins. Girls, Angie insisted.

The flight attendant who twisted her ankle had e-mailed me from the Houston airport. She said Miranda could not be in the apartment when Lanny arrived. He would keep searching for awhile—and his perserverance would pay off. He would discover that Detour Airlines was actually a secret government agency storing all the unfortunate ones in underground caves near the Gaza Strip. Miranda would find an ancient shovel in her cave, tunnel out, then hitch a ride on a camel to the Persian Gulf. There she would sneak aboard a container ship filled with Arabian health food, hide out on the ship for five weeks as it made its way to Jacksonville, then meet Lanny at sunset on Cocoa Beach. They would lay in the surf and kiss as waves lapped over them, just like Burt Lancaster and Deborah Kerr in *From Here to Eternity.*

Larry yanked off his hankie and whispered from between the plants that he liked this ending a lot and wished he had thought of it. Then he said, "No, mine is better. But I could see Hollywood going for this kiss-in-the-surf thing."

I hung up the phone after jotting down the third producer's generous offer; then I thumbed through my Rolodex for Mylan Weems's number. I loved a good bidding war, and now I would give Mylan one last shot.

I was about to call him when Larry balled up the handkerchief and tossed it back at me. It fell short of my desk. "Ned, why don't you read the rest of my ending before you talk to anyone else? My therapist told me that a lot of my history comes out in the end. Plus, it might give you a better sense of my story's worth."

So as Larry sat between my ferns, and Hollywood opened its checkbook, I plucked the pages from my desk and prepared to read. But before starting I leaned down and fed his CD into my computer. Then I e-mailed the file to Angie.

Nuts as it may sound, I wanted her opinion.

25

BUT OF COURSE Miranda's light blue Jetta was sitting in front of her apartment; Lanny himself had driven her to the airport on the day she flew to Orlando. And indeed there was a light on inside the apartment—the rental manager had let herself in after not seeing or hearing from Miranda in a month. She had failed to pay her September rent.

Instead of crossing the doorstep to a blissful reunion, Lanny had stumbled upon a common eviction.

To say that this event sent Lanny spiraling into a deeper level of insanity would be something of an understatement. He had been so sure of blissful reunion—now he literally shook with disappointment.

Lanny stood in the doorway of apartment G3 and looked on as the rental manager—an older woman who seemed to take her job much too seriously—filled out an eviction form. Warm air rushed from the living room, and Lanny wondered why the heat was turned on for such a balmy September night.

"How much does Miranda owe?" he blurted. He would pay the debt himself if necessary.

The rental manager ran a finger down a page of residents. "Is she a fortunate or an unfortunate?"

Lanny motioned for the manager to step outside the apartment, which she did. He then showed her to the rear of his Xterra, parked crooked across two spaces. "See that license plate?"

The manager read the stolen CU N HVN plate. Then, the bumper sticker. Satisfied, she nodded her affirmation. "Very good. This means Miss Timms owes only four-hundred-twenty dollars for September. Will this be cash or check?"

Lanny saw an opportunity. "Check," he said. "But before I write it I'll need you to say the two-word code phrase."

The rental manager nodded as if this was standard zealot procedure. "Triumphant soldiers."

Lanny now knew the phrase—and wondered when he would get to use it—but right now he was most worried about writing a very bad check. Though with a very bad check he could at least buy himself another day or two, enough time to search the apartment for further clues.

Lanny pulled his checkbook from the glovebox and followed the rental manager back inside Miranda's apartment. His lack of funds classified his check as bad; his lack of status classified it as very bad. Lanny was officially dead, drowned off the coast of Boca Raton, and his bank had cancelled his account.

Undeterred, he ripped check number 0817 from its brethren and filled it out on the kitchen counter.

The rental manager looked over his shoulder and said, "Oh, I forgot one thing. For just an extra five dollars per month, I can hook you up with a twenty-four-hours-a-day subscription to TBS."

Larry dated the check and muttered, "But TBS is already included with regular cable."

"Sir, The Blessed Station is now premium content."

Lanny turned away from her, shut his eyes tight. He was approaching his bursting point.

"Could you please leave now?" he asked between clenched teeth, and handed her his check.

The manager left him alone. When she closed the door, the stillness and the silence and the vacancy all melded together, increasing his loneliness tenfold.

It never stops, Lanny thought as he walked into Miranda's bedroom. *It's never going to stop.*

Atop her nightstand he saw the framed picture of the two of them, sitting on a picnic blanket in Chastain Park. For long minutes he stroked the glass. Then he picked up the picture and tucked it under his arm. He opened Miranda's closet, reached for one of her dresses, and drew it to his nose. He sniffed the material long and hard. He reached for the next dress, then the next, sniffing each one. The scent of his woman filled this closet, and as he pulled the fifth dress to his face, Lanny Hooch fell to his knees and wept.

He woke in the closet sometime after 2:00 a.m., carpet creases pressed into the left side of his face. Minutes later he found Miranda's flowery blue journal beneath her bed. Lanny flipped through it and found the last entry. It was dated August 10, just a week before she disappeared.

> Yesterday I got a raise at work! And then I called Carla in Augusta and told her all about it. My own sister had the nerve to ask me if I had a will! I accused her of being greedy. She laughed and told me she was just joking. I told her that at age 29, I had never thought of a will. So, today at lunch I went and had a will drawn up. I split everything four ways: between Mom, Dad, Carla, and Lanny. I love Lanny, and if anything should ever happen to me, I want him to have one quarter of all I have.

Lanny found a copy of the will tucked into the back of the journal. He also found four one-hundred dollar bills tucked into the spine. A note stapled to the bottom of the will described in detail her IRA and savings information, and how to reach her parents and sister.

Lanny figured that this financial data could help fund his search. *I'll pose as the beneficiary of all the intended beneficiaries. And after I find her I'll repay all the money.*

One phone call the next morning flushed that idea. A zealot attorney at Predestined Probate LLC explained the bad news—since Lanny Hooch was officially dead, and there was no changing that, all his monies would go to the state of Georgia. The attorney also explained that even if Lanny Hooch was still living, his bequeathment

would have been small, since a new zealot tax consumed 66.6 percent of all inherited monies.

Flustered, Lanny consoled himself by remembering he still had
the four hundred dollars from Miranda's journal. He stuffed the
cash into his wallet—and solved one minor issue in the process.
With his bumper sticker, license plate, and knowledge of the two-
word code phrase giving him room to roam, and with his ability to
buy gas for only twelve cents per gallon, he now had plenty of dough
to resume his search.

*I'm going to find her even if she's become a zealot herself. I have to
know. . . .*

Certain that he had missed a clue somewhere along his journey,
Lanny lay on the bedroom floor on his back and replayed in his head
his searching, his time in captivity, his late-night escape with his
friends. He remembered what the guard had said when he'd asked
about female captives. He remembered the guard's glance at the sunrise, the subtle nod to the east. And he remembered the auctioneer's
sign propped against the stone wall.

After a quick shower he locked up the apartment and hurried
out to his Xterra.

Suddenly in the wee hours, Lanny knew where to find Miranda.

He just had to pull off a vocational pose in order to get to her.

26

LANNY DID NOT TRUST Atlanta, much less its airport. A direct flight was his preference—and Orlando offered such a flight. He drove for six hours, stopped to refuel north of the city, and barreled on at high speed.

En route he taped a note to his rearview mirror. The note was hardly original. By now he was too crazed, too excited even, to come up with anything more than cliché.

Desperate times call for desperate measures. . . .

Returning to the Caribbean was the desperate measure; discovering the whereabouts of Miranda was the call. Well, that and the news that DJ Ned was back on the airwaves. Sometime in late morning, out of sheer curiosity, Lanny tuned his radio to Fence-Straddler AM.

Lanny recognized the voice booming through his speakers—and this voice caused him to want to pick up his cell phone and call Ned's show. *Even better, if DJ Ned is back on the air, I could pay him a visit, invite him to come along, tell him I'm sorry he got sent back to Cuba. Wonder how he escaped this time?*

Lanny managed a slight smile as he heard Ned's song intro: "This one goes out to an old friend, Lanny, who, if he's still around, is welcome to visit me anytime here in my Orlando studio. I'm DJ Ned Nazareth, coming at you live and revived from Fence-Mender AM."

Lanny jerked his truck to the shoulder and yelled, "Noooo!" at his radio.

DJ Ned continued. "Most of you are well acquainted with the funky guitar in this next song."

Stopped fully and stunned beyond comprehension, Lanny recognized the opening guitar lick to one of his favorite tunes: "Play that Funky Music, White Boy."

DJ Ned spoke over the riff. "In case any listeners are still straddling the fence, I hope the lyrics in this song will prompt you to join the big team. You do want to join the *big team* . . . now, don't you?"

The new lyrics boomed inside the truck, and Lanny flinched at the chorus of "Praise the Zealot Movement, Lost Boy."

Lanny's head dropped against the steering wheel. Eyes shut, his mind in wobbly orbit, he lacked the energy to yell at the radio again. All he could do was whisper, "No, Ned. No, no, no."

He drove in a daze for the airport, but five minutes later the temptation to listen overwhelmed him. As if to sneak up on his own radio, Lanny reached slowly for the knob.

DJ Ned's voice boomed again. "A new superstar is making waves with his debut album, and he and his band are currently on tour across the southeastern U.S. Today, I, DJ Ned, get to introduce this group to you. Please welcome to Fence-Mender AM Radio, MC Deluxe and the InnerCity Rap Ensemble. I'll now play their new single, 'A Skippuh's Nod to God.' "

No! Not MC, too! Lanny couldn't bring himself to listen to the song. He turned off the radio and pulled back onto the interstate and drove slumped in his seat.

I might just be the last poser left on the planet, but I'm still holding out hope for Miranda.

At Orlando International Airport, Lanny parked his truck, slipped deep into poser mode, and hurried inside the terminal. His desperate measure grew mega-desperate as he approached the customer service counter of Detour Airlines.

"Next flight to Puerto Rico," he said to the counter girl. "Economy class."

"Of course," she replied, typing the flight number into her keyboard. "And would you like to be seated in singing or non-singing?"

"Um . . . non."

Lanny paid $160 cash for his ticket, but Counter Girl hesitated to give him his boarding pass. She held it over her head, shook it twice, and said, "Recite the code phrase, sir?"

Lanny cleared his throat and reached confidently for his boarding pass. "Triumphant soldiers."

"Enjoy your flight, sir."

Donald Deacon and Sir Crackhead stood waiting on the warm Puerto Rican tarmac, greeting all arriving tourists. In black fatigues and WWMD bracelets they greeted them. Surprised but not shocked to see his old mates transformed—after the DJ Ned and MC fiascos he expected as much—Lanny descended the stairs from the plane, relieved that Marvin's Lear Jet was nowhere in sight. Halfway down he sniffed warm tropical breezes, then stepped onto Puerto Rican soil for the first time.

Lanny could tell from their blank faces that these former prison mates didn't recognize him. These two were not crucial to his mission, however, so he extended his hand to Donald Deacon and shook hard. "Triumphant soldiers."

"Triumphant soldiers to thee," Donald Deacon repeated in monotone.

"Indeed, thou art in the presence of triumphant soldiers," said Sir Crackhead, shaking Lanny's hand with a limpish wrist. "What bringeth thee to Puerto Rico?"

Aw, man, now these two speak the KJ, too. Lanny kept such thoughts to himself, knowing that these guys could be his best asset. Accepted as their equal, he walked to an observation area and stood with them in the shade of palms, all three sweating in the Caribbean heat.

"I'm here volunteering to help with construction of Marvin's language school," Lanny explained. "In my former life I owned a contracting business, remember?"

"Ah," said Sir Crackhead with a smile. "I hath no recollection."

Lanny figured they were so brainwashed that they didn't remember anything, even their shared imprisonment in Cuba. Neither man had asked about DJ Ned or MC. Thus Lanny played innocent, noting the hilly terrain on one side of the island and wondering if Miranda were hidden there. He wanted to ease in to his big request, but anxiety and excitement merged and produced in him a new-found bluntness. "Would you guys mind if I took a quick look at the resistors who are held captive here?"

Donald Deacon raised a finger of objection. "Um, sir, as thou art a construction worker, does not thou desireth first to see the building site? Bulldozers already cleareth the land."

"I'd really like to see the resistors. . . . Haven't met any in a while."

Sir Crackhead moved closer to Lanny, as if to whisper in his ear. "Can thou keepest a secret?"

"Of course."

"Here in Puerto Rico is where we keepeth the *female* resistors."

Yes! Lanny thought, doing his best not to grin or dance a jig on the tarmac. *I was right. I knew it, I knew it!*

Donald Deacon nodded in the affirmative, pulled a ringing cell phone from his pocket, and stepped away to talk to someone in private. "Thou needest special permission to meet thy fairer gender," he explained over his shoulder.

"I just want one little look."

Sir Crackhead reached for his wallet. "Okay, if thou insist on seeing them, I do owneth wallet-sized photos. But if thou art hoping to meet someone new, thou really did not need to cometh all this way. If thou wouldst subscribeth to the new online dating service, E-Marviny, thou could viewest these female resistors and readeth their profiles."

He handed the first photo to Lanny, who dismissed it with great haste. *A stout blonde in cowboy boots? This ain't Miranda.*

"That blonde," said Sir Crackhead, taking back the photo, "she art a rodeo girl who haileth from Amarillo. Donald Deacon desireth to date her . . . when she becometh legal, that is."

"You mean she's underage?" Lanny glanced anxiously as Sir Crackhead pulled four more photos from his wallet.

"No, I meant that if thou art hoping to marry one, thy must waiteth until total reform hath completeth its course. Then she becometh legal to weddeth. Thou canst also readeth this rule on E-Marviny."

Lanny snatched the four photos from Sir Crackhead's hand and saw four women of various ethnicity, none of the faces familiar. His heart sank again, though determination bouyed it for one last try. "This . . . this can't be all."

Sir Crackhead tapped the third photo. "The Asian woman and I flirteth yesterday during paint detail."

Lanny tried to imagine Miranda sloshing white latex on Puerto Rican graffiti. His hand trembled as he handed back the pics. "Where are the rest of the photos?"

"No more exist. There are only five women here."

Disappointment so welled up in Lanny that he grabbed Sir Crackhead by the shoulders and shook him. "This is all the female resistors you have?! Where else are they kept?"

Sir Crackhead spoke in haste, as if unfamiliar with emotion. "There is nowhere else. All five holdouts were broughteth here. The blonde even earneth her Texas captor a Big Reward! But thou shouldest not worry about their treatment; the women haveth their own loft apartments, 200-thread-count sheets, and a small budget for décor."

Lanny shook him a second time. "This is *it?!* There were never more than these five? Why would Marvin build a language school for just five people?"

"Thou engagest in faulty thinking. The Puerto Rican language school shall be mostly for those who've already joineth the movement. Although the tall woman and the rodeo girl doth showeth a great knack for languages."

Only five? "But this can't be . . ."

Lanny let go of Sir Crackhead. *This cannot be.*

Lanny turned to see Donald Deacon striding over, the pasted-on smile reminding him of zealot fast-food workers. "Sir, the five women remaineth busy painting portraits of Marvin on white canvas. Thou cannot disturbeth them."

Lanny searched his face for any sign of joviality. "C'mon, Don-

ald! Y'all stop kidding with me. Where are the rest of the female resistors? Tell me there are more somewhere!"

Donald Deacon shook his head no and left to greet a second
plane.

Sir Crackhead had no words of sympathy as he walked Lanny
back to the terminal. Lanny sat in the lobby and grasped his hair
above his ears and commenced to rocking slowly. His expression
sank into the spaced-out comportment of one devoid of hope, although to any casual observor he was merely a man mildly suffer-
ing, perhaps having a bad day.

Sir Crackhead looked on with brainwashed confusion, though
after a time he sat beside Lanny and tried to make conversation.
"Thou leavest so soon? What of thy contractor work?"

Lanny motioned for him to leave.

He did not. "But thou just arriveth . . ."

Slowly Lanny raised his head. But he could not look upon any
more zealots, so he just spoke to the lobby window. "I . . . forgot my
tools. I have to go back to Orlando." His words lacked all emotion,
just the residue of conscience.

Sir Crackhead patted Lanny on the back before walking away.
"Thou must worketh on thy memory," he said, tapping the side of
his head as he strolled down the lobby.

For the return flight aboard Detour Airlines, Lanny settled into seat
3F, the lone outbound passenger.

With reddened eyes he stared out his window as the plane took off.

*Miranda is gone. . . . Gone! I'm alone in the world, and every idea I
have leads to a dead end.*

The plane rose swiftly, but neither blue waters nor coastal
scenery had any effect on him. Blank-faced and despondent, he
would not even accept the flight attendant's offer of charismatic
peanuts.

I just want out of this misery.

27

THE NIGHTMARE HAD COME TRUE, and now Lanny figured a downtown Orlando high-rise an appropriate venue for his exit.

The one he chose was still under construction, half completed, if that. The outer shell of the twenty-story building appeared a monstrous gray skeleton, as emotionless as the inhabitants he'd met in Puerto Rico. No glass yet in the windows, few doors hung, and the high-rise's shadow angling across the Xterra's hood.

No workers around on this cloudy Saturday afternoon, just heavy equipment, a crane, a dumpster overflowing with debris. Lanny drove to the gate, got out, and used his pair of bolt cutters to break in. Confident that he was alone, he eased his truck to within fifty feet of the building and sat idling, peering up through his windshield.

Lanny wanted a twenty-story building. He'd already driven around and rejected nine other structures. He left his truck on the asphalt and didn't bother to lock his door. The only item he took with him was a pre-paid cell phone he'd purchased earlier that morning while posing in his *Got Religion?* T-shirt.

He entered the buildling through an unframed doorway. Sand and concrete powder covered the first floor. *I should at least tell somebody, bring some closure to my life. Tell Ned he can have my Xterra to drive to his zealot meetings.*

The inner stairs were of unfinished concrete, the steel bannisters cool to the touch. Wind blew through the north end of the building and whooshed out the far side. Lanny never hesitated as he climbed higher, though between the twelfth and thirteenth floors he paused to look down. *Not high enough.*

Higher and higher he climbed, his thoughts and memories fighting for supremacy, as if they, too, knew their time was short. *We walked barefoot on a golf course at sunset.... I drove her to the airport.... She wrote me into her will ... DJ Ned loved disco before he became a zealot.... I once soaked in Castro's hot tub.... Miranda's mom left her a phone message in Cocoa Beach: "Miranda, we're on our way to the marina to check on your dad's boat. It's 10:20 now, and we'll be back by 10:45 to take you to the airport. There's some turkey and Swiss cheese in the fridge if you'd like to make a sandwich to take on the plane." ... I tried my best to find you, Miranda.... I wanted to marry you.*

Lanny reached the twentieth floor, made his way to a metal door, and stepped out onto the roof. From the south corner he saw Orlando spread before him—office buildings, bridges, lakes, sidewalks, palm trees, the outskirts of Deity World, train tracks—and hopelessness.

A gust pushed him backward off the corner, but he stepped back up and peered down again. After a long moment of meditation, he pulled his cell phone out and dialed a number.

"Welcome, caller, to Fence-Mender AM! I'm DJ Ned Na—"

"Ned, it's Lanny, and I'm just calling to tell you that—"

A short pause. "Folks, I have here on the line a genuine American poser, a man with whom I once—"

Lanny cut him off again. "Ned, even though you're now a zealot, I wanted to let someone know that I'm exiting this misery. Tell your cohorts they won. Tell Marvin he rules the earth. Tell 'em whatever you want. You can even have my Xterra if you want it.... I've decided to ... I just want ... She was all I had ... all I wanted.... It was nice knowin' ya, Ned, back when you were normal.... I'm outta here."

"Wait, Lanny! I'm ... just ... just tell me where you are."

"I'm not telling you where I am ... but I can see the top of your station from here."

And with that, Lanny tossed his cell phone over the side of the building. He watched it somersault for two hundred feet until it burst into fragments on the asphalt.

Lanny inched his toes out over open air. He teetered at the next gust. And the next, and the one after that.

Again his thoughts raced. *All my friends fell victim to the brainwashing. . . . Miranda gone, my golf buddies gone . . . Remember to jump far so you don't hit the building on the way down. . . . There's no afterlife. . . . Life here is worthless. . . . Jump far so you don't hit the building. . . . Nothing here counts for anything. . . . I wish I'd punched Marvin in the geezer. . . . Just five more seconds . . . Miranda, I love you . . . wherever you are . . . Jump far and don't hit the building. . . . New Year's Eve we danced to James Brown music. . . . Close your eyes. . . . No, keep them open. . . . Go headfirst . . . I tried to find you Miranda. . . . Don't look down. . . . Yes, face your fear and do it. . . .*

A figure below ran through the open gate and onto the asphalt, waving his arms and shouting up through his hands.

"Lanny, don't jump!" he yelled. "I'm a poser. . . . What you heard on the radio was just to satisfy the zealots! . . . We're about to head west! . . . We think the zealots lied! . . . There may be millions of us out there! . . . Don't give up on Miranda! . . . Don't jump, Lanny!"

But Lanny could not hear Ned. The same winds that buffeted his shirt and hair restrained the words; the thirteenth or fourteenth floor was their apex, as high as they could manage. All Lanny saw below was a small figure of a man—obviously a zealot—waving his arms in protest.

Oh, so now Mr. Zealot Maintenance Worker doesn't want to have to clean up my mess after I splatter. He probably called the cops on me.

Ned shouted up again. "Lanny, it's me, Ned Neutral! . . . I've been posing for two weeks now! . . . I lied to get out of Cuba! There is *no* DJ Ned Nazareth!"

His words carried upwards again, this time to the fifteenth floor. Lanny peered down over the corner, teetering. *Don't look down again. . . . Yes, do look. . . . You don't want to hit that zealot and have him cushion your fall.*

His next glance down revealed a second figure of a man, this one leaner, darker, waving at first, then dropping to the ground and spinning. *Just another zealot wanting me to join them. But they don't want to know me; they'll always be strangers, just wanting to nail their vinyl siding on my life, put bumper stickers on my car. Would any of them ever admit to a lustful thought? A white lie? A big lie? To cheating on their taxes? . . . Jump far and don't hit the building. . . . Close your eyes. . . . No, keep them open. . . . Go headfirst. . . . I tried to find you, Miranda. . . . I really loved you. . . . Now why is that second zealot on his back, spinning around in circles?*

Lanny clenched his fists, closed his eyes. A gust startled him and he looked down again.

Why is that guy gyrating on the ground?

Lanny leaned out over the edge. Again he teetered with the wind.

His mind was raw mayhem, marinated in chaos and deep-fried in a vat of confusion.

The End.

"That's *it?!*" I asked Larry. Actually, I yelled this at him from across my office. "How can you write an ending that's so unutterably depressing?!"

He was still seated between my ferns, watching me for a reaction. "It's a bit different in tone than Burt and Deborah kissing in the surf as waves lap over them, yes."

I shook the pages at him and said, "Lanny doesn't find her? How can you end it with him not finding her? And why would you leave him on . . . does he jump?"

Larry sprang to his feet. "Does he *jump*?! Is that your big concern? The clue is there, Ned. It's not that hard."

Neither the shifting of my feet on the floor nor the drumming of my fingertips on my desk brought clarity. I must have shifted and drummed for a full minute. "I must be an idiot. . . . Tell me."

Larry remained standing beside the ferns, arms crossed. "No. If you can't figure it out, you're not smart enough to be my agent."

"Please."

He shook his head in frustration. "Close your eyes and think of ABBA."

"ABBA?"

"Yes. What was their big hit?"

" 'Dancing Queen'?"

"And it became . . . ?"

"Um . . . 'Dancing's Wrong.' "

"Exactly." He tapped his skull as he said this.

"I'm not following you."

Larry slumped his shoulders as if he'd lost all confidence in me. "Ned, Ned, Ned. The dark-skinned guy gyrating on the ground is MC Deluxe, doing the break dance. And since Lanny knew that the zealots had banned all dancing—they went hardest after disco, remember?—he would realize that MC was communicating that he, MC, was also a poser."

At last I sat back in my chair and nodded. "And so . . ."

"And so Lanny recognizes that he's really not alone in the world."

I leaned toward him, anxious as a kid asking Daddy if Spider-Man ever dies. "And then he climbs down from the twenty-story high-rise?!"

Larry extended his arms in a gesture of "you got it" and walked to my desk. "In the sequel, he and DJ Ned and MC are on the run again . . . out west, barreling through Arizona in a hippie van. Well, the passenger side is now painted in hip-hop art, at the insistence of MC. Oh, and they now have a dog, a big Lab."

"Dillen?"

"You got it."

Spider-Man lives! Yes, yes! "I'll sleep soo much better tonight."

Larry smiled a most exaggerated smile. "I'm so pleased. Wanna know what their license plate says on the van?"

"Tell me."

"MRVNSKS."

Perhaps this craziness explained the heightened interest from the producers. I had no idea what drove them to hate one project and love the next. But they seemed to move in herds, those slick-haired decision-makers, and they continued to behave like anxious Ebayers in the final seconds of bidding.

I was about to share the latest bids with Larry when my cell phone rang. "Mind if I take this call?" I asked, motioning Larry to sit in my guest chair. "I think it's my wife."

"Sure," he said, perusing the papers on my desk as he sat. "Go ahead."

I leaned back in my chair and held the phone to my ear. "Hello?"

"Ned, it's Angie." She sounded breathless. "I just finished Larry's ending, and it's all tied to the ABBA song. Lanny knows about 'dancing's wrong,' and so he'd surely climb down and embrace MC and Ned when he realized he still had friends." She sighed into the phone as if relieved. "My bet is that Larry will write a sequel."

Maybe I should let Angie be the agent, and I'll organize the protests.

"Yes, honey. We're discussing those very things right now. He's here in my office."

"He's *with* you?"

"Yep. Been here for hours."

"Well then, tell him I think he's done a wonderful job of presenting Miranda as a god . . . a kind of idol worship if you will. And showing how DJ Ned's own idol was music. And tell Larry if his story gets published I'll set up a booksigning for him at Barnes and Noble. My friend Margie works there in community relations. Oh, and invite Larry to share his theological thoughts with Pastor White."

From burger deliverer to the homeless, to booksigning arranger, this was the woman I married—and still loved.

I held my hand over the mouthpiece. "Larry, Angie wants you to explain your theology to our pastor."

He thought this over for a moment, nodded slowly. "Perhaps one weekday morning the two of them can meet me at Starbucks."

I repeated his request to Angie, listened to her reply, then put my hand back over the receiver. "Angie says you should anticipate some light debate."

As if alarmed at the terminology, Larry sat up straight in his chair. "I can handle *light* debate, just nothing heavy. Okay? I'm exhausted from using up my creative energy on this ending."

Angie's next comment sent me further into feelings of inadequacy. "Ned, there's also some kind of hellish theme running through this story. I think Larry is trying to show us his own version of it. But he never goes to church or reads a Bible, so this is the best he can do."

I opened my mouth but nothing came out. Then I rubbed my chin and cocked my head to the side. "Hold on for me, honey, I need to ask Larry something."

Again I held my hand over the receiver. "Larry, besides the music thing, what other themes did you insert?"

"Spiritual themes, of course."

"Please expound."

He spoke to the window. "You have to consider the color of Castro's hot tub, the month of August in Hotlanta, the red M&M's, Cuba, Killian's Red, the sizzling tarmacs, and pushing red buttons, not to mention the very low price of gas. Oh, and if you put the first two letters of Lanny's last name with the first letter of Miranda's last name, you get—" He paused and pointed at his head. "Go ahead, you're a smart guy."

Hooch, Timms. I suppose Larry would tell you that after a few stunned seconds my eyes grew wide with recognition. "This thing is your own take on hell?"

He removed one of his Italian shoes and rubbed his foot atop the corner of my desk. "Correctomundo," he said to his little toe. "And of course, Marvin is—"

"Satan himself." *Yes, I got something right!*

"That is, if you believe in such a being."

"Well, do you?"

He picked lint from his sock and put his shoe back on. "I'm not sure . . . but he makes for an interesting character."

While I ended the call with my wife and offered to pick up dinner—this was a Tuesday, remember—Larry stood and tried to read some notes on my desk.

I hung up with Angie, stood, and put my hand over a stack of papers. "You've been thinking about the afterlife, obviously."

Larry nodded. "My therapist says I think about it way too much."

"You think about hell too much? Or heaven?"

"Both. I mean, the potential existence of both. But I'm not so sure that the whole burning fire thing is how it goes. I mean, what if people like the zealots aren't even aware that they're in hell, but instead they think they're still trying to earn God's favor, and it just goes on and on until the entire planet is one huge, orbiting cheeseball?"

I couldn't resist. "Hmmm . . . My Big Fat Orbiting Cheeseball?"

Larry's eyes widened. "Great title for the sequel, Ned. Jot that on a Post-it note for me."

I did, and handed him the note. "If all this cheese alarms you, why don't you wander into some church and ask a few questions?"

He thought on this for all of two seconds. "Too stuffy. And besides, you've never invited me. No way would I go alone and risk getting smothered by the thumpers. I hear there are tons of thumpers here in Atlanta."

I had no reply; I was too preoccupied with my status in the agent world. I had the potential to be the first agent to sell a project that fit into the genre of *Non-Christian's comic allegory of hell, disguised as apocalyptic spoof.*

"Sorry," I said to him, "my mind wandered. You were saying something about the thumpers?"

Larry stuffed the Post-it note into his shirt pocket and turned to look out my window at the traffic. "What I was saying was that I avoid 'em. I would have asked you a few of my spiritual questions, but you're kinda like Ned Neutral, from what I can tell. You know, somewhere in the middle."

I possessed neither the learning nor the guts to share with Larry any knowledge about the afterlife. Embarrassing, considering whom I was married to. Being a once-a-monther who rarely paid attention, I suppose I was a fine example of neutrality.

He kept twisting his neck and trying to read my papers upside-down. "So, when are you gonna tell me the numbers from L.A.?"

I set my cell on the desk and motioned for him to sit again. "Help yourself to my guest chair, Mr. Hutch. You'll want to be seated for this."

Larry sprawled in the chair, put his hands behind his head, and scrunched his eyes in anticipation. "I just looooove Agent Orange."

I pulled the offers from my desk drawer, where I had hidden them. "When I read you these numbers, you'll be tempted to propose marriage to Agent Orange. But please restrain yourself. I'm spoken for."

Before I read Larry the four competing offers, I pulled his CD from my computer and tucked it into its case, aware that its contents approached legalism from such an odd angle that I should probably ask him to autograph the thing.

Truth was, I should not have been surprised that Larry had attemped some spiritual tangent of a theme. I mean, even his *Aliens Invade Billy Graham Crusade* manuscript had contained a remorseful alien. One little green man out of 14 million little green men—at Philips Arena the little fellow had stood in his chair and confessed his desire to take over the world by the time he reached adult height, which in his case was three-feet, one-inch.

Angie and I did tithe generously to the Baptist church in Buckhead, and even made a cash contribution to Victor, who promised to move out from under the I-85 bridge. After all, fifteen percent of $272,000—an outright buy of the film rights instead of a mere option—was the largest commission check of my career. *Thank you, Mylan Weems.*

Today, however, Buckhead was a long way away. Today Angie and I had sand in our flip-flops, sunblock on our arms and necks—and hammers in our hands. Wielding similar implements out on the porch and inside the sunroom were Larry, Miranda, my son, Zach, and Miranda's twenty-four-year-old sister, Carla, who just happened to be from Augusta.

Surprise, surprise.

We had come to Abaco to renovate and to celebrate. But mostly to renovate. On the southwest side of the island sat an old bungalow, a pastel blue two-story tucked among palm trees. It had four small bedrooms, plus a substantial loft with opposing port-hole windows. On the first floor, all doors and windows stayed open, and tropical breezes blew past our sweaty faces and right out the other side. One year after the deal had closed on Larry's story, and two months after he'd begun writing his next big thing, he was the proud new owner of a Bahamas home in need of repair.

The six of us had been on the island for five days now, helping Larry fix up the abode he had purchased with half of his proceeds from the deal. This was the first home he had ever owned. For the past year he had kept all of his deal monies in a savings account, mostly living off interest and toying with his next manuscript. Then, one day in July, he announced to me via e-mail that he was flying to Abaco to look at real estate, and asked if I would like to go along.

He bought the second place we looked at.

His intention was to rent it out for twenty weeks a year while also using it for, in his own words, "intense writing retreats."

It was now November. The Saturday of Thanksgiving week, in fact. Larry had bribed us all with promises of roasted island turkey garnished with pineapple—if we would only spend a week here helping him fix up the place. An easy decision for all, to say the least.

Filming for *A Pagan's Nightmare* had wrapped in September, and Mylan Weems remained secretive about any edits they had made to the storyline, though Larry said they were few. Larry—asked by Mylan to be a script consultant—had played spectator to several weeks of filming, returning to Atlanta regularly to continue with his twice-a-week therapy sessions.

The gentleman who helped Larry specialized in working with creative people, tapping into childhood traumas and memories, into histories and abuses that might later show up in an artist's work. Here on the island Larry was more open with the details of his sessions, even though I told him he should probably keep them between himself and his shrink.

"I insist that you know, Ned," Larry told me as we donned work gloves and stacked decking boards into his yard. "It'll at least help you understand my work."

Besides the Sunday school teacher who made him hold a chalkboard eraser in his mouth, other issues surfaced that were beyond my ability to predict: Being raised after age eight by step-parents—churchgoers, both—who often left Larry locked in his room alone. A legalistic neighbor who blared religious music into the streets on weekends while pretending to be a DJ. Getting fired from a construction job by a Bible-thumping boss. A childhood fascination with large boats. A spare bedroom filled nearly floor to ceiling with music CDs. He explained that his one happy memory from his early years was being driven to Cape Canaveral to view launches. His stepdad always rented the same little house in Cocoa Beach.

I pressed too hard only one time, as the two of us were taking a break from building the steps to his deck. "Ya think you use your humor to cover up pain?" I asked.

Larry's response was just what I deserved. He tossed his paper cup into the trash pile and said, "Ned, you're an agent, not some psychoanalytical psychology person."

I didn't ask any more personal questions during our time on the island. Whatever had messed with Larry's head was either dealt with, or repressed behind his newfound career, his comely girl-friend, and his island hospitality. My guess was that it was dealt with. Regardless, his sharing of his past helped me deal with my present.

Prior to the sale of his work, I had looked at Larry through the lens of profit, and he likely looked at me in the same manner. He and his creativity were a commodity to be sold for my gain. I had paid almost zero attention to the man himself. Here on the island I had learned that he was as flawed as I was, and whether or not he ended up with Miranda and had his own family, I made sure that he knew he had full access to mine.

I pulled a deck board from the stack and said, "Christmas is at my place this year, Lar."

He whopped a nail into place, then another. "I'll be there, Nedster."

By late afternoon he'd climbed atop a ladder in his kitchen, in-stalling crown molding with an artist's gusto. Angie stood below in the role of helper, handing up each piece, Larry accepting them one after another while sneaking glances at Miranda. She was sitting on the floor painting a rocking chair aqua blue, pausing between strokes to flirt with him.

"I can't believe I'm dating a screenwriter," she'd say.

"Aw, hush."

Zach toiled happily with Carla on another chair, so I joined Miranda in helping paint the last two. Both young women sported tie-dye shirts, denim shorts, and old leather sandals, though Carla wore her hair much longer, grown out to the small of her back. The four of us worked on our knees, scooting around the floor atop newspaper.

I painted one rocker arm as Miranda did the other, and I could not resist the urge to find out what she knew about Larry's story.

"He's told you the plot by now?" I asked in a lowered voice.

She glanced into the kitchen at Larry and wiped a drop of aqua blue from her arm. "All I know is that there's some kind of search for a girl by the main character, and that he has a bit of a problem with some religious people."

"You could say that," Zach offered.

"Yes," said Carla, turning away to hide her face, "you could say that."

Miranda quickly rolled a hand towel into a whip and popped her sister on the behind. "You've read the story, too?"

Carla nodded and started on the underside of a chair.

Miranda shook the hair out of her eyes and glared accusingly at each of us. We all wore serious faces, concentrating on our work.

"How come everybody but me gets to read the story?" she asked.

I removed my glasses and wiped them as casually as possible. "It's a bit evil in places, Miranda. So perhaps Larry just wanted to keep you from having any nightmares."

She looked around again at everyone hard at work, hesitated a moment, and said, "Oh . . . how sweet."

More amusing to me, however, was watching Larry and Angie get along.

I think Larry saw that Angie could appreciate his effort—wacked as it was—to show that many non-believers give thought to the afterlife. To her credit, she only tried once to thump, er, *convert* him.

She did this while discussing with him her idea for bathroom wall-paper. Samples were laid out all over the kitchen and against the walls.

Angie recommended the Last Supper scene.

Larry climbed up four rungs of the ladder and chose sunken treasure beneath a deep blue sea.

And this—just a small disagreement on décor—is what caused their differing views to pop up and debate.

Angie held her preferred sample in both hands and stood facing Larry from across the kitchen. "Larry, I just thought that I should tell you that hell is lonely and totally absent of fun. The only thing you got right in your story was the heat."

Larry tried to humor his way out of the conversation. He came down off the ladder, grabbed his sunken treasure sample, and spoke from behind it. "Oh, yeah? And how do you know the M&M's aren't red? Who's come back and told you for sure? Hmmm?"

"If there are any M&M's, they'll melt. So will the sage green Xterra, the ridiculous billboards, Castro's yacht, and Fence-Straddler AM."

Larry paused, still attempting to hide behind his sample and his humor. "But what if subtropical moisture was pulled in by a hurricane and cooled things off?"

Angie shook her wallpaper sample and stomped her foot. "There is no sub-tropical moisture in hell, Larry."

"You can't know that for sure."

"There's no evidence for it. So you'd better come to grips with how you can bypass hell altogether. If you would only trust—"

And that's when Larry dropped his sample and put his hands up. *No.*

A turn of the head. *No.*

A movement of lips. *No.*

There would be no sharing of the gospel from Angie today. Larry had one firm rule for our free week on Abaco—no Jesus conversations.

Apparently, Jesus was the line in the sand.

*   *   *

At lunch on Day Seven, the six of us gathered around Larry's picnic table. Miranda and Carla brought out twin serving bowls filled with boiled shrimp and centered them between Zach and me. Mid-meal, Larry stood with a jumbo shrimp in one hand and pounded on the table.

"I have some news," he announced. "Well, actually it was a phone call I received earlier today, but that led to my news."

Miranda pointed a three-pronged fork at him and said, "Spew it, handsome."

"How many at this table have ever been to a movie premiere?"

Larry scanned each face around the table. I shook my head no, as did Angie and Miranda, as did Zach and Carla.

Larry picked five more shrimp from the serving bowl and arranged them in his hand, tails up. "Pretend these shrimps are tickets," he said, and handed each of us a large, pink crustacean. "The producer gave me permission to ask five friends to attend the premiere."

The replies came quick and sarcastic.

"I'll be your friend."

"You can rent me."

"I take bribes."

"I just ate my ticket."

"Do I get to meet some actresses?" Zach asked.

Carla reached over and took him by the arm. "No, you get to escort me."

Our last night on the island came much too quickly. After Zach and Larry fell asleep in two of the hammocks—Miranda and Carla had whipped them soundly in a game of Hand 'n Foot—Angie and I stayed out on the porch to talk.

"Funny how this week has been just what we needed," she said, her head on my shoulder.

I could barely mutter, "Mmm," through my exhaustion.

Long minutes and many breezes passed before she spoke again.

"Ned, please tell me I'm not one of those musical do-gooders in Larry's story."

"Nah," I whispered, "you don't even like disco."

We listened to the ocean and spoke between long moments of silence. Topics came and went like fleeting schools of tropical fish, colorful but brief. During a drowsy hour sometime after midnight, we even discussed the fleeting camaraderie between the escapees aboard Castro's yacht. Angie called it a glimpse of community, though one that lacked a true nucleus.

I didn't sleep well that night. I remember her shaking my shoulder at 4:00 a.m. "What's the matter, Ned?"

"I was being chased by men in black fatigues."

She yawned at length and mumbled, "Yes, dear, and Marvin is hiding in the closet."

On the evening of the premiere, Mylan Weems stood at the entrance and greeted each invitee who strolled into L.A.'s Starlit Theatre. He held a silver tray in his hands, serving warm clusters of McScriptures in little red cartons.

"Gracias, Mylan," I said, and reached for a carton.

"Only one per customer, Ned."

Larry entered behind me, arm-in-arm with both Miranda *and* Angie. He tapped me on the back and pointed to the theatre wall to our left. Someone had hung a poster of a Jaws-like shark coming up from the blue to nab a swimming pagan. Larry admired the artwork for a moment and said, "Ya know, Ned, if you ever sell the novel rights, that might make a good book cover."

Little black dresses abounded, and Angie did not disappoint. She motioned to the fourth row, where Zach and Carla were already nibbling away, giggling as they bit into each fry, pausing from their chatter to wave. Larry and Miranda sat directly in front of them; Angie sat next to Zach, and I next to Angie. I had barely settled into my seat when Larry handed a fry back to Carla, who passed it to Zach, who passed it to Angie, who passed it to me.

"But I have my own. . . ."

"I wanted you to have an autographed one," Larry said.

I held it up to the white screen and saw that it was curled into the word *Larry*. "Ah, impressive."

"It's not a stamp or a Wheaties box, Ned, but at least I got my name on something."

We toasted each other with raised morsels, and then the house lights blinked three times and everyone hushed. A waiter hurried in and served us soft drinks—which was a relief, considering all the salt in our mouths.

After shaking hands with studio execs and their spouses, Mylan stopped by our row and asked everyone to please give him their honest feedback after the film ended. A group of actors—Mylan had cast unknowns for all major roles—summoned him back to the sixth row and he went and sat with them.

Mylan said, "Roll 'em," and the theatre went dark.

The members of our triple date peered anxiously at the screen—until Angie shared her speculation on what Hollywood had done to the ending.

"They kiss in the surf," she said. "I just know it. They'll ruin it with a big kiss in the surf."

Miranda, who had opted for the black strapless dress, turned to us and asked. "*Who* kisses in the surf? Will somebody please tell me who gets kissed in the surf?"

On the screen a small circle of light appeared. It slowly widened, revealing at first a section of stained glass, then the top of a baptismal, then the brown hair of a thirtyish man in jeans and a T-shirt. Then we saw that the man was on his knees, on hardwood floors, in front of the baptismal, leaning forward. And finally the circle of light expanded to the full size of the screen—and in the young man's hands a Craftsman cordless drill whirred to life.

Everyone laughed, and the actor who played Lanny shouted from behind us, "That's *me!*"

The film moved quickly: Lanny confused at the BP station, perplexed at McDonald's, aghast at seeing the first billboard. Waiting to merge on the interstate, he turned on his radio—and there was the voice of Paul McCartney, singing "I Wanna Hold Your Tithe."

"How did they do *that?*" Zach whispered to no one in particular.

Larry turned and gave me a thumbs-up, and I returned the gesture in kind.

For two hours and five minutes we sat in silence, absorbing the scenes at Cocoa Beach, inside Fence-Straddler AM, at Abaco, and in downtown Havana. Particularly good was the guy who played DJ Ned Neutral, though I thought him a bit too pudgy. Mylan showed his flare for irony when the soundtrack dubbed a gospel rendition of "Free at Last" during the escape scene, where Lanny, DJ Ned, MC Deluxe, and the Former Donald ran past graffiti-sprayed buildings at midnight, on their way to steal the yacht.

Throughout the screening I snuck glances at Miranda, looking for a reaction. I never saw her blink. She just held Larry's hand and stared zombie-like at the screen, giggling at the funny parts, smiling whenever she heard her name.

I had figured that when Miranda found out Larry had used her name and likeness in his story she might immediately bolt from the theatre . . . or slap him and bolt from the theatre . . . or sue him, slap him, and bolt from the theatre. But that's not what happened at all.

Perhaps I just don't understand how the female mind works.

Watching the scene of Lanny leaving Puerto Rico, crushed and despondent, she stood in the third row and pulled Larry to his feet. "You looked all over the Caribbean for me? You cared that much?!" By the time Ned Neutral and MC showed up below the high-rise, confessing that they were posers and yelling for Lanny not to jump, Larry and Miranda were a silhouette against the screen—and in front of us all she kissed him smack on the lips.

"Down in front," said Mylan. "I wanna read the credits."

"Yeah, down in front," Angie echoed. "I wanna see my husband's name scroll."

The film ended with the hippie van rolling through Arizona, dust flying up behind the tires, DJ Ned driving and singing "Born to Be Wild," MC begging him to switch radio stations, Lanny searching a map for something called Area 51. Then the credits ran against a still shot of the long, dark room in Cuba. The room was empty, and light from the partially opened door slanted across the center. There was no one inside, just a row of reclining lawn chairs set against moist stone walls. The slanted light revealed what was propped against the fourth chair—an old album cover of the Bee Gees, plus a black-and-white photo of Lanny and Miranda seated on a picnic blanket.

I heard Zach whisper to Angie, "I wanna be in the sequel."

"Me, too," she said.

I leaned forward to make eye contact. "Same here, son."

I remained in my seat and watched Larry's name scroll with the credits. He turned in his seat and caught my glance. "Me, too," he whispered.

The screen light faded and the theatre went black.

Applause began immediately. Zach even whistled.

To say that the ending spurred talk of the afterlife would be to minimize the thrust of it. As soon as Mylan stood and asked, "Well, what did everyone think?" I could feel the tension in the theatre.

The house lights came up.

A lean, boyish actor who had played the BP station cashier was the first to speak. From the row behind me he explained that God was everywhere, especially in nature, and that the making and marring of our destinies was nothing to lose sleep over. Whether we viewed the afterlife as a kind of heaven or a kind of hell was irrelevant; we would all possess bodies of light and live forever.

A young actress seated near the back—a redhead named Lauren, who played the counter girl at Detour Airlines—said the rut Lanny was in was very similar to how she pictured hell. But then she added that she was certain heaven was her own destiny, based on her contributions to UNICEF, her volunteer work with Hispanic immigrants, and the peace of mind she attained through yoga.

Angie squirmed in her seat beside me.

I nudged her and whispered, "Please don't say anything. . . . We're their guests."

"Ned, I have to."

"Please don't."

Angie restrained herself so well—for about a minute. After a minute she was bursting with rebuttal. In fact, rebuttal was the very air that filled her.

Perhaps her response came because there was no line in the sand like in Abaco. Or perhaps in California, one need not be ordained to preach.

She stood and faced the back of the theatre. She leaned forward and gripped the back of her seat. "A year ago I was just like those zealots. I even led a protest in my own street—against my own husband for working with this very material. I was wrong, and since then I've stopped protesting Ned and begun praying for him instead"—a glance toward Larry—"and for his clients, as well."

Larry's jaw dropped.

Angie was just warming up. "You can't earn salvation, people. Perhaps some of you think you can earn it, but there's simply no standard to which any of us can point and say, 'So and so has reached the standard of behavior that gets them in,' and then turn and say, 'but so and so is just a few niceties short . . . too bad for ol' so and so.' "

Two brief giggles from row ten were likely as much nerves as humor.

Angie paused, took a breath. "It doesn't matter what religious name or symbols you attach to your surroundings, or what nickname you call yourself, be it DJ Ned Nazareth or Saint Crackhead or Spiritual Scooby-Doo. . . . It's not enough. Even if you change every lyric to every secular song and make disco the object of your personal vendetta, then give every cent you have to UNICEF, it's still not enough. You can call your art a 'A Skippuh's Nod to God' or a 'Bossa Nova for Jehovah' . . . but it won't get you to heaven. Nor will it get you any true peace on this earth."

Another breath, a glance my way. "And by the way, plenty of people will *nod* to God, but what we're supposed to do is *bow* before him, not nod as if he were just our domesticated neighbor out collecting his Saturday morning paper."

More giggles from row ten.

Angie then picked up her empty McScripture carton and set it atop her head like a crown. "Tell me, everyone, does this earn me bonus points? Nope, all this gets me is recognition that I'm a crazy woman from Jawja with a French-fry carton on her head."

No one laughed this time.

Angie gazed with compassion at the audience. "If anyone here would like to bypass hell altogether—whether or not the place involves legalistic do-gooders—then you need to place your faith in the one who conquered death."

Light gasps, one stifled chuckle.

Then Angie uttered the word *Jesus,* and several studio execs and actors added winces to their gasps.

Angie said, "Sorry to be so blunt—and I can assure you that I'm one flawed female—but I hope you'll recognize that pure gold spilled from an imperfect package is still pure gold."

I'll admit, within that setting, around all that diversity of opinion, I even winced a bit myself. But while Angie spoke I had taken out a fine-point pen and written a synopsis on the back of a business card:

> Larry, our options appear to be:
> 1) Hope heaven/hell is irrelevant. (We'll all have bodies of light.)
> 2) Earn it by being nice. (Who says how much is enough?)
> 3) Jesus on cross clears the way (for anyone who accepts, even you).
> P.S. To choose wrong = worst nightmare?

I handed the card up to Larry and he read it. For a moment he appeared pale, as if just now realizing the seriousness of what he'd composed, as if he'd never considered that his showing the triviality of legalism might point him the opposite way, toward the transcendence of the gospel.

Angie's conclusion to her sermon contained both a reference to Marvin and the phrase *false prophets.* This caused Larry, who was now standing behind her in row three, to point at himself and mouth "Is she talking 'bout me?"

I shook my head no. Larry may have been the only screenwriter in the Bible Belt to write a non-Christian's comic allegory of hell, disguised as apocalyptic spoof, but he was hardly a false prophet. Confused, sure; a victim, maybe—but nowhere near prophetic. Except of course for that first day in my office, when he dropped his manuscript, *thwack,* on my desk, and told me we would soon sell the film rights. Nailed that one.

Angie finished her mini-sermon and the theatre fell silent. Someone in back crinkled a carton. I thought it might get tossed at my wife. But no. Restraint won out.

Then my son surprised me with his boldness. Zach stood beside Angie and said, "I agree with my mom."

Carla and her small-of-the-back hair stood next. She put her arm around Zach. "I agree with his mom, too."

Then I felt my family's eyes on me. Then Larry's, as if to ask, *Well Ned, what do you believe?*

Ned Neutral was on stage in front of half of Hollywood—and he was searching for shades of gray.

I felt the heat, the stares. I saw future movie deals crumbling in my fingers. But then I took a deep breath and stood beside my wife and took her hand and brought to the surface what I had always kept so hidden. "I agree with my wife."

Larry sat again and nodded at me, as if to say, "I'm glad you believe what you believe, and I'm glad that the two of us are friends." Miranda offered a wink, then turned to tap Angie on the knee and whisper, "You got guts."

I can tell you this—no one converted anyone else to his or her way of thinking that night. But from the tone and quality of what followed, the afterlife discussions likely spilled over into several L.A. breakfasts and power lunches.

As host, Mylan moved into the aisle and did the best he could to mediate. "Well," he said, clearly sensing the need to intervene, "this has certainly been the most interesting premiere discussion in my memory."

A brooding actor who played the part of Marvin stood in the back and said, "Can we please change the subject from religion back to the film?"

Mylan eased into the third row, put his hand on Larry's shoulder, and smiled a producer's smile. "Why don't we ask our author what he's working on next," he said. Mylan held an imaginary microphone to Larry's lips. "Tell us, Larry, what can we expect from you in the future?"

Larry stood and cleared his throat. He paused and basked in the attention. He even pulled Miranda up beside him. I knew he was working on two different manuscripts, and figured he'd say something about his sequel. Instead he told Mylan and the audience that he was working on a medical thriller with deep spiritual undertones, and that he had titled it *Doctors, Femurs, and Blasphemers.*

Miranda patted him on the back and said, "You go, boyfriend."

No one else said a word. Mylan looked in shock, as did my wife.

I was nowhere near shock; I had already agreed to agent the project. In my orange polo shirt, I would agent it.

Not that I had read any of the story, mind you. All Larry had told me so far was that two of the doctors were named Ned and Angie.

And that was good enough for now.

LARRY HUTCH'S READING GROUP GUIDE

Discussion question for non-Christians:

- Was it wrong to steal Castro's yacht?

Discussion question for Christians:

- If you were given Castro's yacht, would you sell it and give the money to foreign missionaries? Or would you keep the yacht and invite the missionaries to go for a short ride whenever they came home on furlough?

Discussion question for married people:

- Which was Agent Orange's most impressive feat—selling the manuscript or putting up with Angie?

Discussion question for single people:

- Would you go out with someone you met on E-Marviny? Why or why not?

Discussion question for anyone who likes to e-mail authors:

- Should Larry title his sequel *My Big Fat Orbiting Cheeseball?* (If your answer is no, feel free to e-mail your suggestion for the correct title.)

NOTE FROM THE AUTHOR

For years people have accused Christian novelists of using their characters as mere mouthpieces for doctrine, using them to tell the world what Christianity *is*. Last year a friend and I decided that it was high time someone write a novel about what Christianity *is not*. Larry and I did our best, and we welcome your comments via my Web site, www.rayblackston.com.

Blessings to all who can laugh at themselves,

Ray Blackston

P.S. Larry and I confess that our idea for a Broadway musical of *A Pagan's Nightmare* is still in the "Hmmm, should we do this?" phase. But I do know that Larry has already left phone messages for Sister Sledge, ABBA, and Paul McCartney.

ABOUT THE AUTHOR

Ray Blackston is a native South Carolinian and full-time author. He left the corporate world in 2000 to focus on creative writing. He is a graduate of the University of South Carolina, with a degree in Finance and Economics, although this did little to prepare him for life as a novelist. He also serves on the drama team at his church, participates in a weekly men's accountability group, and enjoys playing golf and visiting South Carolina beaches with friends and family. As a sidebar to his time spent writing, Ray has a passion for teaching budding writers, both at conferences and in a local writers group. His first novel, *Flabbergasted,* was one of three finalists for the Christy Award for best first novel and was chosen as Inspirational Novel of the Year by the *Dallas Morning News.* More of Ray's background is available at his Web site, www.rayblackston.com.